OLIVIA HART

Princess of Shadows
A Dark Fae Fantasy Romance

Copyright © 2021 by Olivia Hart

All rights reserved. No part of this publication may be reproduced, stored or transmitted in any form or by any means, electronic, mechanical, photocopying, recording, scanning, or otherwise without written permission from the publisher. It is illegal to copy this book, post it to a website, or distribute it by any other means without permission.

This novel is entirely a work of fiction. The names, characters and incidents portrayed in it are the work of the author's imagination. Any resemblance to actual persons, living or dead, events or localities is entirely coincidental.

First edition

This book was professionally typeset on Reedsy.
Find out more at reedsy.com

Contents

Acknowledgement	v
Prologue	1
Chapter 1	6
Chapter 2	15
Chapter 3	22
Chapter 4	27
Chapter 5	34
Chapter 6	40
Chapter 7	45
Chapter 8	54
Chapter 9	69
Chapter 10	81
Chapter 11	87
Chapter 12	95
Chapter 13	104
Chapter 14	111
Chapter 15	121
Chapter 16	126
Chapter 17	133
Chapter 18	140
Chapter 19	144
Chapter 20	154
Chapter 21	157
Chapter 22	164

Chapter 23	173
Chapter 24	179
Chapter 25	187
Chapter 26	192
Chapter 27	203
Chapter 28	212
Chapter 29	218
Chapter 30	224
Chapter 31	230
Chapter 32	234
Chapter 33	237
Chapter 34	240
Chapter 35	245
Chapter 36	250
Chapter 37	255
Chapter 38	260
Epilogue	268
Get the rest of the story!	270
About the Author	272

Acknowledgement

Cover designed by Moor Books Design

Prologue

Sebastian

The cold obsidian daggers slid into my hands, materializing from gray mist. Lighter than any steel blade, and a hundred times more deadly. They weren't the weapons of a warrior or a soldier. Only one group among all the Fae courts used these. The Assassin's Guild.

A guild that I was not a member of.

A black cloak billowed around me as I stepped through the silver-backed mirror and left the realm of the Fae behind, stepping into the Mortal Realm. The hotel was old and still had silver-backed mirrors. My prey should have known better.

A half-breed. Half human and half siren. She had already caused trouble in the Mortal Realm. A trail of bodies lay behind her as her powers had awoken. I knew her hunger, and I knew it would never be sated. Not while she lived among human men.

A part of me was frustrated by this task. There were already far too few sirens left in either world. Their powers were too dangerous. Much like my own kind.

A deathly silence hung in the air as I followed the siren's scent up the stairwell. Soft mists clung to the floor in my wake, the only evidence I would leave. That, and a beautiful woman's lifeless body.

I found the door to her room, and with a quick exhale, I touched the door. An in-between, it was a natural doorway for all Fae. Unless it had been made of iron or steel, no Fae would be hindered by a simple door. If the siren had known more of the Immortal Realm, she'd have known to ward the door.

The door turned immaterial for the briefest of seconds, and I slipped through the in-between. That same soft gray mist stayed behind in the shape of my silhouette as I stepped through.

The room was luxurious, a perk of being able to control mortals with a single word. Floor to ceiling windows ran all the way up to the vaulted ceiling and looked out over the city that sprawled out below the hotel. A white rug lay under a shiny brown leather couch and coffee table, covering the gold-laced white marble tiles.

And everything seemed to shine. Not as much as the Court of Light. That was born of magic while this was simply nice décor and good lighting.

A blond woman with a body built of fantasies turned physical sat on the king-sized bed. A siren used her body as bait for her prey. Where other Fae had sharp teeth or claws, she had ample breasts, a thin waist, and an unforgettable backside. Strangely enough, sirens were usually more successful hunters

Prologue

than the ones with teeth and claws.

The siren stared at me as I slid through the door. Though her body was the bait, a siren's eyes and voice were the hook. Golden eyes that seemed to draw you into them watched me. The color slowly twisted from deep gold to a pale yellow and back again. Full red lips the color of coral whispered of future pleasures. The scent of a sea breeze over a calm harbor hung in the air. Her scent. No human would have noticed, but for those of the Fae, it was unmistakable.

The huntress wore almost nothing. A matching set of red lace lingerie hid only enough to tantalize the mind. She was not new to the hunt, and she knew her tools well. It was a pity. She could have been an asset to the Dark Court, but sirens were notoriously hard to control and almost impossible to keep fed. Especially when her only prey was humans.

She ran her tongue over her lips seductively. She could taste the power that flowed from me. A buffet compared to the appetizer of mortal men. That dark power that lingered in the air around me should have terrified her. She had no idea who I was. If she had, even a siren would be afraid.

"Good evening," she whispered, seduction filling the air with power. Any human would have lost their free will in that instant. Any Fae would have been drawn to her. Any but me. I plied similar tools of the trade, though mine were far less obvious.

"Not for you," I said from under the cloak, my eyes hidden in shadow.

"Come sit down, assassin. Let me show you your fantasies," she said, putting more force and more power into her voice as she stood up, her body swaying to an unheard song. A siren's song. My lips curved into a smile as I stepped forward, having known all along that this was how things would play out. She was not the first siren that I'd hunted.

She began to slip the red lace off her shoulders as I moved towards her, my footsteps still coated in mists. "Siren," I whispered from only inches away from her, "Incubi aren't affected by your song." Mist flowed from my lips as I spoke and covered her face, making her vision blur and her voice muffled.

She blinked and turned to run, but she felt the bite of obsidian across her back before she'd even taken a step. Crimson dripped from the black edge of my blade, a sharp contrast, as she tried to scream, but the mists covering her face muffled all sound.

She fell to the white rug that covered the floor. Turning over, she tried to crawl backward, away from me, leaving a trail of blood. Her mouth opened as she tried to scream again, but the mists flowed over her face once more as I stepped forward.

"You never had a chance," I said in a low voice as I pulled back my hood. I knew that my green eyes were slowly becoming grayer, becoming more and more cloudy.

She didn't know what she was looking at. She didn't understand why I was different than anyone she'd ever met. The slightly too large eyes, the curved tips of my ears, or my sharper features.

And she wouldn't know why she felt a throbbing between her legs even as she lay in a pool of her own blood. I knelt beside the half-naked woman, and she stopped screaming as I released my own tendrils of seduction through the room. A siren dying under a seductive spell seemed an apt execution.

She smiled as her eyes glazed over with lust even as I raised the obsidian dagger over her chest. Her hips thrust upward,

Prologue

desperate for a pleasure that she would never find. And then she screamed loud enough that even the mists couldn't muffle the sound as my dagger moved through skin and muscle and pierced her heart.

With a single twitch, one of the last half-sirens died, and I withdrew the blade from her body, wiping the crimson on her lingerie and leaving the blade a gleaming black again.

A knock sounded at the door, and I stood up, giving the half-siren one last look as I dropped the daggers, letting them turn back to mist and appearing in their hartskin sheathes at my waist. Turning to the window, I exhaled, and mists flowed from my breath through the room, coalescing into a tunnel. The window, another in-between, turned insubstantial.

I ran through the tunnel, and as I reached the window, I leaped. The black cloak on my back fluttered in the air two hundred feet above the ground as I fell towards the building across the street.

I looked down at it as it raced upward to meet me, and I braced myself exhaling once more. As my boots touch the stone of the roof, the stone softened under me and absorbed my fall. When I stepped forward, I glanced back and saw only the barest of a footprint embedded in the stone.

I reached out one hand and touched a shadow. As I'd known, a warren ran here. A quick glance toward the window almost fifty feet above me showed a man's face. A human face. A face that didn't matter to a creature like myself.

Then I slid through the shadow into another world. I could go home now. Home to solitude. Home to hunger. Home to nothingness.

Chapter 1

Rose

Moonlight made silver halos in the frosty air around the lampposts on campus. The bags of books were heavy as I trudged back to the sorority house. Four days until everyone came back from winter break. The peace and quiet would end.

My sorority sisters felt bad that I didn't have a home to go back to for Christmas. I was supposed to be sad and depressed during the holidays because my parents were dead. What was the point? I'd accepted that I was alone in the world long ago.

My feet moved slowly down the campus streets that seemed like a ghost town. Places that were filled with laughter and antics a month ago were now silent. The lights from classrooms were black. Everything that normally glowed with life and light seemed dead.

And I reveled in it.

Chapter 1

The silence. The darkness. The solitude.

I'd grown up in a world like this. No one had been loud while I was climbing trees in the forest as a child. No one had shouted at me for no reason when I was learning to tie a fishing line. No one told me that I needed a boyfriend when I was learning to steer a sailboat.

A biting wind blew from the North, carrying snow from the tops of buildings through the air. The night was clear, and the moon was bright tonight. Full without a hint of clouds to cover its brilliance.

I let my mind wander and imagined being back in those woods. Instead of pavement, I felt the crunch of leaves on a game trail. Instead of car noises, I heard the swooshing of wings as a nighthawk took off.

Maybe I did miss those days, but it wasn't because of my parents. It wasn't because of Christmas. It was because I'd felt at home there. This city, any city, just never felt like home. No matter how many people I knew. No matter how many parties or events I went to. Not even when I'd joined a "sisterhood".

I came to the street that separated the campus from the neighbors that surrounded it. The street was empty, and I walked across it without waiting for the light to change.

The pedestrian crossing signal began to beep when I was halfway across, a reminder that I wasn't in the woods. There was no natural noise like that. I probably would never live in the woods again. My degree in social services was meant for cities, not cabins in the forest. I sighed.

I needed to get home to drop off the books, and then I could go running through the greenbelt. I needed that run. Tonight, the woods would be beautiful. A picturesque scene of white snow on silver trees as I breathed the free air.

"Girl," a voice called in the silence. I jumped at the unexpected sound and turned. A homeless mature woman who was probably in her fifties stepped from the shadows of an alley. She could have been beautiful once, but now her hair was tangled and dirty, and her clothing was barely more than rags. Dirt smudged her cheeks, and I was sure that she hadn't showered in days.

She still stood tall with more poise than I'd ever seen in one of the homeless that populated the streets around the college. Her steps were slow with no sense of shuffle as she moved away from the alley.

"It's a strange night, girl." Her eyes seemed to focus on things beyond me even though she stared at me. "Don't stand in the dark for the shadows have claws tonight. And eyes and ears. Death comes for the daughter if the mother hears her call."

What the hell was this woman talking about?

Her gaze focused on me, leaving whatever madness behind. "And you will call tonight, won't you, girl? You'll call your mother. Only the mother will call the prince."

"My mother is dead, and I have no idea what prince you're talking about. Have a good night." I turned to walk away from the insane woman, hoping she'd leave me alone to the winter night. I wasn't that lucky, and she called out one more time.

"She left the dark and reclaimed her light. That is not your path, girl. Your heart is dark like your father's."

I ignored her as images of my father came to mind. The kindest man I'd ever known. The only one that had ever cared for me. One that had ignored my oddities like a father should. I barely remembered him, but every one of my memories was of him smiling.

Jet-black hair, emerald eyes that seemed alive, and a smile

Chapter 1

that could fix anything. He was handsome. I knew it like I knew that my mother was beautiful. Both of them could have been models, and I'd been born looking hideous. My eyes were too far apart and slightly too large.

My hair wasn't beautifully black like my father or icy blond like my mother. Instead, I had plain brown hair that was always just a little bit wild no matter how hard I tried to make it straight and pretty.

I pushed the memories out of my mind, but I couldn't help turning to see if the old woman was following me. She was gone, probably back to the alley that she'd come from. Her words reverberated in my mind.

Don't stand in the dark for the shadows have claws tonight. And eyes and ears. Death comes for the daughter if the mother hears her call.

What a creepy thing for someone to say. I guess that's what happens when you listen to crazy old women living in alleys.

The whole experience made me a little more nervous now that my imagined peace had been broken. I hurried along the sidewalk to the sorority house, passing more houses and more alleys.

I heard a noise as I passed one. A scratching noise from behind a dumpster. I froze, the old woman's words running through my mind once again. My heart began to race as I stood there, not sure if I should keep walking or find out what the noise was.

An explosion of movement and howling made me drop my bags of books. A cat flew out of the dumpster, landing on its feet and running straight for me. Right behind it, another cat chased it, screaming like a banshee.

My heart felt like it was about to pound out of my chest as I shrieked. I stumbled over the bags of books as the cats dodged me and ran across the street to the opposite alley.

When the cats were gone, I still lay on the ground trying to convince my heart that I wasn't actually going to die. "What the hell am I doing?" I muttered with a soft laugh.

I stood up and brushed the dirt off my tights. After picking up the bags, I began to walk towards the sorority house again, very ready to be done with creepy stuff for the night.

Still on edge, I checked the alleys that I passed, seeing dumpster after dumpster. This was a strange night. The old woman hadn't been wrong about that. You could feel it in the air that something was off.

When I was two blocks away from the sorority house, I heard a scream from the alley in front of me. Then what sounded like more muffled screams. My heart began to race again as I stepped in front of the alley.

A fat man held a sorority girl against the dumpster while another watched. One hand was held over her mouth as muffled screams tried to escape her. The other hand was pulling at her skirt.

I froze as I watched the scene. I'd never seen anything like this. Everyone knew that this kind of thing happened, but it didn't happen in front of you. It wasn't something that anyone saw.

The woman was doing her best to keep her skirt on, but the second man grabbed her hands. "Shut the fuck up, whore. Don't make me get my knife out." The words were quiet enough that if I weren't standing there, I wouldn't have heard them.

The woman stopped screaming, but nothing was going to stop her sobs. I didn't know what to do. I couldn't fight off

Chapter 1

two men, but I couldn't just ignore it either.

I did the only thing I could think of. I began to scream like someone was murdering me. The two men immediately turned to me, ignoring the woman pressed against the dumpster. The one who had been holding the woman's hands raced towards me. The other turned towards me and zipped up his pants.

As soon as the men turned towards me, the woman slipped by them and ran, leaving them to me.

I tried to turn and run, but my feet felt like they were cemented to the pavement. I should have been able to outrun them. I ran every day, and they were out of shape thugs.

But my body felt frozen. The man who had rushed towards me caught me around the waist. Suddenly, my body began to move all on its own. I kicked at him as he pulled me into the shadows of the alley, trying desperately to make him drop me so I could escape.

He grunted a few times as my feet hit his thighs, but I never connected hard enough to stop him from doing what he was trying to do.

"Fuck Ray, she's a hell of a lot hotter than the other chick," the other man said.

"She kicks a lot harder too," Ray grunted as he threw me to the ground. I tried to scoot backward so that I could get my feet under me, but the fat guy bent over and pushed me to the ground, his hands holding my shoulder against the pavement.

Ray tried to get his hands around the waistband of my tights, but this time he was in front of me, and one of my kicks hit him squarely in the nose. It wasn't a hard enough kick to break his nose, but his hands went to his face.

"Fucking bitch," he said as he climbed on top of me. I tried to kick him again, but he pushed my legs out of the way. As I struggled, I began to scream again, and he slapped me across the face.

It stung, but the pain barely fazed me. I continued to scream as they trapped my body underneath the two of them. Anger overwhelmed the fear that I'd felt moments before. I looked at Ray as I felt something begin to build inside me. A pressure. A fire.

He pulled a large pocket knife from a sheath on his belt and flipped it open. "Shut the fuck up. You should have kept walking." His breath stank like beer and cigarettes. I barely noticed it though as I felt that pressure building.

My skin began to vibrate, almost as though my very skin was just waking up after being asleep. I kept staring into Ray's eyes and stopped screaming.

"That's a good little slut," he said and dug his hands into the waistband of my tights. Feeling his fingers touch the bare skin of my hips was too much for me, and the pressure that was building inside me exploded outward as I put my hands up.

A flash of light brighter than anything I'd ever seen in my life exploded from me. They pulled away, screaming as they pressed their hands against their eyes.

They fell to their knees in pain. I didn't stop to try to understand what had happened. No longer frozen, I ran out of the alley. Books forgotten, I ran to the one place that would be safe. The sorority house.

I wasn't supposed to have someone try to rape me. That happened to other people. I was always so careful. I poured my own drinks. I paid attention to my surroundings.

It had still happened to me.

What had happened afterward, though? What was that light?

Chapter 1

It felt like it had come from me, but that was impossible. And why was I so freaking exhausted? I could have passed out right there, and I might have if there weren't a couple of rapists two blocks away.

When I slammed the sorority house door behind me, I took gasping breaths and leaned against it. I was safe. At least I thought I was.

"What's going on? You're all dirty. Did you fall on that stupid run of yours? I've told you to run on treadmills at the gym like normal people." I jumped before turning toward the sound. Sasha. One of my sorority sisters.

My body still had gallons of adrenaline flowing through me, but when I saw her, I felt a little bit safer. I wasn't alone. She wasn't much being barely five feet tall, but she was something.

"I got attacked," I muttered, finally feeling the sting where Ray had slapped me. My face was probably swollen and red.

"What do you mean attacked?" she asked after taking a sip from a red solo cup.

"I mean some fucking guys dragged me into an alley and tried to rape me." The words came out of my mouth without any filter.

Her eyes got wide, and she put her cup down. "Are you okay? Do we need to call the cops? Did you get away before they…?"

I slid down the door feeling the exhaustion fill me. I was safe. I could be exhausted. "I'm okay," I muttered. "They didn't manage to rape me. I have no idea what happened, but I'm okay."

Sasha picked up her drink and brought it over to me. "I think you need this more than I do. I'll make another one and then you can tell me all about it, and then we'll figure out what to do."

I nodded, taking the cup from Sasha. I'd thought that I didn't need anyone else, that I liked my solitude, but tonight, I didn't want to be alone.

Chapter 2

Sebastian

Seraphina, Queen of the Court of Light stood in front of me with a sneer. She was a bitch, but there was nothing I could do about it. With my own Queen dead almost nine hundred years ago and no one with the qualifications to replace her, Seraphina ruled both courts.

Her ice-blond hair had been made up in a braided crown today with the ends hanging down to her shoulders. Piercing blue eyes that others found attractive stared at me with disdain. I hated her more than anyone I'd ever known. That didn't matter, though. Not when it had to do with a Queen. Especially *the* Queen.

As a Prince of the Dark Court, I was bound by law to do as she commanded. The Fae were not like humans. Our laws were unbreakable with no need for trials. One of the most important being that the Queen of your court could not be

Princess of Shadows

refused anything she demanded. At least not without risking unpleasant things such as banishment or execution.

And this Queen happened to enjoy seeing me do one of the things that I hated more than anything else. Kill half-bloods. Especially since I was mixed blood myself, something she never overlooked.

I stood next to Nyx, the leader of the Assassin's Guild. My mentor. He wore the same black cloak that I wore when I was hunting, but he had earned his. When Catarina, the last Dark Queen, had ruled, he'd worked his way through the ranks of the Assassin's Guild.

I glanced at him, remembering what he looked like under the cloak. Black and red skin covered in thin scales. A throwback to his heritage that was covered in thin, overlapping scars. Trophies of battles won.

"Prince," Seraphina said to me with a sneer. "I have a contract for you." Her eyes never fell on Nyx as she spoke.

"Why not have the Assassin's Guild take care of it? That's their role in the courts after all."

She ignored my question, handing a rolled-up parchment to Nyx as well, still not looking at him. "The contract is for a girl with human parents. Last night, she drew a massive amount of power from the Immortal Realm, and without training, she is likely to draw attention to herself and our world."

"I am giving the contract to you, Prince, but if you do not complete it in three days, Nyx will take care of it."

"Why contract me to do it first?" I stared into her icy eyes, but I didn't waver. The power inside her was immense, and she knew it. It was why she was Queen after everything she'd done.

She ignored me and finally turned to Nyx. "If you find that

Chapter 2

the Prince is disobeying my orders, your contract will extend to the Prince. I am done hearing whispers of a lack of order from the Dark Court. The Prince will either do as he's told and become a model subject, or he will become the perfect example for what happens when someone disobeys me."

Nyx didn't respond for several seconds before a rumbled, "Yes, Lady," came from under his hood. His voice sounded like gravel rolling over pebbles, crushing and scratching away at them.

As he turned, I saw under his hood. Dark red eyes that I knew well shined through the cloth that covered them, shielding him from the brightness of the Court of Light. The curse to his gift of being able to see in almost absolute darkness. Every gift has its price.

Nyx turned and left the room carrying the contract. I glared at the Queen, and she sneered back at me. I didn't respond to Seraphina. My obedience was required, but my politeness was not. I was of the Dark Court, after all, and we were not known for our manners. Instead, I turned and followed Nyx out of the palace.

The very city shined as I followed Nyx through the streets. This was the only place in either world that there was no night. The sun fell behind the horizon, and the moons rose, but the city was never dark. The buildings radiated their own light, pulling their power from the golden throne that Seraphina sat upon.

Even the nobility of the Court of Light glowed. Not bright enough to hurt the eyes, but enough that they could never hide in the darkness.

As we walked through the streets, Nyx in his cloak, and I in a simple silk shirt and leather trousers, people turned to stare.

They knew us by scent. Both of us unique. I, a creature of dreams, and he, a creature of fire and ash, were the only ones of our kinds in either Court and possibly in the entire world.

I could feel each and every one of the people that we passed, their emotions flowing to me unbidden. Lust, fear, distrust. It was one of the curses of being a half-incubus.

We passed the beautiful people that inhabited the city of the Court of Light. A dryad sold the apples from a tree that he protected, his skin a glowing gold. He looked like a beautiful youth except that his skin had a faint bark pattern to it.

A nymph flitted through the market, her transparent robes showing the beautiful body underneath. Long, sky-blue hair fell all the way down her back. She clung to one of the white poles holding up a market stand and talked to an elf who sold shoes. The elf's eyes wandered over her body as he talked to her, and she gave no thought to it.

Nyx, raised his hand, trying to shield his eyes from the light of the city. "Let us run, Prince," he said softly in that gravelly voice.

I nodded, and he began to sprint. I followed, keeping pace with him. This was not our home. These were not our people. We should not be here, but a Queen's demand was not something that we could ignore.

How could Seraphina expect me to kill a half-breed who could draw power from the Immortal Realm? She should have been brought to the Dark Court and trained to use her powers rather than murdered in cold blood because she could expose us to the Mortal Realm.

As we crossed the golden bridge over the Crystalline River that signaled the end of the Court of Light, we began to slow. The forest beyond still glowed, but it was nothing like the

Chapter 2

Court. There were still people there, but nowhere near as many. We were still outsiders, but it was nothing compared to being inside that terrible city.

"Nyx, why don't we just bring the girl to the Dark Court and hide her? If she can truly draw power from the Immortal Realm, she's of value to the court. Catarina would never have had her killed." Nyx silently turned to me.

"Catarina is long dead, Sebastian. Our Queen is Seraphina, and it is not our place to question her demands."

"You'll do as the Queen requires," Nyx said, his words a statement rather than a question. I was his Prince, but he had raised me like a son. That made our relationship more complicated.

"Yes. I know the law. There is no way out of a direct demand."

Nyx nodded. "Good. I do not want to kill you, Sebastian." His eyes glowed from under the hood as he looked at me through the cloth. He was not a soft man. It wasn't in his nature. He was like the stone and fire that he was born of. Harsh and unyielding.

Somehow, he'd decided that I was worth changing for. Not a lot, but enough. Enough to be the rock that I could depend on when the world was just a little too cruel.

I raised my eyebrow. "It's been a long time since we sparred, old friend. I doubt that you would win a bout with me."

"I taught you everything you know, Prince. All of your abilities are ones that I helped hone. And the mists are nothing to me. Do as you're commanded, Prince. I don't relish a battle with you, but I will not dishonor myself and my guild by disobeying an order."

I gave him a grin and said, "I'll do as I'm told like a good little

Princess of Shadows

Prince, but I still think you and I need to get into a sparring ring again so I can remind you just how slow you are."

Nyx shook his head. "I no longer spar. You know this."

I patted him on the shoulder, feeling the denseness that felt almost like stone. "Fine. We should go drinking when this is done, though. It's been too long."

"That would be good. I will see you when all of this is over. When the girl is dead."

He touched the shadow of a tree and seemed to slide into the shadow, the black cloak becoming darker and then slowly disappearing as though light was suddenly shining on the spot he'd stood.

This was not a fair thing for Seraphina to do. She, along with everyone else, knew that Nyx had trained me as a father would. He'd been there when everyone else abandoned me.

He hadn't treated me like a son. That wasn't in him. Instead, he'd given me the tools to survive. He had given me these daggers that hung at my sides, and he'd taught me honor when others had shunned me because of who my father was. Because of *what* my father was.

I was a half-breed, but so was Nyx. He'd raised me to ignore the slurs, and he'd taught me that my twisted bloodlines gave me power that others didn't have. Just as his did.

More than anything, he'd taught me to fight. Of all the men in either Court, Nyx was the one man whom I did not want to find holding an obsidian dagger in my direction. Now, if I didn't kill this girl, that's exactly what would happen.

I sighed. These thoughts didn't matter. The girl had to die, or I'd be forced to fight Nyx to the death, and there was no good ending to that fight.

I touched the shadow and slid into the warren that ran

Chapter 2

between the Court of Light and the Dark Court. I would gather my things, and then I would murder a girl because a woman I hated commanded me to.

Chapter 3

Rose

The repetitive beat of some terrible rap song reverberated through me as I sat at a bar and legally drank for the first time. Sasha, her boyfriend Tony, and another sorority sister named Tiffany danced to the music that filled the building down on the dance floor below me.

The vodka cranberry went down smooth, and I ordered another. It was my twenty-first birthday, and I could get as sloppy drunk as I wanted. That was the ritual, wasn't it? Drink enough that you don't remember turning twenty-one?

I looked into the old-fashioned mirror in front of me. Why was something that old in a place that was supposed to be modern? The silver embellishments that surrounded the mirror face were tarnished and looked like they'd never been polished. Maybe that was the modern take on mirrors. Get a nice antique mirror, let it get ruined, now it's modern. I shook

Chapter 3

my head. Just one more thing that didn't make sense to me.

I saw myself in the mirror and grimaced. I knew what people saw when they looked at me. A toad. Okay, maybe my skin wasn't green, and I didn't have warts, but my eyes were too big, and they were too far apart. There were other problems with me, but everyone I'd ever known had told me just how unattractive my eyes made me.

I wished that I could have just been plain. Not beautiful. I'd given up on being beautiful a long time ago. My parents had been beautiful. Not me. I'd tried wearing makeup, but makeup could only do so much. They couldn't move eyes, couldn't make them smaller. That was life though. We all had our crosses to bear, right? Too bad mine couldn't have been being too beautiful.

I turned around to look at the dance floor. What was the point of it? I had grown up with stories of ballroom dancing, and I'd had little girl fantasies of meeting my Prince Charming while wearing a ball gown and dancing the night away with him.

This wasn't that. This was sex without any of the good parts. Or at least that's what I imagined sex was like since I had seen no reason to partake in it and no men had tried very hard to convince me otherwise. Dirty, sweaty men rubbing against you until they were too tired to keep going. Both of you trying to match a rhythm and failing miserably.

It was my twenty-first birthday, and I was alone at a bar while my friends did things that I had no desire to do. Typical. It was fine. I hadn't wanted to do this to begin with. I hadn't wanted to put on a skanky club outfit.

More than anything, I hadn't wanted to leave the sorority house. Not after last night. Not after the alley.

Princess of Shadows

I sighed and turned back to the bar, sipping the vodka cranberry and enjoying the burn. It wasn't the worst night I'd ever had. At least the music drowned out the people, and I could pretend like it was just me and the bartender who was slower than freaking molasses.

Then a hand brushed the middle of my back, and I sat up straight, turning to snarl at whoever it was.

It was Tony. Sasha's boyfriend. Not my favorite person, and definitely not someone I wanted touching me. I wasn't allowed to yell at him though. It was one of those unspoken sorority rules.

He was officially in the douche club. Or frat club. I wasn't sure there was a difference. He always had that purposefully messy hairstyle, some polo shirt with an animal on it, a pair of jeans that cost at least a hundred dollars, and a pair of retro sneakers because "they were cool" according to him.

Tonight, he wore a salmon polo, and he was giving me creepy looks as his gaze drifted down to my chest. Sasha reached around his waist and grabbed his ass. "You look bored, Rose," he said, ignoring his girlfriend.

She was pretty with a very typical sorority girl look. Long blond hair with obvious highlights and lowlights. A slightly rounder face than she'd like, but still cute. She had a very girl next door look naturally, but she primped enough and wore the right makeup and outfits to look like a sexier version.

"You could come dance with us," Sasha yelled, her voice barely audible over the music. That was nice. I really didn't want to listen to either of them. Tiffany was still dancing with numerous guys crowded around her.

"I think I'm going home soon," I shouted back.

"Come on. We've only been out for an hour. You need

Chapter 3

to experience your birthday. You only get to turn twenty-one once, you know?" She may have been annoying with drastically different priorities than me, but she wasn't a bad person. She'd been there for me last night, and she hadn't told anyone.

"Fine, but can we go somewhere else? Maybe just a bar or something? I don't like dancing."

Sasha chewed her lip and glanced at Tony, but then she nodded. "Yeah, I'll get Tiffany."

She turned and left the bar, grabbing Tony's hand as she left. I ordered another vodka cranberry since it would take a while to get her away from the crowds of people with their hands up her skirt.

I looked into the mirror again, and I saw a man standing behind me. Jet-black hair that hung down below his shoulder, lips that seemed too red to be natural, and features that were just a little off. Beautiful beyond anyone I'd ever met, but off.

More than anything, his eyes were different. Not the shape of them. Not really the placement on his face or even the color. Deep blue that made me think of the oceans. But they seemed to pull me in with an energy I'd only seen in two people in my life.

My mother and father. I'd forgotten so many things about them, but I'd never forget their eyes. They burned with a fire that couldn't be forgotten.

Now, I was seeing that same fire in his eyes. I turned around trying to see the rest of the man who was looking at me. There wasn't anyone with long black hair. I stood up, looking through the crowd. He should have been easy to see. He'd be tall and so different from everyone else.

He wasn't there, though. He'd disappeared in the half a

Princess of Shadows

second it took to turn around. How was that even possible?

I sat back down on the barstool, but when I looked at the mirror again, he was still there. I blinked, but he didn't disappear. He gave me a half-smile, our gaze meeting in the mirror, and I turned around as fast as I could.

Instead of the man, Sasha, Tony, and Tiffany stood behind me. I looked all around just as I had before, trying to spot the man, but he was gone.

"Who are you looking for, Rose?" Tiffany asked.

"A guy with long black hair. Like a clean rock star or something. He's tall." Everyone started looking around, even Tony.

"I don't see anyone like that," Sasha said after a few moments.

I frowned, my lips pressing together as I took one last look around. "I was looking in this mirror, and he was there, but when I turned around, he was gone." I sat back down and looked in the mirror, but he wasn't there.

What was going on? That was so freaking weird. Was I going crazy? Last night, I did something and got away. An impossible thing. Now, I'm seeing a guy in a mirror when he's not actually there.

I left the rest of the drink in the glass and shook my head. I called the bartender for my tab, and then we left the club.

Something was going on. Something strange. Maybe I really was going crazy. I looked at Sasha and Tiffany, doing my best to ignore Tony. I would give them another hour, and then I was going home. I was going to spend that hour drinking enough that when I got home, I would be able to pass out.

They'd had their fun. I'd had my twenty-first birthday. I needed to feel safe now.

Chapter 4

Sebastian

She was part fairy. There was no doubt in my mind. Her eyes had burned with raw magic as all fairies' eyes did. I'd half-expected that. The contract had indicated as much. No other half-breed would have been able to pull enough power from the Immortal Realm. Why would Seraphina want her dead?

Seraphina rarely involved herself in dealing with half-breeds. The siren had been killed because she was dangerous and because she would draw far too much attention. A half-fairy wouldn't. She wouldn't be able to draw power without training or desperate need.

I needed more information.

As I strolled past the buildings that surrounded the club with my hands in my pockets, I thought about the girl. She was beautiful in a very Dark Court way. Her chestnut hair was more than a little wild. Fair skin that had a natural tan from spending time in the sun. She was meant for the woods, not this city.

And that magical scent. Dark power that had no outlet, no direction. It just swirled around her. Intoxicating power that longed to be used. For the first time in centuries, I felt something stir inside me. Not a physical urge. Something more. Something deeper. Something darker.

I sighed. I didn't want to kill this girl. At the same time, I didn't want to force Nyx into a confrontation that only one of us would walk away from. Seraphina had to have known that I'd hate doing this. This had nothing to do with killing the girl and everything to do with pushing me into a position that would give her an excuse to execute me. Then, the Dark Court would rise up against her, and she would have a good enough reason to slaughter them all.

If only Nyx would have let me just hide her away in the Dark Court. Seraphina wouldn't have even looked for her. She hated spending time in the Dark Court.

What a twisted web you weave, Seraphina. You were meant for that damned Court of Light. No one in the Dark Court could be so cruel and vindictive.

I gritted my teeth. No, I would have to kill this girl, but first I would come to know her at least. I would understand her so that at least someone remembered her after she was gone into the void.

Walking into an alley, I touched a shadow and felt the warren beneath it. It was time to meet the girl that had to die.

* * *

Chapter 4

I lay down on the roof above the girl's sorority house. She'd come home several hours ago and would almost certainly be asleep. Especially with how drunk that girl had been. It was almost painful to watch her get hauled out of the car by her friends, and it had been especially painful to see the guy putting his hand under her skirt as he "helped" her.

That was none of my business though. I wasn't here to judge her life, only to understand it. Someone should since her friends most certainly wouldn't. No human could ever understand a half-breed's life. The need to be around others of their kind would be a constant burden that would never be relieved.

It would feel like they were wearing someone else's skin. Especially since she'd never touched the Immortal Realm, never claimed her magic. She would never know what it was like to let all that power loose to change the world before her eyes.

I lay on the roof of the sorority house and closed my eyes, reaching out and searching for the only person in the house with any sign of power. There it was, the shimmering ball of magic inside her. Dark and twisted, it writhed inside her, full of pain and longing.

I built a tie between us out of my own power, a skill every incubus knew instinctively, and I left my body to join her in her dreams.

* * *

A tile floor. Aisle after aisle of racks of food. Boxes and bins filled with produce.

She was drunk and dreaming of a grocery store? I guessed

Princess of Shadows

that her friends decided against giving her anything to eat after getting her drunk. I shook my head softly. Terrible friends.

I approached the girl and noted that she still wore the same outfit that she'd gone to the club in. A corset top that accented her thin waist. A miniskirt that would have made any man want to run his fingers over her legs in the hopes of discovering what lay under the fabric.

"Good evening," I said as I approached her while she filled her basket with produce.

She glanced at me and then turned all the way around to look at me. "You!" she exclaimed. "What are you doing in my dream?"

I raised an eyebrow and cocked my head in surprise. "What do you mean? Why wouldn't I be in your dream? You tried to catch me, didn't you?"

"Yes," she said, giving me another glance. "But you shouldn't be here. I didn't create you. I would never have given you those clothes?"

I glanced down at myself. I wore the same thing that I wore to most human women's dreams, a pair of slacks and dress shoes. No shirt. It wasn't especially creative, but human women were generally appreciative of it.

"What's wrong with my clothes?" I asked.

"You look ridiculous is all," she snipped as she went back to picking up cantaloupes and sniffing them.

"Most women would disagree with you." I stepped closer to her, and I could see her pick up on my magical scent. The same one that drew the Fae to me.

"If you walked into a grocery store wearing that, they'd throw you out. Even with your sexy man abs." She smiled at me and ran her fingers over my stomach. "I'm not going to

Chapter 4

throw you out, but you may want to put something on or he might," she said, pointing at a fat security guard that she'd just created.

I looked up at where the ceiling should have been but saw dark clouds with streaks of purple lightning. She was struggling to build this world. A part of her wanted to build something different, but she was in desperate need of normal. Something she knew.

She grinned at me and a pink sequined corset appeared around my chest. "There, that should keep the guards at bay," she said with a cheeky grin.

I bit my tongue to keep from saying something overly snarly at the girl. I wasn't here to fight with her. I was trying to learn more about her, to understand a girl that would die tomorrow.

"What's your name?" I asked, ignoring her attempt to annoy me.

"Rose. What's yours?" She moved the basket, not paying as much attention to me now that I was "properly dressed".

"Sebastian. Why did you try to catch me tonight?"

"The fire in your eyes. My parents had a fire like that, but nobody else does. I wanted to know what was different about you."

Her parents were both magical? Then she wasn't a half-breed. She absolutely needed to be brought to the Dark Court to find out exactly what she was.

"I'm half fairy," I said, not needing to hide the truth. She'd wake up tomorrow with barely any memory of this anyway. Worst case scenario, she'd wake up tomorrow, remember it, and then I'd kill her. Maybe a little truth before she died would be better for her.

"Uh huh. And I'm a freaking unicorn. Try again, Tinkerbell."

Princess of Shadows

She put one of the cantaloupes in the basket and moved on to the lettuce.

"You might be. Can you tell me about your parents?"

"Why?" She turned around and looked me up and down, and I could tell that she was doing a lot more than taking in my slacks and sequined corset.

"I didn't create you. But you're here. I create my dreams. All of them. So, how in the hell are you here, Tinkerbell? And why are you asking about my parents?"

I blinked. No one acted like this when I dream walked. Well, almost no one. "I'm visiting your dream. Like I said, I'm half-fairy. I need to get to know you."

She smiled. "Oh right. Almost forgot your wings, Tinkerbell. Don't worry, they match your outfit, and I'm sure they'll help you visit other people's dreams like the magical creeper you are." A pair of cheap costume wings appeared on my back, and I tried to pull them off me, but they were attached to the corset.

I gritted my teeth. The corset had been funny. This was a little much.

"When did your parents die?"

"My dad died in a car accident when I was six, and my mom died almost a year later." She smiled as she said it.

"I think you need to go, Tinkerbell." She looked up at the clouds that had grown larger with more frequent purple lightning. "It's about to get bad in here."

I ran my hand through my hair, and was about to say that I wasn't worried, but then I found myself laying on the roof of the sorority house. I reached out to test my tether to Rose and found that it had been cut.

I'd never had a tether cut before. I didn't even think

Chapter 4

that someone could cut my tether other than an incubus or succubus who was stronger than me. How could an untrained twenty-one year old do it?

I tried to reset my tether but found that it wouldn't stick. I could find no purchase in the twisting, writhing ball of magic within Rose.

The original thought was to learn about the girl so that someone would remember her, but now that I'd met her, I knew that I couldn't get any closer. She was too different, too unique. If I found out any more about her, I'd never be able to go through with killing her.

I sighed. Tomorrow, she would have to die. There was no other option. What a waste.

Chapter 5

Rose

That dream had been weird. And who was Tinkerbell? I giggled a little thinking about him in a sequined corset and pink wings. Then I remembered the bit of chest hair that had crested the top of it and how much I'd wanted to run my hands through it. That was almost weirder than him being there. I never wanted to talk to men. Much less touch them.

Those eyes, though. I kept thinking back on them. I never thought I'd see anyone else with eyes on fire like that. But *had* I even seen them? Was I so nostalgic over being reminded of my parents that I was making up people with their eyes?

He hadn't actually been at the club. We'd all looked for him. Why had I seen his reflection in the mirror? Was I going absolutely batshit crazy?

There were just so many things happening that were completely impossible. Either there was someone playing an

Chapter 5

incredible series of practical jokes on me or I was losing it.

It all seemed so real, so impossibly real. I could ignore any one of the bizarre oddities. People had weird dreams. They saw strange things when they'd been drinking. But that night in the alley? How could I possibly have escaped that?

"Ugh!" I muttered as I walked down the street to the bus stop. "It's no use thinking about it. Even if I'm going crazy, there's not a lot I can do about it."

I shook my head and took a deep breath. "I guess I'll just go buy some lunch and try to forget about it all like a normal, not batshit crazy person would do."

I sat down on the bench at the bus stop and noticed a woman for the first time. How had I missed her when I was walking up to the bench? Had she even been there before?

I looked at her, unable to turn away. This was the woman from the other night. The one who had tried to warn me. The crazy one.

She appeared to be homeless. Covered in clothes that looked like they hadn't been washed in months, there was a distinct smell coming from her. Yet, she had a smile on her face like there was nothing wrong in the world.

Sitting up straight, with her hair flowing wild and unkempt from a dirty headwrap, somehow, she looked like she didn't belong with the rest of the homeless that I'd met.

And then I saw her eyes. Just a little bit bigger than normal. Just a little bit further apart. And burning with that fire like the man in my dream. Like my parents. Like me.

In her hand was a small bag, and she dug a handful of birdseed out of it, tossing it to the pavement in front of us.

Birds of all variety flocked to the seeds, and she turned to me, giving me a wide smile. "Good morning, sweetheart," she said in a full-bodied voice. No hint of the cracking voice of an addict or smoker. And no hint of the crazy from the other night.

If this woman was homeless, she certainly wasn't the typical homeless woman, and she might have answers to all of the questions that were racing through my mind. I turned to face her and tried to figure out which of the million questions running through my mind to ask first.

"What did you mean two nights ago? The stuff about shadows having claws."

She reached down, seeming to ignore the question, and put her hand out, and I watched in complete surprise as a dove that had been eating the seeds walked over to her. Reaching down as if it were the most normal thing in the world, she picked the dove up and put it in her lap.

I rubbed my eyes and blinked several times as she petted the dove. It began to coo as though it were completely happy with the situation.

"Why is that bird letting you hold it?" I said it softly, as though my voice would scare the comfortable bird.

"We are all connected, my dear. Even the birds. You just need to know how to pluck the cords that run between us, and you'd be surprised at what will happen."

With an almost childish grin, she tossed the dove into the air. It flew upward, and I watched it, my eyes following its flight as I wondered what it would do. I felt like an idiot, expecting it to do something special, but after watching the woman pick up a wild bird and pet it, I wasn't sure what was possible.

Especially after the last few days.

"Morning," the woman said, drawing my attention away from the bird. Two frat boys wearing typical douchey

Chapter 5

sweaters and jeans walked by and glanced at the woman before laughing.

The boys tried to kick the birds eating the seeds as they walked by, but the birds moved out of the way just as they normally would have. "How do you sit next to that creature?" one of them said to me, but then he got a look at my face and noticed how different I was.

"Oh, I'm sorry. I thought you were a person and not that witch's pet frog." I felt my cheeks warm as a blush came over me, and I looked down. I'd been mocked my entire life for how I'd looked, but it never stopped hurting. I felt tears beginning to well up, but a strange compulsion made me look back up at them.

The one who had called me a frog began to laugh, throwing his head back. Something flashed in the air above him. He immediately began choking and fell to his knees. I didn't understand what I was watching, but I couldn't turn away as the asshole began vomiting on the grass beside the sidewalk.

I glanced at the homeless woman who was smiling even wider than earlier and beginning to giggle. The guy still standing was laughing at his friend as he vomited, and I heard his words more clearly than I thought possible.

"How did a bird shit in your mouth?" I blinked, knowing somehow that this dirty woman that sat next to me had done this. It was crazy. Completely insane. There was no way that anyone could have made that happen, but the coincidence was just too much.

"Dear," she said, reaching out and taking my hand as she looked me in the eye. "The world is about to become a very strange place for you. Very strange, indeed. Remember this moment."

At that moment, the bus pulled up, brakes squealing slightly, but I couldn't think of anything except the woman's words as they filled my mind. I couldn't look away. I couldn't turn away from the woman with eyes that held a flicker of the fire that the man in my dream had.

Then she began to speak. "The Prince is a friend in search of a secret that only you possess. He is death, but he will be your life when he finds your secret. Trust the Prince. Only he will be true."

The bus waited a few moments with the door open, and then it pulled away in a cloud of exhaust. The old woman released my hand as soon as the doors shut, and I felt like I could move again.

I yanked my hand away from her, confusion winding its way through me. What had just happened? How had this woman kept me still like that? I almost felt like I'd been stuck in place.

The words rang through my mind over and over again. *Trust the Prince. Trust the Prince. Trust the Prince.*

And then a crash filled the air. It was louder than anything I'd ever heard. Not an explosion. Like a massive can being crushed and shredded. Whatever had caused that sound had been terrible.

I jerked toward the sound and saw a plume of dust rising into the air a mile down the street. I didn't know what to do. The sane part of me said to run away, but a different part of me, a part that had gotten me into trouble too many times urged me to find out what had happened so that I could help somehow. It was the same part that had been stupid enough to become bait for rapists.

Still, those words echoed in my mind. *Trust the Prince.* I turned to the woman to see what she was doing. When I

Chapter 5

looked, she was gone. Somehow, without a sound, she'd disappeared in less than a second.

The sane part of me lost again as it normally did. I stood up and began running down the street. My heart raced, and that part of me that needed to help people surged, pushing the logical side of me away. I knew that regardless of what had happened, I was going to do whatever I could to help the people that had been hurt.

As I got closer, the dust seemed to clear, and I realized what catastrophe had happened. People had begun to gather around the edge of a wide hole that had opened up in the earth in the middle of the street.

A sinkhole. Supposedly, they were caused by leaking water slowly eating away at the rock underneath roads, but when I looked down at the twenty-foot deep hole, I couldn't believe that it was natural. It was so perfectly circular. Pipes sprayed water into the hole that held an entire bus.

The bus that I was supposed to be on.

Screams came from that bus. The people standing around the hole murmured quietly. People were on phones calling in to 911. But no one was helping.

I couldn't just stand there. I didn't know what I could do, but I couldn't listen to those screams without moving. I got down on my hands and knees and lowered myself over the edge of the hole. The concrete had plenty of handholds, and there had never been a tree that I couldn't climb.

One step, one handhold at a time, I began the descent into the hole that should have been my death.

Chapter 6

Sebastian

Why wasn't Rose dead? How could she possibly survive a crash like that without any wounds? I'd watched her all morning. She'd been at the bus stop.

Now she was climbing out of that hell hole? Climbing. Out. Not being rescued like all the other people. Covered in dust and blood, but otherwise unhurt. What in all the realms could she be to make it through that without any training? *And*, without using magic.

If she'd used magic, I would have known. I was keyed in on her scent and it still writhed around her with no outlet, no purpose.

I sat on a balcony overlooking the sinkhole that I'd created. I hadn't been able to watch the whole thing. I'd needed to be on the ground and nearby to create the hole. It was one of the limitations of working with stone.

Chapter 6

Maybe she hadn't got on the bus? But why would she be climbing out of the hole, then?

I turned away from the carnage below me. I'd already counted over fifteen dead. Whatever Rose was, there was no way that I was going to kill her from a distance.

I hated the idea of being close to her. It would allow the temptation to ignore my command. That close proximity to her, the knowledge that I would gain being within arm's reach of whatever she was. I was already struggling with the command, and if that bitch Seraphina hadn't sent Nyx to finish the job tonight, I would have already taken her to the Dark Court and hid her somewhere.

I ran my hands over the hartskin sheaths around my waist. Unlike a siren, Rose would be able to heal from a cut, but the iron dust that coated the inside of the sheath would be embedded into any wound that I caused with them.

It wouldn't be permanent. Slowly, a fairy would push the iron out of them, and then would be able to heal from the wounds, but it would keep her from healing instantly during a fight. I normally wouldn't worry about this with a half-blood, but this girl had surprised me at every turn. I couldn't take any chances.

Thinking about that made me even more confused. A fairy that had embraced her powers shouldn't be able to touch iron without physical discomfort. If she'd managed to somehow embrace them, she'd be lost in this world. Everything was made from iron and steel in the Mortal Realm, and it was one of the reasons the Fae had created the Immortal Realm to escape into.

Fairies were immensely powerful, but humans were plentiful. They reproduced a thousand times faster than fairies, and armed with iron and technology, the Fae would have become extinct hundreds of years ago.

I sighed and walked inside the apartment. The man who lived here was asleep on the floor. He would wake soon, and I needed to prepare for tonight. All of these questions would find no answers because, by midnight, she would be dead.

* * *

I sat in a condemned house. The walls smelled of mold and mildew, and the roof sagged. I'd had to run the vagrants living in the place out, and their belongings, along with empty bottles and cigarette butts, littered the floor.

I didn't need anything nice. I needed discreet and dark. I needed a place where I wouldn't be bothered. I needed to be close to Rose. And I needed this mirror. Silver-backed and large enough that I could crawl through it.

I closed my eyes, gathering my strength, and I built a tether between the two mirrors. With a muttered incantation, *droch*, I built the bridge that would allow me to both see and travel through the mirror gateway. Very similar to the one I'd used while she was at that club with her friends.

Rose was already asleep. I could see her snoring softly in her bed. Tanned legs lay just outside the white comforter that she curled up in. There was still dust in her wild chestnut hair from the crash.

I felt that same stirring inside me, and I gritted my teeth. This had to be done, and it had to be done soon. Nyx would be here. I touched the mirror and felt the pull. The bridge wanted to be used, wanted to be crossed, and its desires pulled me through to the other side.

Chapter 6

I stepped out of the mirror, the surface of the silver and glass rippling as I passed through. Mist covered my black boots, silencing them as always. Creeping across her room, I covered the distance in seconds.

As I approached, I saw her face. Eyes too large. Too far apart. No elongated features. No sharp features. She'd never claimed her magic. How had she done these things?

Yet, just as before, her scent filled the room. Like a campfire hidden in the woods, soft cedar slowly turning to ash. It was intoxicating. I'd never felt this way during a hunt, never met a being who stirred this part of me, a hunger for more than her power.

I needed to know what lay inside this woman, what power she held. I'd never felt this way before. Not in a thousand years. Leaving my daggers in their sheaths, I reached out to touch her. My bare hand crossed the space between us, and with a touch as light as the breeze, I built the connection between us that let me touch the tightly wrapped ball of magic that rested inside every Fae.

This was not a tether, this was a personal connection, more intimate than any physical touch could be. I was letting my soul touch hers.

And I pulled back immediately, shocked at what I'd found. "Gods damn you Seraphina," I hissed. Stepping backward, I moved away from Rose. It all made sense now. All of it. Especially why Seraphina would give me this contract.

I couldn't kill this girl. Regardless of the cost, I couldn't let her die. I began to turn around, to get back to the mirror. My foot caught on her desk chair, and I stumbled, sending the chair racing across the room to hit her wall.

Terrified that she would wake up while I was still in the

room, I leaped toward the mirror and managed to hit it directly in the center, sending me across the bridge and back to the abandoned house. Landing in a roll, I stood up.

I took a few deep breaths as my mind raced. Staring at a large swathe of mold that darkened the thirty-year-old wallpaper of the opposite wall, I tried to decide what to do.

Nyx would be coming for her. Soon. Seraphina knew that I wouldn't be able to kill Rose. She'd given me this charge for a single purpose: to kill me. Finally, she'd found a way to force my hand.

Rose wasn't a half-fairy. She was full-blooded. Half from the Dark Court and half from the Court of Light. The most difficult to fill requirement in becoming Queen of the Dark Court.

Chapter 7

Rose

I woke to the sound of a crash, and I sat up immediately, my heart pounding in my chest. My desk chair was still spinning against the opposite wall, but that wasn't what terrified me.

Black strips of cloth that looked to be part of a long coat were flowing into my mirror. Into my fucking mirror. The mirror rippled as the last bit of black went through it, and then everything was as it had been other than the slowly spinning chair.

"What in the holy hell?" I cursed. It had been a very long and confusing few days, and I was done with it.

Something was going on. I'd been a loner for most of my life. I'd gone day after day of feeling like an outsider. I was used to that. This was different. Things were happening that I didn't understand, and I was done with just accepting them.

I rolled out of bed and walked over to the mirror. I looked at

Princess of Shadows

it, and everything seemed normal except that instead of seeing myself, I saw the black cloth that had fluttered through my mirror.

It was part of a cloak. A cloak that some thief from a fairy tale would wear. Strips of tattered black cloth had been sewn together in an odd pattern rather than being made of a single piece of fabric.

It hung from the back of a man who stood looking away from the mirror. A matching hood covered his head, but there was no doubt that the person under it was male based solely on how large he was. He had been in my room. I hadn't dreamt that.

There had been far too many oddities these past few days. Too many things that were impossible. I reached out to the mirror and felt something, almost an emotion, coming from the mirror. A pulling. It begged me to just let it pull me forward. To let my hand slide through the glass into another place.

With only the slightest bit of pressure, I pushed against the mirror, and my hand slipped through the glass creating ripples across the surface. Inside the mirror, I could see it sticking out the other side. Surprised, I pulled back and looked at my hand.

Nothing was wrong. It was exactly as it had been. The mirror hadn't hurt me. It was just... a portal? I had a freaking magic portal in my room? I started thinking about what that meant, but then I stopped myself. Not now. I could think later. The man on the other side of the mirror knew what was happening. If I didn't talk to him now, he might disappear forever. Then, I would never find out what was going on.

With a deep breath and a prayer to whoever was listening, I

Chapter 7

stepped through the mirror.

And tripped on the edge of the mirror on the other side.

I let out a little shriek as I fell into the man in the black cloak, grabbing the edge of the cloak to keep from falling. He pulled away from me, and I slipped to the floor, falling face-first into a pile of old fast-food wrappers.

A soft growl came from the man, and I scrambled to my feet. He was holding two black glass knives in his hands as he crouched. He looked ready to get into a knife fight with me. The knives gleamed in the dim light of what looked like a crack house.

"Hold on!" I said, putting out one hand as if I could stop him from whatever he was planning.

He just stood there, silently watching me as I wiped the disgusting mess off my face. My heart was beating so fast that I wasn't sure if I was going to die to those wicked-looking knives or a heart attack.

"What are you doing here?" he growled. I tried to see his face, but it was shrouded in shadows by the hood.

I started taking steps back toward the mirror. "I saw your cloak in my mirror. Then... then, the mirror wanted me to touch it."

What in the holy hell had I been thinking going through that mirror? This guy had used some kind of spell to walk through a freaking magic mirror in the middle of the night. He was wearing all black, and everyone knew the guy wearing all black was the bad guy. This must be what those blondes in scary movies felt like right before they were eaten by the monster.

He slid the knives into strange white sheathes on his belt and stood up straight. That made me feel a lot better. I was sure he could still do very nasty things to me if he wanted to, but those knives were more than a little terrifying.

"I guess this was bound to happen," he said with a sigh. Then, he pulled his hood back, and I saw the man from the club. The man from my dream. It had all been real. All of it. Or I was completely off the reservation, and this was all some kind of schizophrenic nightmare.

Jet-black hair that hung down to his broad shoulders. Small strands of it crossed his face as though a wind were constantly blowing around him. A long face with a sharp jawbone and no facial hair at all. Dark red lips that seemed to curl in a smile even though he was pissed. Lips that somehow begged me to kiss them. Lips that called to me.

But his lips were nothing in comparison to his eyes. Piercing blue eyes that burned white-hot. Impossible to forget. Even more impossible to look away from. It was like he could see inside me, like he could touch my soul without moving his hand.

And yet, I managed to speak. Poorly. "Tinkerbell?" I asked hesitantly. As soon as I said it, I realized that this was probably not the right time to call him anything even remotely funny.

"No. But yes." I blinked, and he seemed to understand my confusion.

"My name is Sebastian, but you called me Tinkerbell in your dream." He leveled those piercing blue eyes at me and sighed. "Now we're officially fucked, Rose. There might have been a way out of it all before, but not anymore."

"Why? What's going on?" My heart had started to slow down when he'd put those knives up, but now that the big bad guy seemed scared, it kicked on the turbos, and I was positive that the heart attack was going to win out.

Chapter 7

He looked like he was about to say something when he moved to the mirror. I followed his eyes and saw my room from this side. So weird. This guy had been watching me while I was sleeping. I could see my bed from here.

The thought was gone almost as soon as it flashed through my mind as I realized what Tinkerbell had been interrupted by. A man dressed almost exactly the same as Sebastian was in my room. He held the same black glass knives in his hands, except his were already covered in blood.

Whose blood was that? Only Tiffany and Sasha were still in the sorority. Had this guy freaking murdered my sorority sisters?

"Fuck," he whispered in a voice barely audible even to me. I began to ask him what was going on, but he put his hand to my mouth, his other hand going to the back of my head.

All I got out was a squeak, but that was enough. The man in my room turned around almost instantly and began stalking towards the mirror. My eyes got wide as I realized that he was about to jump through the mirror just like both of us had.

Sebastian realized it at the same time, and without saying a word, he lifted me up and threw me over his shoulder. I began to scream, but it didn't seem to matter to Sebastian what I did at this point.

He reached out and touched the ground next to us. "Hold on," he whispered, and I immediately gripped his cloak in both hands. What kind of madness was I about to get into now?

He exhaled deeply, and then he hopped into the shadow that lay underneath us. He didn't hide in it. He literally jumped into a hole in the floor that wasn't there.

For a half-second, I felt a heavy pressure surrounding my entire body. Darkness and silence filled my senses. Darkness and silence that was so intense, it was blinding and deafening at the same time.

Then everything came back into existence. It was like when a movie or a song stutters for just a moment, and that silence or darkness is impossible to miss. But then everything starts back up like it never happened.

It was like that, except instead of the stutter happening to a movie or song. It was my very existence that stuttered. For that half-second, I was sure that I was as close to being dead as possible. There was this nothingness everywhere.

Then it was over, and there was no mistaking it. If I'd had a cute little dog with me, I'd have told him that we weren't in Kansas anymore. Instead of being in my room or a crackhouse or even a forest somewhere, Tinkerbell and I reappeared into something out of an alien movie. We were in a cave filled with a dim light that seemed to come from the very rock itself. I hesitated to think it, but it felt almost magical. A perpetual gray twilight. No color. No smell. No sound.

There was a mist, though. Barely noticeable, it filled the tunnel we were in. I took a deep breath and tried to calm down, tried to stop the panic that threatened to make me freeze again, and I felt the mist move against my lips, soft and damp. Like fog on a cool morning.

I was still hanging over Tinkerbell's shoulder, and I tried to wiggle off him, but his arm clamped down tightly over my waist, holding me tightly against his shoulder like I was a bag of flour.

"I'll explain everything soon, but we have to move," Sebastian said as he began sprinting down the tunnel.

He took a deep breath, and the mist gathered around him. When he exhaled, a mirror image of us appeared. It kept pace

Chapter 7

with us, and when Sebastian ran his hand along the walls of the tunnel, the mirror image did the same thing.

I started to yell as what was happening started to click into place. Some crazed, knife-wielding, bad guy was abducting me and running through a magical cave after I'd teleported through a mirror into a crackhouse. As soon as any sound left my lips, Tinkerbell slapped my ass hard enough that the sound carried through the caves, echoing over and over again. "Shut up or you're going to get us both killed," he whispered.

Then, the copy of us that had been running next to us somehow flowed into the rock. Sebastian kept running, and I looked down, realizing that mist had surrounded his boots, becoming almost solid. His footfalls should have made noise, but they didn't. Somehow, that mist was keeping his footsteps completely silent.

Once more, he created a copy of us and began to run his hands along the wall. The entire time, he continued to sprint, and I thought of how much I'd run in my life. How could he possibly still be sprinting while carrying me? I would have been dead a mile back if I'd tried to do this.

My awe went away pretty quickly as the minutes passed. I wanted to scream, but I knew that he'd just hit me again, and maybe he was right. Maybe that other guy with freaking *bloody* knives was the actual bad guy.

The longer that he carried me, the more the questions that had no answers plagued me. Where were we going? Where were we? How'd we get here? How did I walk through a magic mirror? Who was chasing me? And, more than anything, who the fuck was Sebastian?

The copy slid into the wall just as the last one had. Sebastian still ran. The tunnel was eerily silent as we moved. No footsteps. No panting. No dripping water. No noise.

He put his hand against the tunnel wall again as he ran, letting his fingers trail against the strange gray rock. We ran into a fork in the tunnel, and he stopped.

Then I heard a sound. The first one since we'd gotten to the tunnels. Footfalls. Far away, but definitely there. Did the mist not cover the other man in black?

Another copy of us formed from the mist, and it began running just as we had. The copy of Sebastian began to run his fingers against the stone, and then he stopped, sliding into the stone, becoming a shadow as he did.

I could feel Sebastian's heart pounding, but his breathing hadn't changed. I knew instinctively that silence was our best friend in these tunnels because our tail could hear us just as easily as we could hear him. I would trust Sebastian just long enough to take me away from bloody knives guy.

Sebastian turned down the split, making another copy of him as we ran. The copy slid into the stone. We moved just a little further down, and Sebastian made yet another copy, sending it much farther down the tunnel.

I watched it, still amazed at how realistic it was. Fully solid. Identical in every way. It moved just as we had. At one point, a copy had turned around, and I'd seen the copy of Sebastian's eyes, and that was when I realized the difference. There was no fire in them. None at all.

I smiled to myself when I realized that I could see the difference. It only brought those same questions back to me. Questions that couldn't be asked here. I would get answers though. And soon.

The homeless woman's words echoed in my mind. *The world is about to become a very strange place for you.* She had been more

Chapter 7

accurate than I could have imagined. How had she known? That was the second time that she'd predicted something no one could have known. A shiver ran through me. What else had she said? I didn't have long to think on it, though.

A second later, Sebastian touched the wall in front of us, and then we slid through the nothingness.

Chapter 8

Rose

When we left the nothingness, I was immediately confronted with the fact that we still weren't in Kansas anymore. Not even close. I'd thought the tunnel was weird. I was wrong. This place was even weirder. Like, pinnacle of weirdness.

I glanced up at the night sky and realized that two moons hung in the sky. One white, like moons are supposed to be. The other was purple, not at all like moons are supposed to be.

And the grass was weird. Also pinnacle of weirdness. Unlike normal grass, this was green and purple. The colors swirled in each blade in different amounts. And it didn't crunch when we walked. It seemed stronger, yet softer as I walked on it with bare feet.

Even the air seemed weird. Little sparkles seem to pop in and out of existence like lightning bugs. Except that when one

Chapter 8

popped into existence right in front of me, it was nothing but light.

When we'd arrived in this land of the bizarre, I'd had a whole list of questions. Now I had two. Where the fuck were we, and who the fuck was Sebastian. Okay, there were three questions. How do I get home?

A wide field spread out before us. There was a small pond, and beyond that, a forest. It was beautiful. Almost normal. A scene from a storybook if you ignored the purple moon, invisible lightning bugs, and weirdo grass. It even included a beautiful, pure white horse grazing in the middle of it.

With a freaking silver horn sticking out of his head.

"Is that…" I asked, pointing at the horse, "is that a fucking unicorn?" Sebastian set me down and turned around, giving the unicorn a glance.

"Yeah. Never seen a unicorn before?" The tone of his voice told me that he gave absolutely no shits about the unicorn. None. I mean, I guess unicorns were normal for people who lived in purple moon land. Like crickets or something.

"No, Tinkerbell. Not a lot of unicorns in my area. I think they got put on an endangered species list a few years ago."

He looked at the ground and shook his head, not responding to my sarcasm as he headed towards the pond.

"Hey," I said, trying to catch up to him, "Sebastian, I'm sorry. I get snippy when I walk through magic mirrors and get carried through weird tunnels by strange men in black cloaks. And, of course, when someone is trying to kill me."

"I guess those are new things for you," he said softly. He pulled his hood back over his head as he walked.

"Please stop. Talk to me, please. I don't know what's going on." I reached out and grabbed his arm and was surprised

Princess of Shadows

at just how large it was. My hand didn't even get close to wrapping around it.

Sebastian pulled away immediately, but he did stop. "You're a fairy like I told you in your dream. We just traveled from the Mortal Realm through a tunnel between the realms called a warren, and now we're in the Immortal Realm where your kind rule."

"I was sent to kill you, but I decided not to for reasons of my own. Now, the leader of the Assassin's Guild is hunting for both of us. The Queen of the Fae wants both of us dead, and I have to get you to a safe place before I can deal with her. Is that enough of an explanation before I get a drink of water?"

I just stared at him, and I guess he took that as a yes because he turned back to the pond. When he started walking, I started following. What else was I supposed to do? I guessed that I was in fairy world with someone who was hired to kill me, or I was a schizophrenic nutjob and this was my life now. The unicorn chomping on purple grass a few hundred yards away seemed almost normal in comparison.

"Why does this Queen lady want to kill me?"

Without turning around, he said, "Because you have bloodlines from both courts. That means that there's a slight possibility that you could be a rival queen, and there's no way that she'd let you claim your place in the courts if that were a possibility."

"Hold on there. Let's back up a second. You're telling me that my parents were fairies? How could they be fairies? Fairies have wings, and I distinctly remember them both being wing-free. That's one of those things even a kid would remember."

We were nearing the pond, but Sebastian answered anyway. "Almost certainly. There's an extremely unlikely possibility

Chapter 8

that both of your parents were half fairies, and you somehow came out as full-blooded, but that's far less likely than the possibility that you simply didn't know about your parents' magic."

"Full-blooded fairies all have wings. Your parents probably just hid them or gave up their magic to live a mortal life. It's not unheard of."

"Then why don't I have wings?" I turned to show him my back. "If I'm a fairy, then where are my wings?"

He chuckled. "You're a fairy, but you have yet to claim your magic. You've never been to the Immortal Realm, so you couldn't have claimed it before."

He knelt down and put his hand under the placid water, scooping it into his mouth. I sighed and began to pace.

How was I a fairy? Wouldn't I know? Wouldn't I be able to do magic or something? Then the night in the alley flashed through my mind. I'd thought it was a miracle, but maybe it was magic. It was when everything had changed.

"How did you find me?" I whispered.

Sebastian took another drink of water before he stood up. "You pulled power from the Immortal Realm. That happens rarely enough that we track it. The Queen's seers recorded where and when it happened, and they made this." He reached into a pocket of that cloak, and he pulled out a sheet of weird paper that had been rolled up.

He slowly unrolled it so that I could see what was on it. A painting. Of me. But not me. My face was different, a prettier version of me, full of sharp angles where my eyes didn't look weird. Kind of like Tinkerbell. It was me, though. No doubt.

I took a deep breath. I had two choices here. I could either curl up into a ball of disbelief, or I could run with it. Even if I was batshit, living in my own fairy dreamworld couldn't be that bad, could it?

"Alright, Tink, I'm in. What do we do now?" I was out of my element. I had no idea what the rules of this game were or who the players were. All I knew was that I was in a field with a unicorn and some weird, sexy assassin, and I happened to be a fairy. I needed some guidance.

"Like I said, I'm going to get you someplace safe. Then I'm going to find a way to deal with the Queen. Somehow. All while trying not to die or get you killed. Does that sound like a good enough plan to you?"

"Hold on. I just walked through my first magic mirror about an hour ago, and that's the first unicorn I've ever seen, but I've heard plans before. That one happens to be terrible. No details. No actual plan."

"I'm being hunted by a magical assassin and the Queen of fairyland. Somehow, you, the other assassin she hired, is going to save me from both of them. I don't know, I kind of feel like a plan is slightly necessary."

"Then make a plan. If that makes you feel better, you can plan for the next few hours since we need to stay here and make sure that we're not being followed."

I crossed my arms and realized for the first time that I was still wearing what I'd fallen asleep in, a pair of booty shorts and a tank top. How was I getting chased by an assassin while wearing clothes I wouldn't be caught dead in public in?

I guess that it didn't matter. Tinkerbell was wearing a death eater cloak, so I wasn't sure any of my clothes would have been "appropriate" for fairyland travel. I just wished that I had my running shoes. "What happens if we're being followed?"

"I'll kill him. He works alone, so if he's dead, then we're

Chapter 8

mostly safe. I'd rather that it didn't come to that, though."

Sebastian lowered his hood and walked over to a tree, and I followed him. He sat down and leaned against the trunk, continuing to look to where we'd come through the... what did he call it? A warren?

I sat down next to him and began to pick at the grass. It really was strange stuff. It didn't have the same stiffness that human grass had. Instead, it was almost like really thick hair. Full of bounciness, but flat like grass. Weird stuff.

A picture of fairyland being on the top of a guy's head popped into my mind. I had to bite my tongue to keep from laughing out loud at what he'd look like with weird purple and green hair and little bugs fighting wars on the top of his head. And unicorns nibbling his hair.

Strangely enough, it almost sounded like a plausible myth. Wasn't there a Greek myth about how we all lived on top of a titan's body or something? Then there was the Iroquois story about how we all lived on the back of a turtle.

"So, we just hang out and wait to see if a murderer stops by?" I asked.

Sebastian nodded and kept watching the spot.

"We could chat," I suggested. "You could tell me some more about all of this instead of the 'I'm annoyed' version."

He sighed and ignored me.

"Look. I don't know how long we have to stay together, but we might as well make this as pleasant as possible. I need to know more stuff. And you look like you're about to pass out. Let's chat."

"What do you want to know?" He turned his attention to me, and I felt those eyes on me, but they seemed different. Were they grayer?

Princess of Shadows

"First off, if I'm a fairy, how do I get my wings?"

He pulled his dagger out of his sheath and began to toss it into the air, letting it spin several times before catching it. He didn't look at it while he did this. His eyes never followed it or left my face. It was disconcerting to say the least.

"You simply have to say, 'I, Rose, claim my birthright.' That's it."

I raised an eyebrow in question, but instead of saying anything, I shrugged. What's the worst that could happen?

"Well, here it goes. I, Rose, claim my birthright." I waited a few seconds. No flash of light or harp played. No ray of light shining on me like a Harry Potter scene.

"That's it?" I asked. "No fanfare?"

He pursed his lips and shook his head. "Nope. You'll notice the changes soon enough though."

"Okay, next question. Where are we going to after you decide the other stabby guy isn't going to show?"

"The other stabby guy is named Nyx, and he happens to be a decent guy with terrible orders. We're going to a safehouse of mine. Then we'll wait out the night there. Tomorrow, we're going to get you a new scent."

"My scent is just fine, thank you." Sebastian shook his head in annoyance.

"Your magical scent, little girl. You have a very distinct magical scent. It comes from the blending of your bloodlines and your uniquely human experiences. Anytime you use magic, you leave your scent behind, and it's trackable. Kind of like a dog pissing on a tree."

I blinked at him. "Did you just compare me doing magic to a dog pissing on a tree?"

He shrugged. "It's a good analogy."

Chapter 8

"Have you ever talked to a woman before?" I asked, shaking my head.

"I've done a lot more than talk, Rose. I learned a long time ago that women really don't care what you say to them as long as you do things that other men can't. So I stopped caring about their delicate sensibilities."

"Well Tinkerbell, I've got news for you. Most women that I know care about what men say to them."

He grinned at me. "Like Sasha? She certainly cared about what Tony said, didn't she?"

"How do you know about Sasha and Tony?" I asked in surprise.

"They were there the night of your twenty-first birthday. I watched all four of you the entire night. Tony is a far bigger ass than me, and he's not nearly as big in the ways Sasha claims."

"Well Sasha's a slut, and he's rich. That doesn't count." Sebastian just stared at me with the edge of his lip curled in a smile.

"What woman isn't a slut when it comes to the right man with the right looks and the right amount of power?" he asked as he arched his eyebrows while somehow maintaining that infuriatingly sleepy expression.

"Not me. I'm a virgin," I said, getting fed up with his obviously misogynistic view of women. "I've never put up with a man talking to me like that." I stood up and began walking away from him. He had managed to convince me that being quiet was better than talking to him.

Suddenly, I felt his presence behind me. Somehow, he'd stood up and moved behind me without making a sound. The thought of him running silently through the tunnels of the warren flashed through my mind, but they were overshadowed by a feeling I'd never had before.

It was like my stomach had twisted in knots, and my skin seemed extra sensitive. My breath came out more quickly, and everything felt just a little bit warmer than it had.

I turned around slowly, knowing what I'd see. I was wrong. The man in the black cloak was gone, the cloak in a pile on the ground. Instead, Sebastian stood in a black, armless silk tunic that seemed to meld to his body and a pair of linen pants that tucked into the bottoms of his black boots.

The whole outfit hugged his body in a way that didn't seem natural. It showed off every muscle in his body, and I knew how he could have run for so long. His body was perfect. Tight, strong. Fiercely male.

Dangerous.

His black hair hung loosely around his neck and shoulders, and he felt so big. I wasn't short, but he seemed to tower over me. And those lips that were just faintly redder than normal. A vision of those lips on my body in ways I'd never dreamed of flashed through my mind.

All of that was insignificant in comparison to his eyes. Icy pale blue eyes stared down at me as he put his hand to my cheek. They claimed me in their sight, demanding that I accept his touch. A demand I was more than happy to accept. I felt just as helpless as I had when I'd talked to the old woman on the bench, except that the last thing I wanted to do was turn away.

His touch was like lightning. Lightning that ignited my body with a sensation that I could never have explained. Bliss. Excitement. Energy. Need.

Lust.

For the first time in my life, I knew what lust was. He moved his hand down my neck towards my collarbone, and

Chapter 8

as he made the curve toward my shoulder, I wished that he'd gone lower. His fingers never did anything but graze my skin, turning it red hot and desperate for more.

My breath came out in short, shallow bursts like my body wanted to move as little as possible so that I wouldn't disturb him, wouldn't stop him. He craned his head down to my neck, and as his hot breath touched my skin, I had to bite my lip to keep from moaning.

Then he stopped moving, just letting his breath run over me. I could feel the antsy feeling course through me. I wanted his touch, and I wanted those lips on me. Those brutally beautiful lips.

"I guess that you're a slut just like Sasha," he whispered in my ear and pulled away, gliding backward inhumanly fast on boots coated in mist. As soon as he was away from me, I felt all of my old emotions racing back to me, and it was good that he was further away than he had been.

"You used magic on me!" I screamed.

He chuckled and threw his cloak back on. "No," he said as he pulled the hood down, letting it hang behind him, "there was no magic. You would have been begging me to do less than appropriate things if I'd used magic on you at all."

I couldn't prove it, but I knew that he'd used some kind of weird fairy magic on me. That was the only reason that I could have felt like that. I'd never felt so... so slutty in my life. And there was no way that it was just because he was big and sexy.

"You're a liar, Sebastian. Now I know that I can't trust anything you say." I stomped away from him, infuriated with how vulnerable I'd been to him, but even more angry at the fact that he might have been telling the truth.

I glanced at Sebastian out of the corner of my eye, and he

Princess of Shadows

was sitting with his back against the tree again, looking at the spot where we'd come out of the warren. I started walking, hoping that simply getting some distance from that obnoxious fairy man would help soothe the feelings that still coursed through me.

They didn't make any sense. I was pissed at him. More pissed than I'd been in a long time, yet my body seemed to thrum with the need for his hands on me. At least my breathing wasn't coming out like some panting puppy anymore.

I began to run. Running had always helped to clear my mind, and this place, although it was different than anything I was used to, was still the wild. The weird springy grass felt like a wonderful carpet under my bare feet, and for some reason, I felt like I was home.

Even then, I couldn't help but look back at Sebastian against the tree. His eyes had turned towards me, but he didn't get up. He knew that there was nowhere for me to run. It wasn't like I could hop on a bus bound for humanland. At least not that I knew of.

I was so lost in this world. So lost about myself and about that damned man. Somehow, even knowing there was an assassin who was supposedly going to try to kill me just didn't compare to the feeling of lost.

I closed my eyes before I even turned away from Sebastian and let my other senses open up. I heard the soft buzzing of some kind of insect. They had insects in fairyland? The scent of cinnamon floated in the air. Where did that come from?

Then there was a very loud snort. I opened my eyes immediately and saw just how close I was to the unicorn. I stopped abruptly, almost falling as I realized that I'd come within fifty feet of the massive creature. I'd been wrong. This

Chapter 8

wasn't a horse with a horn on its head. It was a Clydesdale with a horn on its head. My head wouldn't even reach its back.

The unicorns that humans had memories of must have been foals. Normal sized and nice. I'd been around horses a time or two, and I knew the pawing at the ground and snorting for what it was. A warning.

I wouldn't be able to pet the thing much less come even an inch closer. He, and I was sure it was a he, was extremely unhappy about my proximity. I turned around and ran back the way I'd come. Back towards Sebastian. For all his frustrating attitude, Sebastian was the closest thing to a protector that I had in this place.

And if that unicorn decided to charge me, he would be my only hope of escape in a field this large. I didn't want to think about what that horn could do even ignoring the fact that he was a beast that every human knew would have powerful magic.

I looked behind me and saw him barreling towards me, hooves pounding the ground and throwing up a cloud of sparkling dust behind him.

"Help!" I screamed as I looked at Sebastian who was still sitting against the tree several hundred yards away.

The unicorn was getting closer and closer by the second, and Sebastian wasn't even moving. He just stared at me, his head resting against the trunk and his hands flat on the ground.

My lungs felt like they were going to give out at any moment, but I kept sprinting away from that terribly sharp horn that I was sure would pierce my back at any moment.

And then a fog began to rise around me. I didn't stop running, but I changed direction as soon as it covered my vision. And I felt hands wrap me in an embrace, one arm around my chest, and the other around my mouth, silencing the scream that instinctively tried to escape my mouth.

"Silence, Rose." Sebastian's voice. I listened, hearing a trumpeting and snorting as the unicorn searched in vain for me. Hooves pounded the ground again, and I knew that Sebastian had saved me from yet another brush with death.

His hand moved from my mouth, and I felt it wrap around my hand. It was strangely cold. Maybe that was what happened when you used magic? I was blinded by the fog that was so thick that I wouldn't have been able to see my hand in front of my face. Yet, the light seemed to pass through the mists easily enough because it wasn't dark.

Sebastian tugged on my hand, and I followed him. How had he gotten to me so quickly? I didn't trust this man, but I trusted myself even less at this point. How was I supposed to know that a unicorn would be so aggressive? I hadn't tried to hurt it. I hadn't even really gotten that close to it.

A horse would never have acted like that, even a wild one. It may have rushed me, but it wouldn't have pursued me like that. Then again, a horse didn't have a giant horn on its head to gore people that annoyed it.

The fog began to fade, and I found myself back at the tree that Sebastian had been sitting in front of. He was still sitting there. The hand that had held me was fading just like the fog, and I blinked.

He'd seemed so real, but he'd been just another copy. Like the ones in the tunnel. "Why didn't you tell me that unicorns were so aggressive?" I asked accusingly, my hands on my hips even though I was still shaking from my brush with death.

"You didn't ask?" he said with a shrug. "It's generally a good idea to expect everything in the Immortal Realm to

Chapter 8

be aggressive. Then you'll be pleasantly surprised when something isn't. But, unicorns are one the worst since they don't die easily, but they're easy to aggravate."

I blinked a few times trying to register what he'd said. "Have you killed a unicorn?"

"No. As I said, they're tough creatures to kill. Especially when they're in a herd, and they're almost always in a herd. He's young, and it's mating season, so he's probably trying to find a mare to breed. The older males in his herd wouldn't have let a young stallion like him anywhere near their mares."

"I never would have stopped here if there'd been a herd, but I'm not worried about a solitary young male. They haven't learned enough magic to deal with mine."

He stood up and smiled, and his eyes seemed even mistier now, as though there were almost transparent clouds beginning to cover his pupil.

"Your eyes change color," I said softly, completely ignoring the comments about unicorn mating. My mind wasn't ready to think about things like that.

"So do yours. It's a Fae thing. But it's been long enough. Time to go. There's another warren just a short walk away from here that will lead to a safehouse where we can spend the night. Tomorrow, we need to make you smell like another woman."

He grinned and glanced down at me before chuckling to himself, "And maybe pick up some clothes that don't make you look so terribly human." I glanced at my clothes and realized that being in the mists had made all of my clothes damp. Especially my shirt where his copy had held me.

I'd felt at least a little embarrassed because of them before, but now I felt more humiliated than when I'd had to wear that skank outfit to the club.

"Some clothes and *shoes* would be nice," I said in agreement. "Though, the grass is nicer here."

He nodded and began to walk away from the pond we'd sat down by. Into the woods. I glanced at the unicorn who was still grazing in the same area as he had been. He looked up and watched me as though he was trying to decide whether or not he should pursue me again.

After a second, he put his mouth to the grass, and I felt just a little bit better. Who knew that a freaking unicorn would be the first thing to try to kill me?

Then I realized that it wasn't. Sebastian was. He'd come to kill me, and I still wasn't completely sure he wasn't going to. All I knew about him was that he'd stolen me away from my life and brought me to a world where, according to him, everything was going to try to kill me. Even unicorns.

Everything else was based on what he'd told me. The assassin could be trying to rescue me. I had no proof that I was anything other than human. All I knew was that everything had turned insane the moment that I'd seen him.

I followed him anyway. What else was I supposed to do?

Chapter 9

Sebastian

I was not a fan of this woman. Queen or not. She talked incessantly. Every moment that we finally had a moment of silence, she began jabbering. I'd never met another fairy who could manage to annoy me as much as her. Except maybe Seraphina. Maybe. At least I had never had to travel with Seraphina.

"So, can all fairies do this whole mist thing? Or is that just a Tinkerbell thing?"

I pulled my hood up trying to keep from showing her just how annoying she was. If, on the very unlikely chance, she was a Queen, the last thing I wanted was for her to realize that I disliked her this much.

"My name is Sebastian. Please stop referring to me as Tinkerbell if you want me to answer any more of your idiotic human questions."

Princess of Shadows

I gave her a moment to respond, and she seemed to consider it before nodding. I'd saved her life while putting mine in jeopardy, and she struggled to say my name. This is why I didn't deal with the Mortal Realm or humans.

"All fairies have powers, but they differ based on bloodlines and other things. Most of them tend to have power over a specific element or piece of the world. Some are natural gardeners because they can help the plants grow more quickly or more distinctly. They'll build entire homes out of living plants."

"Others can command water and tend to work on or around the water, creating currents where there aren't any or sensing fish hiding far below the surface."

"The mists are mine. It's an uncommon power, but that's probably for the best. There aren't a lot of ways for the Fae to make use of the mists other than for murder."

"Interesting. So, what's mine?" she asked like I was some kind of seer capable of reading the soul.

"I have no clue. You'll have to figure that out yourself or maybe with the help of a seer. Maybe we could just be quiet for a little bit? The warren is close, but I have to sense it, and it's a lot easier without all the talking."

She finally shut her mouth for more than two seconds, and I was grateful that she believed that fairy truth. As with all fairy truths, it wasn't a lie. It was easier to feel the warrens hidden beneath the surface of this Realm if I was able to concentrate. Once upon a time, a thousand years ago when I was learning how to shadow walk with Nyx at my side, I would have needed quiet. Now it was nearly as easy as running.

Rose continued to look around us as we passed through the forest. The trees were different than her human ones.

Chapter 9

Little berries hung from the limbs in small rings. Half were poisonous and half were delicious. If you saw only the berries, you'd never be able to tell the difference, but underneath the berries, the leaves of the poisonous rings were edged in white. The edible ones had leaves edged in black.

A blue-skinned pixie sat on one of the trees picking berries out of a ring and shoving them into its mouth. It began to scream at us as we passed, and Rose jumped, her body brushing against mine.

I inhaled sharply as my body reacted instinctively, catching her before she fell over me. The touch of her skin sent sharp reminders of what she could be. Dark and light mixed in a weaving, twisting blend of powers that was intoxicating to a being such as me.

She jerked away from me, and I knew that she felt the attraction to me that all Fae felt. Somehow, the only time that she'd ever shown me anything even close to what other Fae had shown me, she had been angry at feeling those emotions. No one else had ever been angry that they'd lusted after me.

The memory of how she'd reacted was burned into my mind because unlike the thousands of other partners I'd had throughout my life, when I pulled away, she didn't beg me to keep going. Instead, she'd turned away as well.

Maybe it was just because she didn't know my reputation. Maybe it was because I hadn't used magic. Maybe it was because she had that twisted bloodline. It had been a very long time since I'd had any interactions with someone from both sides.

I found the warren and stopped. Rose waited patiently as I took her hand and made the transition into the tunnel. When I stepped into the tunnel and pulled her along, she managed to stay upright, a surprising feat from someone not used to shadow walking.

She quickly gave me a smile to cover up the discomfort of sliding between realms. It wasn't like using a portal. Portals were permanent bridges between the worlds. There were no gaps like there were when using the shadows to cross over. Many people believed that the space between the worlds and the warrens was where people went when they died.

I listened, letting the mists enhance any sounds. Warrens were excellent places to stage an ambush, though the number of people capable of shadow walking made it difficult to overwhelm an enemy. Slipping in and out took almost no energy, and unless the traveler was extremely wary, it was easy to be caught from behind.

Luckily, we didn't have far to go. I didn't relish the idea of carrying Rose again. If I hadn't been so focused on fleeing, it would have been difficult to touch her like that without becoming inflamed with hunger with no possibility of sating it.

Thinking about that forced me to realize that I'd used far more magic than I should have. Normally, I'd have enjoyed a relaxing night with one of the many female Fae who would welcome me. They were always more than willing to let me feed on them in return for giving them a night they'd never forget. For some reason, I didn't feel like I could do that with Rose near me.

I turned around and began walking. A small squeak came from Rose, and she covered her mouth. She already understood the dangers of these tunnels which was slightly impressive. Humans, and half-bloods who had grown up as humans were notoriously stupid. She pointed at her feet, and

Chapter 9

I nodded. Mists coated her bare feet, cushioning her footfalls and protecting them from any jagged points in the stone.

I hadn't told her that I would do that, and it must have surprised her. I made a mental note to explain what I was going to do. I rarely traveled with other people, so I wasn't used to having to explain each and every thing that I did. It would be much better once I could get her stashed somewhere so I could deal with the real problem of what to do about Nyx and Seraphina.

She recovered well enough at least, falling into step behind me. My fingers trailed the rock, sensing picture after picture of the shadow that I would step through if I slid between the realms.

Some went to the Mortal Realm, but the vast majority went to the Immortal Realm. These tunnels were connected to both, but the warrens were closer to the Fae.

After only a few minutes, I took Rose's hand silently, and I made the transition. We stepped out of the shadow of a tree, appearing from the ground as though we were floating out of a hole. This time, Rose stumbled slightly, but I caught her, my hood slipping off my head in the process.

"You did well," I said softly. Her eyes stared into mine, and her green eyes slowly turned a bright amber. I felt her desires stirring inside her as my hands held her bare arms.

Lightning bolts of power began to flood my hands, and I felt the hunger growing. That power teased me, tempting me to push her into something she would regret. The hunger of an incubus was not like an earthly hunger. There was no growling stomach, no hunger pains.

Instead, it was a slowing of the body. A slowing of the mind. Pains in the extremities.

Princess of Shadows

I wasn't there yet, but I needed to be careful. My body knew it. I'd spent the majority of my life with a topped-off tank of power, and I'd become careless. I shouldn't have made the replica yesterday. I should have simply run and caught her. Even a unicorn would have retreated from me. He would have smelled my power and backed off if I had made no aggressive moves toward him.

I'd been showy, and now I was feeling the hunger returning. It would be many days before I would be able to feed again. I glanced down at Rose, and the thought flashed through my mind. *Unless she were willing...*

No. She was too inexperienced. Regardless of how annoying she was, no one's first time should be with an incubus. It would ruin their experiences for the rest of their lives. And there was no way that an incubus could be monogamous.

I pulled away from her and pointed at a cottage in the distance. Simple and small, no one would expect a man of my power and prestige to stay in a place like this, much less own it. I'd even told the gardener to let the flowers that grew inside the cobblestone wall stay a little overgrown.

"That's beautiful," Rose said, her voice more chipper than I'd expected. "Is it yours?"

"One of many, but I happen to like this one more than most of the others. It's where I would choose to live if I had the option."

She nodded, surprisingly quiet as we began to walk towards the cottage. The wooden gate squeaked as I opened it. Rose glanced around the front of the house, smiling at the flowers that grew along the wall and the statuaries that had been placed throughout the flowers.

The statuaries were simple stones that had been carved by a

Chapter 9

local stoneworker into the shapes of various animals from both Realms. A small rabbit sat amongst the vines of a honeysuckle and a boggart was perched in the split of a rose bush.

Others found homes in the plants while several stood like sentries in front of the door. Large and imposing, a stone gargoyle stood opposite a lion on either side of the door. Rose smiled at them and ran her fingers over them.

The door swung open without the hint of a creak. The home's caretaker was meticulous in his duties, and he was paid well for it. The last thing I wanted to do when I came here for a moment of peace from the Courts was to find chores.

I opened the pantry and pulled a few small bags out. Travel rations. Nothing to be excited about, but it would do until tomorrow when we went to town. I set them on the wooden table of the one-room cottage as Rose closed the door and latched it.

We were in the Dark Realm, the half of the Immortal Realm that the Dark Court ruled over, and so more than half the hours of the day were dark. Only a thin period was truly lit by the sun, and even that seemed dim compared to the Light Realm.

The darkness was at its peak at this point. Even the moons didn't truly illuminate the world. It was the point in the night when only the darkest of beings felt completely comfortable. The rest would take a nap or even sleep during this period.

"Food's on the table. Eat what you want, and I'll eat what's left. We'll get breakfast in town, so don't worry about saving anything."

She nodded, and I saw her glance at the bed. The single bed that was meant for me and no one else. I sighed. No one else had ever slept in that bed. If I had been hungry, I would have taken my companion for the night somewhere else. Her bed or an inn.

"So, who's going to sleep on the floor, *Sebastian?*" she asked, putting more than a little emphasis on my name.

"I'm sleeping in my bed. I already saved your life twice now. I've already met my chivalry quota for the week. You can sleep on the floor or next to me in my bed, but I must warn you that I snore. And probably drool."

She sneered at me. "The floor will be fine as long as you don't have rats. The bed probably has bed bugs anyway."

I ignored her jab since I was getting what I wanted and obviously didn't have bed bugs. Whatever those were.

Rose sat down at the table and began to open the bags. I lit an oil lamp and let it burn low, a soft light in the room. No need to make my eyes hurt just for her benefit.

I sat down across from her as she pulled pieces of dried meat from one of the pouches and put them in her mouth. "These are really good," she said between bites. A part of me wanted to snarl at her as she ate more than half of the meat. This was one meal for me. All of it.

She moved to the bag of dried fruit and began to shovel it into her mouth like an animal. I had to grit my teeth as I watched her. How could someone eat like that? She wasn't some vagrant who hadn't eaten in days. The more I looked at her, the more I doubted that she could ever be a Queen. Just by watching her move and talk, her lack of respect and poise annoyed me.

I stood up, unable to stand watching her eat. Going to the cabinet, I pulled a bottle of wine out. I poured myself a glass of the deep red liquid, and then I glanced at Rose who was eyeing me and the bottle.

Chapter 9

Snarling, I got another glass from the cabinet. *Great. She's going to eat all my food, and now she's going to drink all my wine. She'll probably slurp it like a mug of ale.*

I handed her the glass, and she took a sip before I'd even sat down. "This is really good. What kind is it?"

"Are you really asking about the type of Fae wine you're drinking? Would you know the difference between a Bhaldraithe and a Talún?"

I smirked when she shook her head. "I guess that since you can't really go back to the Mortal Realm, you should start learning these things. It's a Talún. Not my favorite, but it's local to the region."

"It tastes like a darker blush, but it's more... intense? Like the flavors are stronger without any of the chemical tastes."

"They're grown in the Immortal Realm, so magic is infused in their very essence. That's the intensity you're tasting."

I took a sip of my wine as I leaned back in the chair and let out a deep breath, feeling the stress of the day lighten just a little bit. I still needed to get Rose to a safe place before I returned to the Courts to deal with Seraphina, but at least we'd survived the day. More than that, I needed to figure out how exactly I was supposed to deal with her. I'd gone against her commands, but those commands had gone against the morals of the Dark Court.

Against my own morals.

That didn't matter when Seraphina was Queen of both Courts though. I glanced at Rose and asked the question that had stopped me. Could she fill the empty seat? Was that why Seraphina had put the contract out on her, or was it simply because she knew that I'd never kill someone who had even the slightest chance of filling the seat?

Princess of Shadows

I sighed. There was no way to tell. Not unless I brought her to the Dark Court and allowed them to test her. And I couldn't do that until I dealt with Seraphina. The last thing I needed right now was to waltz into Court with my mark beside me. It might save her, but it would doom me.

Rose was staring at me and sipping her wine as I thought about our predicament when, out of nowhere, she dropped her glass with a crash and began screaming. Her arms reached behind her, trying to get something in the center of her back. I jumped up from my seat and leaped over the table to see what she was clawing at.

"It hurts!" she screamed as she turned so that I could see. When she turned around, I couldn't see anything.

"My skin. It's like something is cutting me open. Make it stop!" she groaned. In an instant, an obsidian dagger appeared in my hand, and I ran it under her shirt, slicing the thin fabric in two and revealing her spine. The dagger faded to mist as I released it and pulled the shirt off her.

Two large bumps had formed near the spine and just below the shoulder blade. Something writhed underneath the skin, and a bit of black smoke seemed to rise from them.

I sighed as Rose continued to try to scratch at the bumps. "Stop," I commanded, and she turned to look at me. Pain wracked her face, and I gritted my teeth. This shouldn't have happened yet.

"What is it?" she groaned.

"You got your fanfare is all." I settled down in the chair next to hers and realized that I'd spilled the wine in my glass.

"What do you mean!" Her voice was pitiful, and I began to feel a little sorry for her.

"It's your wings. You claimed your power, and now they're

Chapter 9

trying to grow. You asked about fanfare, and this is it."

She continued to try to claw at her back, her hands getting nowhere near the two bumps. "God, I hate this fucking place." She grimaced and finally gave up, putting her hands on the table as tears welled in her eyes. I could feel the pain and frustration running through her.

"I was human until two days ago. I don't know anything, and all you do is get annoyed when I try to understand things. I'm sorry that I didn't grow up in fucking fairyland, but I didn't even know it was a place until you brought me here. I didn't ask for this. I didn't ask for you to do anything. All I want is to be able to go back home and live out my miserable life."

Helplessness flowed from her, my empathy letting me feel exactly what she was feeling. I took a deep breath as I realized that I had been more than a little callous. I wouldn't have known how to function in her world either.

"I'm sorry, Rose. This is part of the process of claiming your power. All gifts require sacrifice for the Fae. This pain is the sacrifice."

"Yeah, well I didn't know." Tears began to run as she gritted her teeth.

"I should have told you that this was what would happen. Now that it's happening, there are a few options. They'll eventually burn their way out of your back, but that will be about two weeks of agony. Or, I can cut them out with my knife like I was cutting out an arrow. That's a night of rest and thirty minutes where you think you're going to die. Unless…"

I didn't want to say it. For anyone else, I would have taken them into their dreamworld and locked them there in fantasies until the worst of it was over, but for some reason, I couldn't push that on her.

Princess of Shadows

"Unless what?" she demanded as she winced again.

I let out a long breath and made a decision. "Unless you let me use magic on you. Unless you let me seduce you in a dreamscape while I let your wings out. For all intents and purposes, you'll barely notice the pain, and as soon as your wings are free, you'll heal."

"It's the right decision, logically, but you're... inexperienced."

I turned around, unable to look at her as she realized what that meant. I glanced down at the spilled wine. I picked up the bottle and took a long slow drink directly from it.

"What are you?" she whispered.

It would eventually come out. I'd known it would, but I hadn't wanted it to. How stupidly mortal that sounded.

"I'm half fairy and half incubus. I feed on sexual energy both in dreams and in the physical."

"And... you'll feed on me?"

"I would. I won't lie to you, Rose," I didn't turn around to face her, not wanting to see the horror on her face. "I also won't force this on you. I should, but I won't. It has to be your decision."

Chapter 10

Rose

Another wave of pain raced through my body, and I whimpered. God, it hurt. Excruciating, white-hot pain that sent my back into spasms. I would never be able to survive two weeks of this.

I didn't want Sebastian digging around in my back, but I would die before those two weeks were up. The tears were already flowing steadily, and my nails dug into the table as a fresh bit of misery ran through me.

"Which hurts less?" I asked through clenched teeth.

"The dreamscape will be painless," he said softly as he stood up and removed his cloak.

"Then do it. Whatever you have to do. Fix me." Another wave of pain coursed through me, and I shut my eyes as I tried not to scream.

When I opened my eyes, Sebastian was standing in front

of me, staring at me. Those blue eyes that had slowly begun turning more and more misty seemed to pull me into them, and gray mists filled my vision.

I felt myself falling, but for some reason, I didn't try to catch myself. The mists whispered to me. Peace. Calm. Rest.

And then they seemed to burn away, leaving me in a room that had to be part of a palace. Ebony posts rose up around the bed that seemed like a cloud made solid. I sank into it, and every muscle in my body relaxed.

The light was dim, barely illuminating anything else. Candles burned in black and gold sconces on the walls, the light flickering so that shadows danced everywhere I turned.

The scent of lavender and lilac filled the room like a scented candle was burning somewhere nearby, but underneath it, I smelled something different, something that no candle could put off. I inhaled, and it felt like I was stepping out the front door on a fall morning, fresh dew on the grass. The air still. Such a strange scent.

I was pulled away from my thoughts as I looked down at my body. Instead of wearing the sleep clothes I'd been taken in, I was covered in a silk nightgown, so elegant and expensive I would never have worn it. Deep blue, it shimmered in the light, and the shadows danced on top of me.

I felt strange like I'd been given a drug at a doctor's office.

Then Sebastian stepped from the shadows, wearing only his pants. His eyes were made of pure mist now. Not even a flicker of blue. He took a step towards the bed and seemed to materialize above me, appearing from a puff of mist. This time, the mists didn't dissipate. It hovered around me as he rested his weight on one elbow and ran his fingers over my cheek.

Chapter 10

I took a gasping breath as he finally touched me. Somehow, I knew that this was the true Sebastian. This place of mists and luxurious beds was his home, and everything else was just where he existed.

Lightning seemed to flow from his fingers, igniting my body wherever he touched with warmth and something more. My body seemed to pulse in time with his magic touch as I stared into those mist-filled eyes.

I inhaled his scent. Not the way he smelled, but his magical scent. I understood what he had been trying to explain before now. It engulfed me. It couldn't be described. Not truly. Like the dew on a fall morning. It was so strong, I could almost taste it.

It overwhelmed my senses, and I seemed to lose track of where I was. A luxurious bed filled with mist? The silvered floor of a moonlit forest? A boat on the open ocean, rocking to the peaceful waves of a gentle sea? It didn't matter. Only he mattered. His body on top of mine. His eyes gazing into mine.

His hand running down my neck.

He craned his neck down, and for the first time in my life, I felt lips on mine. Lips of passion. Lips of need. Lips of hunger. They spoke to me. Breathing their desires into me. A fire exploded inside me, and I wrapped my arms around him, feeling his bare skin for the first time.

Hard muscles hidden under the flesh rippled as he shifted. His lips left mine and found the crook of my neck. Passion and need flowed through me as I'd never known possible.

My breathing came out in little gasps as he kissed his way down my neck. His hand moved to my nightgown, and it seemed impossibly thin. His grazing touch seemed to move

Princess of Shadows

right through the fabric, igniting my skin.

I ran my fingers over his back, exploring his skin in ways I'd never done before. His lips found the top of my nightgown, and the pulsing inside me grew even stronger. God, everything inside me wanted this. My mind. My body. My very soul craved his touch and everything he could give me.

He whispered, "Tell me what you want, Rose."

"Please," I moaned. "Please don't stop."

I looked down as he gripped the top of the nightgown and, without any effort, he split the gown down the middle, tearing it all the way to my waist. His lips left a trail of soft kisses towards my breast as his hands wrapped around me. He pulled my body upward, forcing me towards those lips that were desperate for me.

And I felt lightning inside me, flickering bits of desperate need. I needed more than this. More than kisses. More than his touch. There was something more, but I didn't know what it was.

His fingers dug into my back hard enough to hurt, but it was nothing compared to the pleasure that raced through me. I moaned as he showed me how strong he was, and I dug my nails into his back hard enough to draw blood, but he smiled down at me.

A flicker of light behind the mists in his eyes told me something was changing, but I was consumed by the pulsing need flowing through my body. I arched my back and pressed my breasts towards him.

His strong arms pulled me upward as he moved into a kneeling position, pulling me with him. I stared at him as I wrapped my legs around his waist. His hardness pressed against me through his pants, and I groaned.

Chapter 10

That was what I needed. That was the more that I craved. He stared into my eyes as he pulled my nightgown down around me, ripping the straps off it as though they were nothing.

He pulled me to him, my naked breasts pressed against his chest as he pressed his lips against mine. I could feel his hunger again. More pressing. More desperate. He was going to consume me. Every ounce of my being.

And I didn't want to stop him.

As long as he didn't stop kissing me. As long as his hands never stopped running over my naked skin.

His hands moved down lower. My nightgown was still wrapped around my waist, and he ran his hands down to my butt and pulled me against him, against that hardness.

God, it was ecstasy. The world could explode, and I wouldn't turn away from his kiss. The mists began to swirl around us, and it was like he was touching me everywhere, igniting every inch of my body with a fire that only he could soothe.

His hands edged lower, and he brushed that part of me that had never been touched, and everything else paled in comparison to the lightning that begged to be released inside me.

One hand moved to my back while the other pressed against that throbbing, desperate spot, and he broke away from the kiss, holding my gaze in his. With a single finger, he pushed through my resistance, finding the spot inside me that had craved his touch since the beginning. The more.

And I exploded with a scream. A flood of pure bliss raced through me, and as he withdrew his finger, I saw that his eyes were a soft blue again.

His arms wrapped around me, and he held me tight to his chest as the waves of pleasure slowly calmed inside me.

Princess of Shadows

Something had changed inside me at that moment, but I didn't know what it was.

My body was naked from the waist up, and I should have been ashamed as the mists cleared, but I wasn't. The steady rise and fall of Sebastian's chest began to lull me to sleep as I snuggled tighter to him, pressing my head into his shoulder. At that moment, I wanted nothing more than to feel him.

Chapter 11

Rose

I woke slowly. I'd had no dreams other than that very inappropriate and strange one with Sebastian. My body ached, and yet it felt so much more alive than it had yesterday.

As I opened my eyes, I realized that I was curled up on Sebastian's shoulder, and I jerked away from him. He was already awake, and he gave me a half-grin. "Strange dreams, Tinkerbell?" he asked.

"Tinkerbell? You can't steal a nickname. It's against the rules of nicknames." I yawned and sat up. It took me a second before I saw that Sebastian's gaze had drifted lower than my face, and I realized that I was topless. Quickly covering myself with the blanket, I felt my cheeks warm intensely.

"What did you do?" I exclaimed. "Did you... did that dream really happen? Did you put... your finger...?"

Sebastian laughed and got out of bed wearing only those

leather pants that showed off the pieces of him I hadn't experienced in the dream. God, after that dream, I had so many thoughts about what he could do with that body, and a part of me wanted to see what lay under that leather. "No, Tinkerbell, I certainly didn't put my finger anywhere. It was a dream. That's all."

"Then why am I freaking topless?" I asked, verging on shouting.

"Had to take off your shirt if I was going to let your wings out. Seeing your tits was just a bonus." I snarled at him, but something pulled at the edges of my mind. I reached behind me with one hand while pulling the blanket tighter against my breasts with the other. I felt something stuck in a line down the middle of my back. It came off easily enough in little broken pieces.

I looked down at the almost black flakes and realized what had happened. Everything last night was so cloudy. Pieces were missing. I remembered drinking and hurting. The only thing I really remembered clearly was that dream that was so real.

This piece of red turned black reminded me of what had happened. Sebastian had taken me to a dreamscape while he'd cut my wings out of me.

My wings.

"Do I have wings? Is that why you're calling me Tinkerbell?" My voice was barely a whisper. Sebastian turned from where he was pouring water into cups and grinned at me.

"Want to see them?" he asked, not sassy in the least. "They're beautiful."

I nodded, and he said, "Then you're going to have to get out of bed. Mirrors are quite a bit less common here than in your

Chapter 11

world, and I'm not going to rip this one out of the wall."

I glanced at Sebastian who was holding two cups of water in his hands, and I sighed. He may have played with my body in a dream, but that didn't mean that I wanted to be naked around him.

I wrapped the sheet around me like a towel, covering myself and dragging the sheet across the ground. I had to take little shuffling steps so that I didn't step on the sheet and fall over, embarrassing myself further, but I slowly followed Sebastian to a little corner next to the stove. It was a full-length cabinet with a lock on the door. Not big enough to stand in, I understood the purpose.

I'd walked through a mirror before. I knew that they were gateways. No one would be able to sneak into his house through the mirror in such a small space. At the same time, he could step through it when the doors were open. His own fancy little portal maker that he could lock up tight.

He stepped back and let me get in front of the mirror. I gasped as I looked at myself. Everything about me looked rough. Wild hair that still had bits of gravel from the sinkhole. There were smudges of ash on my cheeks. Everything about me made me look like some homeless girl.

Except the shiny black wings rising from the center of my back.

They looked to be made of shadows that seemed to repel the light flickering from the oil lamp that was still burning.

They were darker than shadows, yet they shined like obsidian with a black fire inside them. Rising almost a foot above me, they made me seem taller. An unfelt wind seemed to make them ripple, making their dark light flicker against Sebastian who stood behind me.

They were nothing like the fairy wings on postcards. Thin veins of what I could only assume were magic ran through them and seemed to pulse with my heartbeat. Living wings made of pure magic.

Reaching a tentative hand out, I touched the edge. I felt it then, the power that Sebastian had talked about. There was no shock of electricity. This was a different kind of power. Deep and slow, it seemed to pulse.

When I pressed on the wing, there was a bit of resistance, and then my fingers slipped through it. I frowned, and Sebastian said, "They're newly formed. Eventually, you'll learn how to make them solid. You'll also learn how to make them completely ethereal where they'll be invisible and impossible to touch. It's important if you want to go to the Mortal Realm.

I set my jaw. This was real. Not just a lie that Sebastian had told me. I really was a fairy. One of the Fae. Immortal.

Then I saw my face and jumped in surprise. The wings were something brand new. Something supernatural. My face was different. I'd been born with one face. A face that was "wrong". I'd grown up hearing that I was odd, that something was off about me. That I looked like a bug or a frog.

Now, I understood. My face hadn't been right because I hadn't claimed my magic, hadn't become the person I should have been. Now, instead of having eyes too large and too far apart, my face had shifted slightly. Just that little bit was all that had been needed. Now, my face was thinner and slightly longer.

My nose had narrowed, and my eyes had shifted into place as well. Everything about my face was now built on angles. Angles that humans tried their best to make for themselves with makeup. Contours that were impossible for a human to

Chapter 11

ever have. A sharp jaw and high cheekbones that seemed to have been sculpted.

The eyes that had been slightly too large fit my longer face perfectly now. Everything that I'd hated about myself for so long had been *almost* right which had made me look hideous. Now it had all slid into place, and I looked more beautiful than anyone I knew.

Sasha would have nothing on me. She'd have tried to build a face out of makeup so that she could look half as perfect as me now. I turned to Sebastian and saw the same elements in his face. A man's version of my face.

"I'm beautiful," I whispered.

"You've always been beautiful, Rose. No different than a child who has to grow into their body. Anyone who thought differently had no idea what you'd grow into."

I felt a tear begin to form at the corner of my eye, and I blinked it away. I'd hated my face for so long, and now I understood it. If my parents had survived long enough, they'd have explained it to me. They'd have taught me. But instead, they'd died, and I'd gone through life thinking I was a hideous toad.

I smiled at Sebastian, and my lips quivered as I tried to keep from crying in joy. "Thank you," I whispered.

I reached around him and hugged him, not quite so worried about covering myself up. I needed to say thank you to him. For bringing me to the Immortal Realm and fixing the part of me that I'd always thought had been broken. For showing me who I was meant to be.

"Let me see if I can get your shirt fixed up," he said. "Then we need to go." His hands wrapped around me, and his fingers touched my bare skin. He wasn't trying to seduce me with that

Princess of Shadows

touch, but I wasn't sure his touch would ever be anything but seductive. It seemed to ignite the same feelings that I'd had in my dreams, and a throbbing between my legs woke inside me.

He released me and gave me a half-smile as he turned around. "Lock the door when you're done," he said. I looked at myself in the mirror one last time and noticed the final change. My ears had sharpened just as much as my face had. The tops ended in sharp points rather than the naturally rounded ears of most people.

I really was a freaking fairy. I took a deep breath and giggled a little bit before I shut the cabinet and locked it, leaving it as it had been when we'd arrived.

When I turned around, Sebastian was holding up my shirt. The back had a giant slice from top to bottom where he'd cut it off me. Sebastian sighed and said, "No, I don't think I can patch it. Let me get one of my shirts for you to wear until we can get you some clothes."

He tossed the shirt on the bed and turned to the small chest of drawers next to the bed. I didn't know what to say. I knew that I was going to look ridiculous no matter what I wore since I'd basically been wearing sleep clothes this entire time. The thought of wearing a shirt like that silk one he'd worn yesterday made me shiver.

In movies, it was the sign of a girlfriend sleeping over. Something she would put on after they'd had a long night full of hot, dirty sex. I thought of the mess my hair had been in when I'd looked in the mirror and knew that this was even worse than bedhead.

The thought of a shopping trip during my first "walk of shame" made me want to throw up. Especially walking with Sebastian. I shivered.

Chapter 11

He pulled a linen tunic from his drawer and tossed it to me. I held it up to myself, keeping the sheet around me with my elbows, and I realized that it was almost dress length on me.

I grinned at him. "You're really big."

"That's what most women say," he said with a wide grin, and I wanted to slap him. Had a fairy sex god actually just made a "that's what she said" joke to me?

"So funny. Turn around so I can get dressed with some bit of modesty."

He raised an eyebrow that seemed to say, "You weren't very modest last night," but after a second, he sighed and turned around.

I dropped the sheet and hurriedly pulled the linen tunic over my head. It was huge on me and looked like I was wearing a potato sack, but at least it didn't make me look like a whore like a silk shirt would have.

I realized that it shouldn't have gone over my wings, but it had. "Done yet?" Sebastian asked.

"Uh huh," I muttered as I reached behind me to figure out if it was stupid looking. Just before I turned to go back to the mirror, Sebastian said, "It looks fine. Until you can make them solid, clothes will pass right through them."

How did he do that? It was like he could read my mind or something. "Oh," I muttered, putting my hands back at my sides.

Sebastian picked up his shirt from yesterday and put it on. He slipped on some socks and then his boots. Then he began rooting around in cabinets until he pulled out a big leather bag. He rolled up his cloak and put it inside the bag which he slung over his shoulder.

I ran my fingers through my hair, trying to get the tangles

out, but it was hopeless. I was destined to go on my first shopping trip in fairyland looking homeless.

I caught Sebastian grinning as he watched me. "What?"

"Oh, I was just thinking of offering you the use of one of the most important Fae inventions."

"And what would that be?" I asked, every ounce of my frustration flowing into my words.

He walked over to a cabinet next to the mirror and pulled out a brush. "We call it a brush."

He held it out to me. "How was I supposed to know that you had a brush? I figured that you just wiggled your nose, and your hair was styled."

"Once again, you didn't ask, little fairy. You may need to start working on that."

I snarled at him, but he ignored me as I opened the cabinet once more to look in the mirror. I tried to brush my hair as best as I could, but I needed a shower. It had been a rough couple of days, and my hair was not behaving in the least. I put the brush up and locked the cabinet.

Sebastian was still grinning when he asked me if I was ready.

I nodded, my fingers still trying to convince my hair to be a little less wild.

He chuckled at me and walked out the door, a pack on his shoulder. At least I would have some shoes again after I was done with this shopping trip. What would it be like to go shopping in the Immortal Realm? What kind of Fae would I meet? And when was breakfast?

Chapter 12

Sebastian

It felt good to have fed at least a little bit. I was nowhere near sated, but at least I wasn't starving. My body didn't have the same aching sensations, and I could fight again.

With anyone else, I wouldn't have gotten that much power from the little bit of foreplay that Rose and I had shared last night in the dreamscape, but she was far stronger than I'd have expected.

First times were always more powerful though. That could be it. I thought about the alternative. This naïve and inexperienced girl being a Queen of the Dark Court? How would she survive?

Seraphina would kill her just as she'd done with the previous Dark Queen. Just as she'd done with the previous Queen of the Light. There would be no one to help her. Within the Fae, murder was not illegal. Even the murder of a Queen. A Queen had to be able to protect herself. Other people could help, but Seraphina would destroy them without a second thought unless Rose was capable of fighting on her own. Not even I could go toe-to-toe with Seraphina.

Her guards were for protecting her from assassins and armies, not from fighting another Queen. At least not for fighting a High Queen. I sighed. It would be better for Rose if she could just go into hiding even if she was a Queen.

We stepped into the yard, and I locked the door to my cottage. I was sad to have to leave. Regardless of where we went, people would know what and who I was. At least our shopping trip today would be amongst friends.

We got outside the gate, and I took Rose's hand. "I thought we were going to a town near here?"

"We are. It's just in the Mortal Realm. A quick step into the warrens and then out again, and we'll be there."

She seemed surprised. "Oh. I just thought that we'd buy clothes from this side."

"The people that I have to see work in an illegal business. They forge scents. It's far easier to hide in the Mortal Realm."

She nodded in understanding. "So the Mortal Realm is like the ghetto. Got it."

Not entirely sure what she meant by that, I shrugged and touched the shadow that lay across the ground. Slipping into the warren, I called for the mists. They covered our feet as always when I walked through the warrens, and Rose didn't make any screams.

Good. She's learning. We moved silently through the tunnels for only a few minutes, and I reached out to touch the wall. Yes, this was the right place. The image of a small alleyway between two imposing buildings came into my mind.

Chapter 12

I stopped walking and glanced at Rose who nodded. She was beginning to impress me with how quickly she learned. She was even beginning to be a little less annoying.

I pulled on the image in my mind, and we slid through that space between the realms. Stepping out of the shadow, Rose tensed. Darkness blanketed the alley. She was not comfortable in a city. Especially in a dark alley.

The thought made me chuckle. If she only knew that there were very few creatures that lived in this Realm that could actually hurt a full-blooded fairy, she would probably be a lot less nervous.

I whispered to her, "Calm down. We're in your world. You don't have to be afraid. I have a friend who's going to take care of you while I get something to hide your scent. She lives in this building, but you really shouldn't leave the shadows until she gets here since you have wings now."

"How will she be able to help hide my wings?" Rose asked, running her hand behind her to touch the midnight wings again.

"She's a full-blooded succubus and extremely good with illusions. I need to leave you here for a few minutes while I get her."

Rose seemed to think for a moment, but then she took a deep breath and nodded. "Fine. I'll be okay, but try not to take too long."

"It may be a few minutes if she's with a customer, but I'll try to hurry." I stepped out of the alley before she had a chance to ask questions. The last thing that I needed was to try to explain that one of my better friends happened to be a whore.

The brothel was as close to an old-world feel as was possible in this age. Everything was made of wood. No paint. Even the floors were wooden and creaked slightly. It was made to be simple. No one was coming for the décor. They were coming for her. For the experience that they'd never get from a human woman.

Slipping inside the building, the sound of men drinking at a bar filled my ears. Humans. Food. How Ast managed to leave them living after she had fed on them was still beyond me. I'd tried time and time again, but they were so fragile, so easily drained completely.

"Look at what the storm brought in," a waitress said. Barbie. I had no idea what her real name was, but that was the only name I'd ever heard anyone use. The first human that Ast had hired for this brothel and bar almost fifteen years ago. Immortals couldn't stay anywhere too long, or people would realize that they didn't age. This particular brothel was fifteen years old, but it was probably her hundredth.

Barbie was a pretty woman, but she was getting older. Her blond hair and round face were still very youthful, but the rest of her body was showing the signs of age. She ran the place when Ast was busy with supernatural things. Or when she was busy with her own clients.

She also happened to be one of the only mortals that Ast trusted enough to share her secrets with. It wasn't that uncommon to have mortal confidantes for the Fae that lived in the Mortal Realm. Even the Fae needed to share their lives with others.

"Evening, Barbie," I said with a smile. "Is Ast around?"

Barbie grinned. "She's upstairs with a guy. I'm sure that they'd both like the company if you're a little low."

I shook my head. "I think I'll pass. I tend to overindulge, and bad things happen, but I do need to interrupt her."

Chapter 12

Barbie just shrugged and handed another beer to one of the men. It didn't seem as though Barbie was struggling with finding customers because, as she leaned over the bar, nearly all of the men stared at her cleavage.

It was almost sad how easily mortals were seduced. Leaving Barbie behind, I climbed the stairs up to the 'hotel' above the bar. Each of the doors would have a woman servicing a man. I needed to find the right one, and I took a deep breath, inhaling the smells of sex, cigarettes, and cheap beer. And power. Only one person in this building had anything more than a spark of power, and she was the one I was looking for.

I opened the second to last door, not bothering to knock. Ast was already getting dressed. The man she'd been with was fast asleep, drained of a fair amount of his life's energy.

He'd recover it. All beings slowly regenerated their energy. Fae took longer unless they had a source to feed from. It was one of the most important weaknesses of fairies and one of the most important strengths of many of the other Fae. Fairies could not feed on any other source of power while most of the rest of us could draw life from our surroundings.

Bright red hair that seemed to glow ran to her shoulders. Made to stand out, Ast's features were all slightly more obvious. Like a siren, her body was the bait. Her back was to me, and I could see everything that wasn't covered in her black lingerie.

Another man would have been entranced by her curves, but I waited patiently, completely unaffected by her body. When she turned to me, I smiled at her. Like her hair and backside, her front was just as obvious. Large breasts, bright red lips, a thin waist. And green eyes that almost seemed to glow.

In actuality, they did glow, but the glow was so subtle that a human would never pick up on it. That subtlety was enough to draw a man's attention away from the body and let her weave her spell over them.

"What do you need this time?" Ast questioned. Her tone was annoyed, but she had a smile on her face.

"I can't just stop by to see an old friend?" I replied, giving her a wide grin.

"I'd hope not. Especially with what I've been hearing. Is the Assassin's Guild really on your tail?"

"I was hoping that they weren't actually still hunting me. Should have lost them yesterday."

Ast pulled on a pair of tights that hugged her body. Then, she pulled a silver sequined top on. She caught me looking at her pants and turned to shake her ass towards me.

"New 'exercise' leggings. Greatest perk of being around mortals. They make the best clothes." She certainly wasn't trying to seduce me. Neither of us could feed on the other, and sex was rarely ever for more than to sate the constant hunger.

We were both creatures born to seduce the world, and as one professional to another, I had a hard time denying that the leggings looked good on her.

"Worst perk is that you're only allowed appetizers," I noted, giving the naked man in the bed a glance.

"Not all of us want to play in the Courts, Bastian. Come to my office and tell me what you need since we both know you need something. You wouldn't have come here without a purpose."

"We don't need to go to your office. I need you to take a friend of mine shopping. Keep her busy for a little bit, but make sure she has plenty of clothes. And maybe you could do something to hide her wings."

"Are you fucking kidding me? The rumors are true? You

Chapter 12

deliberately disobeyed Seraphina's orders to kill the half-fairy?"

"She's not half. She's a full-blooded fairy with both light and dark bloodlines."

That stopped Ast. She put her hands on her hips and very slowly said, "Is she strong enough to fill the void?"

I shrugged. "I can't tell. Maybe. It looks more and more like it every day, but what I know is that I fed on her only once, and she brought me from the beginning of mists to this."

Ast crossed the room and stared into my eyes, seeing the light blue. "Only once?" she asked as she stepped backward, shaking her head.

I nodded. "It was her first time, but yes, only once."

"I'll take her to Elora's. Won't be much shopping, but I'll get her some clothes. Don't let Damian know, though. That fucking vampire talks too much."

"Show me where she is. Please don't tell me you left the poor girl out in the alley."

"I can't shadow walk into the building. I made sure of that when you bought the place."

She huffed and said, "Fine. Introduce us and get on with your business you unchivalrous ass." I chuckled and led her to where Rose was waiting for us in the alley.

"What in the hell are you wearing, child?" Ast said as she reached for Rose's hand. Rose pulled back immediately.

"Rose, this is Astriel. She's the friend I was talking about. She needs to touch you to create the illusion."

Rose glanced from me to Ast and sighed as she put her hand out. Ast touched her and closed her eyes for a few seconds. Then the wings seemed to disappear. Every once in a while, they would flutter, and I'd catch a glimpse of a shimmering light. If you knew what to look for, you'd see them, but otherwise, they were as good as invisible.

Then the rest of her began to shimmer slightly, and the tunic transformed into a simple black dress. Her feet became covered by shoes that weren't there. Her hair transformed from the tangled mess into a long straight braid that ran down to the middle of her back.

None of it was real. That was the thing about succubi. Everything was illusions with them. Unlike my abilities, Ast's were unable to interact with the world.

She let go of Rose's hand and said, "Rose, I'm going to take you to get some clothes. Then we'll get you all cleaned up. And I'll brush your hair for you."

Rose glanced at her with a frown and took a deep breath. "Okay. I think I can manage to brush my hair though. I may not be a million years old like you two, but I'm not a toddler. I just need a shower."

I had to bite my tongue to keep from laughing at the way that Ast's motherly tendencies were shattered. "She's a sassy little fairy, isn't she?" she said.

"Alright. You can shower and brush your own hair. But I will be getting your clothes for the Immortal Realm. This is an embarrassment."

Rose nodded, and I said, "I have to run an errand, but I'll catch up in a bit. You're safe with Astriel, Rose. Listen to her. Please?"

Rose gave me a half-smile and said, "Fine. But only if we can have some breakfast. I'm starving. You do eat normal food too, right? Not just humans?"

Ast raised her eyebrows. "Come on little fairy, there's a cafe down the street that's got the best late-night breakfasts I've

Chapter 12

found this side of London."

Chapter 13

Sebastian

The immortal side of London was hidden deep in the city, set in shops with marks on windows and doors to let the other immortals know that they dealt in magic. There was no law against immortals living in this Realm. Except that they were required to keep it hidden from humans.

It had been the law since the very beginning when the realms had split. We had left the Mortal Realm when the humans had begun picking up iron and steel and turning it into weapons. We were far more powerful, but they were so numerous that our numbers dwindled quickly in the wars that followed.

Most types of Fae have only a handful of children over the course of millennia. Fairies were no exception, and as the ruling class, they decided early on that our casualties were far too numerous to stay here. They requested that everyone travel through the portals that were set up and

Chapter 13

hidden. Requested, not required.

Many refused due to their prey being on this side. Others because they liked living with humans. And then there were the ones that simply disliked fairies. Like vampires.

Like Damian. I stood in front of his shop, glancing up at the symbol. Jewelry. No mark of which Court he associated with, so he must be plying his trade with both sides these days. Glittering gold and silver filled jewelry cases just inside the shop's windows. I glanced to either side to make sure that no one was on this particular cobblestone street, and I tried to shift through the doorway.

Pain shot through my body as a hidden sheet of steel stopped me. I cursed and tried the door. The handle turned, and I walked into the shop just as any human would have.

A thin man walked down the stairs dressed in a suit minus the coat, tie neatly clipped to his vest with a burgundy silk shirt underneath.

His steps were silent. One of the perks of being a vampire was complete control over the physical body. They were one of the deadliest predators if you didn't know they were there and would have made the perfect assassins if they had been able to shadow walk.

I'd known Damian for a very long time. And he was one of the slowest Fae to adapt to this world when it changed. Glancing at the register, I noted how old it was. It looked to be at least a century old, kept in pristine condition. Made of brass, one of the metals that the Fae could touch without pain, the entire machine was mechanical.

"Good evening, Sebastian," Damian said as he ran a pale hand through his short black hair. He kept his nails long. They were hard as diamonds and one of the most important weapons a vampire had. Unlike other Fae, they used little actual magic. Instead, they relied on physical strength and speed. Very few creatures were as effective as a vampire when magic was taken out of the equation.

"I was expecting you, so I left the door unlocked. I hear that you're looking to hide a recent acquaintance."

Damian was well connected with the immortals on this side, but I was still surprised that he knew so much about what I was doing. If he knew, then that meant that Seraphina and Nyx might know as well.

"Not in the mood for small talk?" I asked stepping closer to Damian. "It's been a century since we last talked." His eyes flared, but his expression remained unnervingly flat.

"I'd prefer that you left my shop as quickly as possible. Nyx has a reputation for leaving a trail of blood in his wake, and I happen to prefer not to be a part of it."

"I wouldn't have come here with a tail if it weren't important. You know that." I didn't turn away as he walked around the counter even though a compulsion flowed through me. A generous Fae must have gifted him a compulsion trinket that he'd just tried to use.

It wasn't uncommon for Fae to pay Damian in favors, but feeling the strength of that compulsion surprised me. Few powerful Fae lived in this Realm, and I knew of almost all of them. Most had a tie to one of the Courts. Whoever had made this for him was someone new or someone from the other side.

He didn't seem to notice that the trinket hadn't worked, but he did hesitate. I waited patiently as he moved just a little bit slower, not wanting to show his secret hiding place for magical jewelry.

Chapter 13

Finally, he turned to a cabinet and pulled a drawer out. All the way out. He reached behind it, into the actual wall, and slid another drawer out. I watched him set it on the glass counter without making a sound.

He held up a simple necklace made of a strange silver metal I'd never seen before. The chain seemed slightly thicker than most jewelry he made. Hanging from the chain were medium sized circle-cut sapphires with diamonds set around them in a sunburst pattern.

In the very center hung a massive diamond that was also cut in a circle. It hung from a long chain made of that strange metal. Gleaming in the perfect light of the jewelry shop, the entire thing sparkled like a necklace that royalty would wear.

This would cost just as much as something royalty would wear. Unlike simple necklaces, this was an illegal one. Those sapphires would have been filled with the magical essence of another being, and it would slowly let out the scent like an oil burner set on a very low setting. The diamond in the center would be used to trap Rose's scent before it left her body. The entire necklace would hang slightly lower than most so that the diamond would rest right between her breasts.

It wasn't meant to be beautiful even though it was. It was meant to hide Rose. Only a skilled artificer like Damian would know how to make this and infuse it correctly. Damian didn't have any magic of his own, but he knew how to work with distilled magic like a scientist from this world would work with various chemicals.

"Tell me about it," I said. "Then we can talk about price."

He nodded. "The diamond will hold the essence of the person until it is filled. For you, it would take almost a hundred years to fill that particular diamond. I do not know how long it will take for her to fill it."

"The sapphires will slowly release the scent of a Selkie. They're common enough, and they live on land regularly, so that shouldn't arouse suspicion. You'll obviously need to relocate her near a shoreline, but other than that, there are minimal limitations on her placement."

"And how long will the sapphires last?" I asked.

"At least a hundred years. At least. I don't want to have to refill them any more than I have to. If she has the eye of Nyx and Seraphina, they won't stop hunting her anytime soon."

I nodded. "Understandable. What is it going to cost?"

Damian didn't hesitate. "A dagger."

The words hung in the air. It was a well-known secret that I held a set of Assassin's Guild daggers, given to me by Nyx.

They were special and one of my most valuable possessions. Just making a dagger from obsidian was an easy thing to do. They also were nearly worthless. They were easy to break and more than that, they were no different than any glass dagger.

The difference was in the power that they'd been enchanted with. An enchantment that only one man had ever learned how to do, and he'd only been able to do it to something made of obsidian.

Obsidian could hold magical power just like a crystal could. These particular daggers were able to siphon the power from any being struck by them. This caused the magical power to flow from a wound into the bearer of the dagger, giving them more strength while draining their enemy.

This made them some of the most powerful weapons in the Immortal Realm. "There has to be something else," I said. "Be reasonable."

"No. That is the price of this piece. If you believe it's an

Chapter 13

unreasonable price, find another artificer."

I stared him down. No woman was worth an obsidian dagger. Except for a Queen. A Queen that could stand up to Seraphina. If I'd been sure that Rose was that Queen, I'd have given the dagger over without question. But I wasn't sure.

I gritted my teeth and held out my hand, the dagger appearing from mist. "Why shouldn't I just kill you and take the necklace?" I snarled.

"I thought we were friends, Sebastian," he said, not showing even a slight anxiety at having that dagger pointed at him. At the same time, fire glinted in his eyes as his muscles prepared to react.

"That's not a friendly price. I'll give you nearly anything you ask, but you ask too much this time, Damian."

"That is the price of the necklace. Take it or leave it. Or kill me and deal with the difficulty of finding an artificer to handle that diamond when it is full. Those are your choices."

An instant later, I tossed the dagger onto the counter. "Take the damned dagger. I will be finding another artificer, Damian. One who knows not to push me too far."

He nodded and slid the necklace across the counter, and I snatched it up. I stalked out of the shop, and when I glanced back at Damian, he was holding the dagger as though it were some kind of crystal vase, terrified that he would break it.

That dagger would allow him to protect himself better than almost anything else. He was already faster, stronger, and stealthier than most of the Fae. Even me. If he could drain his enemy as well, it would make him a force to be reckoned with.

I hoped that Rose was worth it. I was at a severe disadvantage if Nyx finally caught up to us. I stepped out of the shop, breathing in the misty air and tried to reconcile the loss of a weapon that I'd held for a thousand years.

It would be worth it. At least I hoped it would.

Chapter 14

Rose

"Two full English breakfasts," Astriel said to the waitress, a younger woman who looked like she had experienced more than a few of the less than pleasant parts of the world. The waitress gave her an odd look, and Astriel smiled seductively at her. The waitress seemed to jump at the smile and said, "That may take a little bit. We don't get a lot of breakfast orders at this time of night."

"I know, hon. Run along and get the order in. We're going to sit and talk a bit anyway."

The waitress nodded to Astriel and scampered off. Then Astriel leaned forward. "How long have you had wings? Most of your kind learn to hide them quickly enough."

"I woke up with them a few hours ago," I said nervously. This was a friend of Sebastian's that he'd said to trust. I tried to remind myself that I should be less nervous around her, but

Princess of Shadows

everything about her pushed me into a fight or flight reaction.

She walked with the confidence of knowing that every person who saw her was drawn to her. It was obvious why. She was probably the most beautiful woman I'd ever met, and she made me feel like a troll next to her. Granted, I'd lived my life thinking I was hideous. I was always the ugly friend. Next to Sasha. Even next to Tiffany.

The one who couldn't convince a guy to date her in three years of college.

I knew that my face wasn't odd anymore. I was pretty. I told myself that for the hundredth time since I met Astriel.

I still didn't have those curves. I was normal, not some mix of pornstar and high fashion supermodel like Astriel. Was she normal for Fae?

"Oh..." she said. "So, what'd you think of the *Immortal Realm?*" she asked with a smirk. "I'm guessing that Bastian took you there, and you claimed your power?"

I nodded. "It's kind of weird. We saw a unicorn, and it tried to kill me."

She grinned. "They tend to do that. I've always wondered if they grew that horn because they're such giant dicks that they needed a second one on their head."

I couldn't help but giggle at the remark. "Tell me about yourself, hon. You've managed to get one of my best friends into a hell of a lot of trouble, so I'd like to know at least a little about you."

"I'm just a normal girl. I grew up in the foster system. I studied hard and got into college. I don't know what else you want to know."

"Well, first of all, you're anything but normal. Wings of shadow don't grow on normal girls. You're full-blooded fairy.

Chapter 14

That means that you were born to rule over half of the Fae. Born to rule over people like me. That happens to be one of many reasons I don't get over to their side very often."

"Why do fairies rule over the rest of the Fae?" I asked.

"Because they're the most numerous and most powerful of the Fae. There are maybe fifty full-blooded succubi like me. And we're mostly useless when it comes to battle. There are even fewer incubi. Vampires don't have the juice to rule. Shifters don't want to. Each and every group has at least one reason why they couldn't or shouldn't rule. Except fairies. Plus, fairies like to get up in everyone's business. It's natural for them."

"Oh." I paused realizing what she'd said. "You're a succubus? Like, you have sex with people and they die? Kind of like Sebastian?"

"No. I don't kill my food. Keeps them from coming back. They just feel really really tired. Most attribute it to the mind-blowing sex, but others don't even notice the relationship."

"And Bastian and I are different. I don't do the dream thing very well. I can do it, but it's a pain. He, on the other hand, doesn't have the natural beauty that I do, and he can't control himself as well. It's a lot of give and take, but almost everyone agrees that it's easier to be a succubus, but incubi are much more powerful. That happens to be why there are so few of them left."

"And remember that Bastian is only half incubus. I assume that you've experienced his powers in dreams?"

I nodded, feeling a blush come over me. "Hon, stop getting embarrassed around me. There's no need. I feed on sex and desires. I have been the literal fantasy of nearly every desire the human race has come up with. Talking about sex with me is like talking to your doctor about a scrape on your elbow."

"Anyway, a full-blooded incubus can twist a person while in dreams, and they'll wake up different. Even the Fae are vulnerable to the words spoken by a full incubus. Women have murdered their families after being compelled. Kingdoms have been ruined. They're some of the most powerful and most dangerous beings."

"So they're hunted?"

Astriel nodded. "To the brink of extinction. The last Queen of the Dark Court tried to stop it. Her consort was an incubus, and she knew that just like other dangerous beings, they needed to be punished for crimes, but not punished for their existence."

The waitress came to the table and set our plates down. Massive plates of food. The waitress glanced at Astriel and began to get a strange look in her eyes as she stared at her.

"Thank you," Astriel said. "You can go now. Don't come check on us."

The girl nodded with a smile and walked away.

"You used magic on her, didn't you?" I whispered accusingly.

"Sweetheart, I use magic on everyone. It's what I am. It just doesn't work quite as well on you fairies if I'm not expending a significant amount of energy. Yet another good reason for me to steer clear of you."

"So you could whisper in my ear all sorts of things, and I would do what you say?"

"No, I'm not a siren. That's out of my realm of possibility when dealing with full Fae. Humans are easy to control, and half-bloods are possible with enough power."

"I have so much to learn," I said feeling more and more lost. There were so many different kinds of Fae. So much to learn

Chapter 14

about magic. So much to learn about myself. I felt like all I did was ask questions and try to learn as fast as possible.

And something inside me told me that I wasn't learning nearly fast enough. I didn't know why, but it pushed me to be ready for whatever was coming.

"Yes, you do," Astriel agreed. "But it's okay. At least for now, you have Bastian to lean on. He's one of the few people in the world that I would trust to save my bacon. On that note, how about we eat a bit because if I have to look at a pretty girl like you wearing a paper bag like that any longer, I might start throwing things."

I looked down at the illusion of the little black dress. "You can see through the illusion?"

"Of course, I can see through my own illusions. Wouldn't be very helpful if I couldn't tell what I'd glamoured, would it?"

Just one more time where I felt stupid. I was beginning to get used to being an idiot. I looked down at the breakfast and wondered how anyone could eat all this. "That's a lot of food."

"You'll be surprised at just how much food you need now that you've claimed your magic," Astriel said as she began to eat.

I picked at the food, not used to this kind of unhealthy eating. Two links of sausage, two fried eggs, some kind of beans, hash browns, several slices of grilled tomatoes, sauteed mushrooms, and what looked like burnt sausage patties.

Astriel picked up a sausage link and began biting pieces off it, not bothering to use a fork and knife.

I reached out to pick up the fork, and it felt like I'd just touched a hot stove. "Fuck," I whispered.

"It's steel, sweetheart. Use your fingers or start carrying around your own silverware. You're a fairy now that you've

Princess of Shadows

got wings, and you can't go around holding steel or iron."

I blinked at her. "Seriously? I can't touch metal? How am I supposed to drive? How am I supposed to function?"

She grinned. "Carefully. Or wear gloves. It's one of those few cons that comes with being able to do things that humans couldn't dream of doing. And not aging. That's a pretty big plus in my book, so I'm happy to wear gloves and carry my own silverware."

I nodded. "I guess that's true." I picked up the paper napkin and tore it in half, wrapping one half around the fork handle and the other half around the knife.

"There you go," she said as she continued eating her food.

I dug into mine, and though it was one of the greasiest breakfasts I'd ever had, I felt like I couldn't get enough. The more I ate, the more I wanted. I could have eaten another plate with how hungry I was.

"I'd skip the black pudding," she said pointing at the burnt looking sausage patties. "It's an acquired taste, and you're American." She said it as if that was a good reason.

I glanced at them and shrugged. I was hungry. They were food, and I wasn't going to turn down food right then. I cut a bite off one and put it in my mouth and began to chew. The flavor was stronger than I'd expected. Like a heavily seasoned steak with the texture of a soft sausage.

Astriel stared at me with the hint of a smile as though she expected me to make a disgusted face. "Not half bad," I said as I cut another bite of the black pudding.

She shook her head and finished her plate, leaving the black pudding untouched.

Standing up, she pulled out a stack of money and put several bills on the table. I had no idea what anything cost here. Not

Chapter 14

only was I having to deal with all of this fairy magic stuff, but we were in a country where I didn't understand anything. Even the breakfast had been strange.

As we walked, Astriel began to talk. "This area of London is known by the immortals as being a gathering place for those of the Fae. Many of the shops are owned by immortals, and they cater to the less human needs as well as the human side of things.

She pointed at a clothing boutique. In the corner of the door, a strange symbol had been drawn in black paint. "That means clothing with the added notice of dark," she said. "The Court of Light lives during the day, and so they'll only shop during daylight hours. This one caters to the Dark Court and will open at twilight and stay open all night long." She opened the door, and we stepped into a room that looked like a costume shop.

A silver bell above the door rang signaling our entrance, and a middle-aged woman wearing a beautiful silver dress that brought to mind the image of a starlit sky stepped out of a backroom behind a curtain.

The shop was exactly what I'd thought a tailor's shop would look like. Mannequins held men's and women's clothing in various styles that looked distinctly out of today's social norms. Capes and cloaks hung from the walls. Dresses that looked like they would touch the ground. Tunics and trousers like something that Robin Hood would have worn.

The walls were plain and unadorned except by the clothing. There was no computer to keep track of sales. I didn't even see a cash register. Just a counter with a notepad and pen.

"Astriel," the woman said, seeming to flow across the floor, "here for another set of lingerie? I'll have to order more spider silk if that's the case."

"Not tonight, Elora. My friend here is looking for a brand-new wardrobe." Astriel pushed me forward a step, and Elora glided to me, her feet making no sounds on the wood floor.

"I'd say so if that's what the rest of your clothes look like." Her voice reminded me of a wind blowing through trees, and when I looked in her eyes, they were almost void of color. At the same time, they seemed to burn just like everyone else that had magic.

"What kind of clothes are you looking for, my dear?" she asked softly.

"She needs mostly traveling clothes, but throw in a dress or two as well." Elora glanced at Astriel and then turned back to me.

It was hard to look her directly in the eye. That lack of color made me think that she was dead. "Is that what you'd like, child?"

I nodded. "Yes, please. Do you need to take my measurements?"

She shook her head, her head moving just a little slower than most people. "I've been doing this long enough that I can tell your measurements from looking at you." She paused before saying, "Though that sack you're wearing makes it slightly more difficult."

She turned to Astriel and said, "Give me two hours. Her clothes will be ready by then."

Astriel nodded and took my hand. A sense of dread had fallen over me the longer I'd been near Elora, and when we stepped out of the shop, I felt it fading. "What is she?" I whispered.

"She's a Draugr. Extremely sad story, actually, but she's

Chapter 14

made the best of things." Astriel took my hand in hers as she began to lead me through the streets.

"She was a dark elf that was killed when she made her Mistress an unfashionable dress and embarrassed her to an extreme level. It wasn't actually unfashionable, but her Mistress was an idiot who thought they were laughing at the dress when in actuality, they were laughing at the fact that her husband was sleeping with her sister."

"Because she was unfairly killed for a crime she did not commit, she didn't leave to go to the void. Instead, she stayed to feed on her Mistress, slowly making her weaker and weaker until she died. Afterward, she decided to stay a part of the world and to continue her trade."

"Well, she kind of creeped me out," I said softly, still shaking off the effects of being in the room with Elora.

"The Dark Court is filled with all sorts of magical beings. Most of them are the creatures that fill the nightmares of humans. We aren't the good guys, but neither is the Court of Light. We just don't try to hide who we are."

I nodded. I thought that I could accept that. Maybe. There was nothing in the world that was black and white. No clear-cut good guys and bad guys. But was the Dark Court even remotely close to being "good"? I glanced at Astriel and knew that she had killed men while she fed. Just as Sebastian had killed women. Was that too far?

I needed time. Time to think. Time to try to wrap my head around the fact that nothing in my new world was as simple as my old world had been. Somehow, I doubted that I would get that time. Things were moving too quickly.

"Come on, little fairy. I think you could use a nice hot shower, and we've got two hours to kill."

"That sounds like a good idea."

Chapter 15

Rose

I stepped out of the shower and felt like a brand-new woman. I dearly hoped that the Dark Court was up to human standards in terms of showers if I was going to end up spending any time there. I wasn't sure there would ever be anything as refreshing as a good hot shower.

Astriel had laid out a set of clothes that she thought would fit me. They wouldn't. At least not in the bust area since she must have been two or three cup sizes bigger than me. They were still a lot better than the linen tunic of Sebastian's that I'd worn.

I put on the top and was pleasantly surprised to see that it mostly fit. It was certainly not a Fae top since it was made of a stretchy T-shirt material that seemed to fit no matter what the shape of the person wearing it. It was a simple black. I put on the matching black yoga pants and finally felt like I wasn't running around looking like a homeless person doing a walk of shame.

I quickly brushed my hair, realizing just how wild my hair had gotten. When that was done, I felt alive again. The feeling of it all being a fantasy mixed with a nightmare had faded, and after thirty-six hours on this adventure, I finally felt awake.

Long black socks and a pair of running shoes were the last pieces of the ensemble. Now I wouldn't have to worry about where I stepped. Who knew that a good set of clothes and shoes could make such a difference in the way you viewed your situation?

I looked in the mirror and smiled. I didn't look half bad. Even with wet hair, I looked better than I ever had when I'd been human. Yes, I was ready for the adventure now.

I stepped out of the bathroom and found Sebastian talking to Astriel. She had a look of horror on her face, but Sebastian seemed nonplussed.

"Let's try this necklace on you," he said.

He walked up to me and pulled a ridiculous necklace out of a pocket in his trousers. I looked at the necklace that had to have been worth more than most cars.

"Turn around," he said sternly. There was definitely something going on, and he was trying to remain calm.

I turned around and lifted my wet hair for him. As Sebastian's fingers brushed my neck, I recognized the feeling for what it was. Lust. With just a touch, he had turned my mind away from the situation towards him and what he could do to my body.

With a soft, almost inaudible click, he latched the necklace in place. "That should keep your scent hidden from everyone," he said softly. His fingers trailed down my neck, and I shivered

Chapter 15

before he stepped back.

"Let's see it on you." I turned around and looked down at the wealth of gemstones wrapping around my neck.

"It's gorgeous," Astriel said. "Though, I doubt that it's worth the cost."

I ran my fingers over the central diamond, surprised at just how big it was. It was at least as big as my thumbnail. The smaller sapphires were the size of my pinky nail. They were all so massive.

"This must have cost a fortune," I said softly.

"More than a fortune," Astriel said with a snort.

Sebastian crossed his arms and assumed a defensive stance as he glanced at Astriel before turning to me. "It cost what it cost. You needed it, and there was no getting around the price."

Astriel stomped towards the stairs. "She may have the right bloodlines, Bastian, but is she really worth this? Is she worth the risk?"

"Anything is worth it if she is what I believe her to be." Astriel turned to him, one foot on the first step, and they stared at each other for a few seconds, neither of them willing to accept the other's argument.

The tension in the air was thick enough to cut, but then something interrupted it, shattering the silence.

A cracking sound. Beginning as a soft crack, like when an ice cube is put into a glass of water, it grew, and I glanced down at the diamond. A tiny crack in the center slowly grew outward, and both Astriel and Sebastian's eyes were trained on the stone.

The crack slowly grew until it finally reached the surface of the stone, and with a resounding pop, the stone broke in half, both pieces slipping out of the setting and falling to the ground.

The scent of a campfire began to fill the room. I could almost hear the crackling logs. A scent of power. My scent. This was what I smelled like?

Sebastian and Astriel's eyes both got wide as they stared at the stone on the ground.

"What does that mean?" I whispered, my voice the only sound in the room.

"It means that you are more powerful than anyone I've met other than High Queens," Sebastian said, a wry smile crossing his lips.

"It means you could be the next Dark Queen," Astriel said softly.

I didn't know how that was possible. I was just a girl who happened to have parents that were fairies. I couldn't even do magic.

"I can't be a Queen. I've seen what you can do, and I can't do anything like that. A Queen is supposed to be powerful, isn't she?"

Sebastian nodded. "You need training. That's all. You've had magic flowing in your veins for less than two days. You just need training and time to understand your powers."

Suddenly, the scent of a smoldering fire wafted into the room, and both Sebastian and Astriel's bodies went tight. This was nothing like my scent. This was polluted by the faint scent of rotten eggs, of sulfur. "Get her clothes and get her to the portal. I'll meet you there." His tone was commanding, and Astriel ran to me, pulling me across the room to a cabinet next to her dresser, and when she opened the door, I saw stairs leading down.

Chapter 15

"Come on," she hissed, pulling me into the hidden stairwell.

"Whose scent is that?" I whispered back as I followed her, closing the door behind me.

"Nyx."

Chapter 16

Sebastian

I walked down the stairs where Barbie smiled at Nyx in his assassin's cloak. A cloak exactly the same as the one in the pack on my back. She was a nice girl, and she knew a few things about immortals, but she didn't know that she should have run and hid the moment that anyone in this cloak walked into the room.

Nyx turned away from her, ignoring the fact that she was still trying to talk to him.

"Sebastian." A greeting. A warning. "Where's the girl?"

"Gone." I reached into the pack and pulled my own cloak out. Tossing the pack aside, I pulled the cloak on. I may not have been part of his guild, but he respected me enough to give me the professional courtesy of allowing me to dress for the occasion.

"Where?" The people in the bar stared at us. One man

Chapter 16

started laughing so hard that he spit his beer out. "Nyx," I said softly, but he didn't respond. Instead, he turned to the man.

He didn't use magic. He didn't need to. He simply walked up to the man, and as the man stood up, he slipped the dagger out of its sheath in a reverse grip, and, in a single graceful movement, sliced the man's neck clean to the bone. Without saying a word, he turned and walked back to where he was standing.

For just a few seconds, there was silence other than the gurgling of blood as the man tried to breathe through the blood that blocked his windpipe. His hands tried to clamp around his neck to stop the bleeding, but then he fell over.

When he hit the floor, everyone began to scream including Barbie. They all ran out of the bar while we stared at each other. A human life was nothing to Nyx. Truthfully, it barely mattered to me.

"Where has the girl gone?" he asked again in that gravelly voice. A voice that sounded tinged by smoke and ash.

"Away. Stop chasing her. Tell Seraphina that she is dead, and everything can go on as it was."

I shifted, putting my hands on the sheaths that held one dagger instead of two. Nyx didn't know that I was without one of my daggers, and I wanted to keep it that way.

"I can't do that. My honor does not allow it. I will follow the Queen's commands as you should have done."

"She's a full fairy, Nyx. Of both bloodlines. She could be the next Dark Queen. I can't kill someone that could fill the empty seat."

He seemed to think for a moment before speaking as was his way. "Then step aside and let me do it. I will lie for you, Sebastian. This time."

Princess of Shadows

I shook my head. "I can't do that either. I don't want to fight you, but I will if you force it upon me."

Nyx withdrew his daggers, and I gathered my strength, grateful that I'd been able to feed on Rose. This was not going to end well for either of us. Or for this city.

Without hesitation, I flicked my hand towards Nyx, and a dagger materialized from mist and flew towards him faster than a human eye could have seen. He shifted his head slightly, and the dagger didn't even graze him.

As soon as it had passed him, it dematerialized once again. Nyx crossed the room in half a second, faster than any human could have done. Jumping backward, I dodged his first swing, but there would be another and another.

I would lose a knife fight with this man. His skin was thicker than mine, almost like a natural armor. And he was drastically stronger than me.

I turned and ran towards the simple glass window. I didn't have time to shift through it, and I covered my head as I threw my weight against it. The window shattered, and I rolled on the ground, shedding most of the broken glass that had attached to my cloak.

Now that I was out of Ast's bar, I touched a shadow and slid into the warren. As soon as my feet hit the tunnel floor, I was running, not bothering to wrap my boots in mist. There would be no hiding. Nyx was just as effective a shadow walker as I.

He entered the warren a half-second later, and my fingers grazed the wall. A rooftop. A place where my powers would be stronger, and there would be less damage during our fight.

I reappeared in the Mortal Realm next to a metal pole, slipping out of its shadow. I ran to the edge of the building

Chapter 16

and leaped, soaring through the air towards the next one. I smelled Nyx as I jumped, his scent impossible to mistake.

The scent of fire filled the air, and I had to twist as a spout of flames singed the side of my cloak. Mist cushioned my fall as I hit the next rooftop, becoming nearly water as I forced it into a tight block underneath my feet. Turning, I watched Nyx spray the roof with fire to slow his fall.

Pure fire left the palms of his hands. Bright orange, it filled the darkness around us with light, and I had to shade my eyes from the sudden brightness.

"You cannot run from me, Sebastian. Either stand and fight me or tell me where the girl is so that all of this can be over."

"I won't let you have her. She could save the Dark Court from Seraphina's rule. Don't you remember when we didn't have to take orders from that bitch?"

Mists began to rise above the rooftop, and flames sprayed out from Nyx, burning them away. "You're going to tear the Dark Court apart, Sebastian. When I kill you under Seraphina's orders, they'll rise up against her."

"And they'll die. All of them," he continued. "You and I both know that there's no other end to that battle."

I snarled. "Then stop trying to fucking kill me, Nyx. They're your people, too. Your guild is Dark Court. They'll die just like the rest of them."

"Seraphina has given my guild her protection. She will shelter us in the coming battle if I fulfill her command. I do not want this, but I don't have any other options."

I growled in frustration. She'd laid the trap well, that bitch. "Then I'd better not let you kill me," I said.

I ducked behind a chimney, and fire hit the brick with a concussive explosion of heat and power. Closing my eyes, I combined my powers over mist and stone, shaping the mist into three exact replicas of myself.

Their daggers wouldn't have the power that mine would. They would still be sharp, but Nyx's wounds would heal almost instantly. I gave them the simple commands to rush him. One to run around the chimney, one to climb over it, and the third to sneak around.

As soon as they moved, I slid into the shadow that ran behind the chimney. It would take Nyx a moment to realize what had happened. He would figure it out soon enough, though.

I needed something that would keep him from following my scent. Raising my arms, I filled the warren with mist. He would burn the mists away as soon as he slipped into the warren, but that wouldn't change where my scent was. Everything would smell like me as my magic coated the very walls of the warren.

I ran down the tunnel, my fingers trailing against the wall. Images of London popping into my mind. Finally, after almost a minute, I found the place with the portal I was looking for.

The portal that not even Damian would think to look for me at. Only Ast would know where I was taking Rose.

I slid through the shadows and found myself in Hyde Park at almost three in the morning. I took a whiff of the misty London air. Rose's scent was nearby. They'd be waiting at the portal. A portal I had made and hidden years and years ago.

I began running, not wanting to use any more magic than I'd already used. This chase was very possibly not over, and I had already used almost all of the power that I'd drained from Rose.

Thinking about Rose brought even more questions. Damian had said that it would take a century for me to fill that diamond.

Chapter 16

Rose had filled it in minutes. That was High Queen levels of power. Levels that I didn't even think that Seraphina had.

She was still untrained, so it was nearly worthless to her. Nyx would have killed her in seconds. I understood now why Seraphina wanted her dead. If she had this much power without holding a seat, she would be terrifying when she finally took the throne.

Strong enough that Seraphina would be no match for her.

I found Ast and Rose standing around a simple oak tree. It was old. Far older than most of the trees in the area, but not ancient.

"Are you coming with us, Ast?" I questioned, feeling slightly out of breath.

She shook her head. "You're going to have enough trouble keeping Rose safe as it is. The last thing you need is another person you have to keep safe from Nyx. I'll be fine. I've been thinking about moving anyway."

I nodded. "I'll see you when this is all over. Don't go back to your place. Nyx killed a human in plain sight. And, if he can't track me through the portal, he'll wait for you there. Might want to warn Damian as well since that diamond is still on the floor. I may be pissed at him, but I don't really want him getting tortured by Nyx."

"I'll take care of myself and warn Damian, Bastian. Don't worry about us. Get her out of here, and keep her safe."

I gave her a quick hug, knowing that there was a very distinct possibility that one of us wouldn't survive this. Then I picked Rose up and climbed the tree. At the top, a small piece of silver wire had been wrapped seven times.

I touched the silver and felt the pull of a permanent bridge, the portal to the Immortal Realm. No trail through the warrens for Nyx to follow. He'd have to find my trail to Hyde Park. Then he'd have to find the portal.

I prepared myself. If he found us, I wouldn't be able to run again. Not with where I was taking us. No, if he found us, I would have to pit myself against a man who had never lost a fight. And I'd have to do it with only one dagger.

Chapter 17

Rose

We appeared in the middle of a field. It wasn't all that different from the one with the unicorn. I took a deep breath and smelled flowers blooming and the soft smell of pine. We were on the edge of a thick forest.

The grass was different here. More like the grass from the Mortal Realm. Except that it was darker. A deep purple rather than the mix of purple and green.

For the first time, I saw the Immortal Realm in the light. The sun hung on the horizon, turning the world orange. It felt like I hadn't seen the sun in forever.

I reached behind me and felt my wings. They seemed more real now. Like they'd finally become solid. Astriel's illusion must have worn off when we stepped into the Immortal Realm.

Sebastian stood beside me in his assassin's cloak, and he looked me over, noticing my new outfit and the bag on my

Princess of Shadows

back full of new clothes. Why had he been worried about my clothes when he was getting chased by Nyx?

"How'd you get away from Nyx?"

"It's complicated, but I'll tell you later. Right now, we have a very short man to talk to."

As if on cue, a man in a full beard ran out of the forest. "Sebastian!" he yelled as he ran on short little legs.

"Come on. It hurts me to see him run like that." Sebastian grinned down at me as he pulled his arm away. He began to run, and I followed, happy to have my new clothes and especially my shoes.

The forest wasn't even a mile away, but Sebastian began to slow much earlier than I'd expected him to. This man had been able to sprint for almost thirty minutes when he'd taken me through the warrens for the first time. Now, he could barely make it a mile? What was wrong?

He was panting softly when we finally reached the short man in the beard. I looked down at him and couldn't help but smile. This was a gnome. No question about it.

He wore a soft hat over a bald head. His beard went down almost to his waist. And he barely came up to my waist. Wearing brown linen pants and a green linen shirt, he looked like he belonged in the woods.

He had big bushy eyebrows, and under them, his eyes sparkled with energy. His lips were thicker, and small wrinkles creased his smiling face.

"Sebastian! It's been so long!" He was out of breath, but his excitement must have been more important than breathing because he didn't stop talking long enough to catch it.

"The village is doing so well. So very well. And we've kept it safe. This whole time."

Chapter 17

"Calm down Enivyn. Catch your breath, friend." Sebastian smiled down at the gnome as he took big gasping breaths as fast as he could so that he could start talking again.

"Before you begin, Enivyn, this is Rose. She's a friend."

Enivyn looked up at me, and his brow furrowed. "But she's a fairy. With wings. You said no fairies."

"She's a different kind of fairy, Enivyn. Trust me on this. One that will help rather than harm."

Enivyn crossed his arms and glared at me, and I almost giggled. "I'll be watching you, fairy. I trust Sebastian. I don't trust you."

"Come on Enivyn. Let's get back under the trees. When is your brother coming to relieve you?" Enivyn turned and began walking back to the trees while we followed him, making sure that our steps were shorter than usual so that we didn't pass the gnome up.

"Morning. It's Sinivyn. He'll have goodies. He always has goodies." He paused and then turned back to look at Sebastian. "Did you bring goodies?"

"Not this time, friend. I was in a bit of a rush to get here this time." Enivyn sighed. "We don't get many goodies. And we never get chocolate. Or coffee. Or sugar. Or new silver needles. Cara says she only has two needles left. We need some goodies, Sebastian."

Sebastian chuckled. "When this is all over, I'll make sure to bring the village some supplies. Maybe even some chocolate."

That made Enivyn smile, and his little legs moved just a bit faster. I felt like I should know what was going on a little more than I did, but I didn't blame Sebastian for that.

It scared me that Sebastian had run from Nyx. After watching what Sebastian could do, I hated to think of how powerful Nyx must have been for Sebastian to decide that running was the better option.

"So what's new with the village, Enivyn?" Sebastian asked.

"Lots. Kasia had her foals. She had two. A girl and a boy. They're loud. And rude. But cute too. That's how babies are. Even centaurs. They like to fight a lot. Thalena always makes Oreus cry. Thalena is the girl. Oreus is the boy. Anyway. That's the big news."

He seemed to talk in a rhythmic way, like every word was a tiny piece of a song that only he could hear. His body rocked back and forth as he walked in time with the words.

"You have horses?" I asked, confused.

"Centaurs. They escaped the Court of Light's war pens. Centaurs are considered a far superior war mount in comparison to normal horses for good reason, so many of them have been enslaved for various 'crimes'. I helped them find a home here instead of killing them as my contract stated."

"Yes, Sebastian rescued all of us. Each. One. Of. Us. Except Cara. She was just his friend."

"Sebastian sure has a lot of lady friends," I said with a smirk.

"That's because he makes ladies happy." Sebastian winked at me, and I had a hard time not laughing. Enivyn was so serious about everything that it was hard to take any of it seriously.

When we got to the edge of the forest, Enivyn led us to a hut that had been made of grass and leaves in a way that it would be impossible to see from the field.

"Won't Nyx just be able to follow our scent if we stay this close to the portal?"

Sebastian glanced at Enivyn, and Enivyn stood as proudly as the little man could. "I am a half-gnome with all the powers of the gnomes inside me. No one will be able to smell us. Not

Chapter 17

even a fairy bloodhound could smell us."

He nodded as if that was that. I glanced at Sebastian and he grinned. "Gnomes have an instinctual ability to cover the magical scent of everyone in their area. Half-gnomes like Enivyn aren't able to hide as much of an area, but they're still incredibly helpful. They're the only reason that the village is able to remain hidden in the Immortal Realm."

I heard a soft humming coming from somewhere, and Enivyn jumped up. "Sinivyn and his snacks are here!" he announced. "We will eat well this morning!"

Enivyn opened the door to the hut, and Sebastian found himself a spot against the wall to sit. He leaned his head back, closing his eyes as he had done when we'd been at the field with the unicorn.

I sat next to him, watching as Enivyn and another half-gnome walked into the hut. "This is Sinivyn!" he announced.

Sinivyn wore similar clothes, but there was a darker look in his eyes. He had many more wrinkles, and they seemed to cut deeper in his cheeks and forehead.

The other half-gnome was not nearly as outspoken as Enivyn. He seemed more serious, and he dragged a bag nearly as large as himself behind him. "Sebastian, who is the fairy? Fairies aren't supposed to be here." He frowned just as Enivyn had.

"Sebastian says that she's okay," Enivyn said. "I don't trust her. I trust Sebastian."

Sinivyn nodded and walked into the hut, dropping the bag in the center of the room next to a ring of stones that was almost certainly a cookfire. Sinivyn sat down in a tall chair next to a window facing the area of the field that we'd appeared.

"That's a big bag, Sinivyn," I said, trying to build some kind of rapport with the half-gnomes.

"Not a bag, fairy. It's a snatchel. A satchel for snacks." He didn't turn around, focusing all his attention on the field.

"Oh."

Sebastian's eyes cracked open, and he grinned at me. He was really enjoying how uncomfortable I made them. The minutes passed quietly, and Enivyn began building a fire in the ring of stones.

"Why are you staying?" Sinivyn asked. "You should go to the village."

"Someone may be coming after us this time. I don't want to be surprised."

"Because of the fairy?"

"Yes. And because I disobeyed the Queen."

Sinivyn turned around in the chair, his brow furrowed even more. "Why?"

"Rose may be able to fill the empty seat, and Seraphina wants her dead."

Sinivyn's eyes moved from Sebastian to me as though he were really seeing me for the first time. "She has very dark wings," he said softly. "And she smells strongly."

"This is dangerous. Very dangerous. Why did you bring her here?"

Sebastian finally sat up and opened his eyes. "Because this is the safest place I can think of. I'm not asking you to protect her. I just need her away from everyone else so that I can begin training her before I bring her to Court."

Enivyn had stopped building the fire, and he was staring at the two of them. Sinivyn stood up and reached into the snatchel, pulling out an apple that had small splotches of purple on it.

Chapter 17

He took a bite as he continued to stare at Sebastian. "I understand. You saved us. You're saving her. Each of us brought danger to the village. Not this much, but that does not matter. We will not be angry." He nodded to Sebastian and then to me.

"I will trust you a little, fairy," he said and turned back to stare out the window, quietly eating the apple that was nearly as big as his head.

Sebastian closed his eyes again and leaned back against the wall as Enivyn went back to building the fire.

This was the strangest experience I'd ever had. Even compared to everything else that I'd gone through. Even compared to being hunted by an assassin.

I didn't know how I felt about Sebastian saying that he was going to bring me to the Dark Court. I hadn't agreed to that. I'd agreed only to being brought somewhere safe, and from everything, and I mean everything, that Sebastian had said, the Dark Court was one of the least safe places in either of the Realms.

I set my jaw. That warning that had been screaming at me since I'd grown my wings told me that if this was what it took to learn how to use my powers, then this was what I needed to do. No matter what, I had to do that in order to survive in this new world. This world of purple grass and apples. A world with two moons. A world where half-gnomes telling me I smelled strongly was not unusual.

A world where one man hunted me and another fed on me.

Chapter 18

Sebastian

I was already so drained. Nyx would be at nearly full strength. I truly hoped that he wouldn't be able to find the portal, that he would have to report to Seraphina that he lost us.

I doubted that it would be that simple, though. I thought back on my mentor, on the only man whom I'd ever looked up to. He was the best. Even better than myself. There was a good reason that he was the leader of the Assassin's Guild. He was an excellent duelist as well. Plus, he had two daggers where I had only one.

If I were at full power, I would have been the expected winner. I was nowhere near full strength, and if I were a betting man, I wouldn't bet on me. I had to conserve my strength. Every drop of it.

So I rested, my head against the wall as Rose, Sinivyn, and

Chapter 18

Enivyn talked. I didn't pay very much attention. Eventually, Sinivyn handed me a plate of food, and I ate it, not caring what it was. The fairy part of me could still regain my strength through eating, though not nearly as fast as full-blooded fairies could.

I glanced at Rose. I knew what I would have done with nearly anyone else. I couldn't do that with her, though. I'd already forced one experience with her. It wouldn't be enough to tip the scales anyway. No, I didn't have the time to feed the way that I needed to.

And if Nyx found us while we were in the middle, before I'd actually fed, then I'd be even weaker than I was now. I sighed and asked for seconds. Sinivyn loaded the plate up again. He narrowed his eyes at me, realizing just how weak I was.

I ate silently as the rest of them ate and talked. Rose seemed to enjoy Enivyn's antics and hearing about the village. She would love it there. She'd feel more at home there than anywhere she'd ever lived, and she'd finally have a moment to get her bearings.

I let out a slow breath before getting off the ground. I put the plate on the stack of dishes that Sinivyn would end up doing today. I glanced around, seeing that everyone's eyes were on me.

They all recognized that I was conserving my strength. Enivyn and Sinivyn would be wondering why I didn't feed on Rose, but they wouldn't question me. Not the gnomes. Of all the people in this sanctuary, these two and their brother would never question me.

I closed my eyes and tried to rest as I sat back down, letting the food become strength. It was nowhere near as good as sexual energy, but it was better than nothing, and I'd take what

Princess of Shadows

I could get right now.

* * *

It felt like I'd slept for only moments before I heard Sinivyn whisper my name. My eyes snapped open. There was only one reason that he would wake me.

Nyx.

I jumped to my feet and peered out the window. Yes, Nyx stood in the middle of the field. Directly where the portal had led. Sinivyn seemed to shake next to me. I patted his shoulder and saw that Rose was awake as well.

"I'll be fine," I said. "Stay here. Whatever you do, don't leave this hut. Nyx will abandon the fight to kill you."

"Isn't there anything I can do?" she asked. Concern filled her green eyes. They'd changed colors as all fairy eyes did.

"Be patient, and don't leave the hut unless you see me fall. If that happens, the gnomes will get you to the village so that they can warn everyone. There's a backdoor out of the village. It will take time for Nyx to find the village as long as everyone stays near the gnomes."

I turned to Sinivyn. "You know what to do. Keep everyone safe, but don't leave unless I die. If I survive, I'll need help."

Sinivyn put out his hand, and I took it. I could feel the fear and sadness flowing from him, but he stood tall. At least as tall as a gnome could.

Enivyn ran over and hugged my leg. I patted his back, and he looked up at me. "Don't die. We'll miss you too much. And no one will bring us goodies."

"I'll do my best, friend," I whispered.

Rose stood up, and I walked towards her. She wrapped her

Chapter 18

arms around me and whispered, "Don't die." Then, she pressed her lips against mine and every emotion that she felt flowed from hers into mine.

Passion. Fear. Sadness. Lust. Even now, she lusted after me. I pulled back and smiled at her. "I'll try."

Then I turned from all three of them and stepped out of the hut feeling nearly as ragged as I'd felt when I'd got here. The sun was shining. One thing that was in my favor. The wind blew through the trees, and I took a deep breath. I'd thought I would live forever, but all things must end. At least this would be in the pursuit of fixing things, of protecting someone that mattered. That mattered to the world. That mattered to me.

I took another deep breath and began to walk to the field where Nyx was waiting. I walked towards the battle and, almost assuredly, to my death.

Chapter 19

Sebastian

"You're hungry, aren't you?" Nyx said in that voice made of ash and smoke.

"I could eat," I said, smiling under my hood.

"You know you're going to die, don't you?" He wasn't going to enjoy this fight. Neither was I for that matter. Unlike most of the battles I'd been in, I genuinely respected Nyx.

He was nothing like me. Descendent of dragons, he was my opposite. He was a murderer, but who wasn't in the Dark Court. Unlike me, his honor was unshakeable. His reputation, infallible.

Yet, he respected me for the things that I'd done. Things that others had condemned me for. And I respected him for his skills and strength. For training me when no one else wanted to be near me because of my father.

"Once again, I don't want to fight, Nyx. I just can't let you

Chapter 19

have the girl. She matters more than your honor and even more than either of our lives. Even if it takes my life to protect her, I won't let you have her."

"That's too bad, Sebastian. I'd hoped that if it was going to come down to one last fight between us, at least you'd make it a good one."

I took a deep breath and let it out slowly, centering myself. Letting my awareness expand and take in all of the sounds, all of the feelings. Even from Nyx. Being half-incubus allowed me access to the emotions of people. Not exactly the same as mind reading, but the closest I could come to it.

Confidence. Sadness. Readiness. And a strange fear. Keying in on it, I explored the fear. He was afraid that I was right, that he was doing something that was actually against his own code.

I didn't want this fight. I was sure that I was outmatched. I would not make the first move. Not this time.

Nyx knew that this was the way that things would happen, and he didn't wait for my move even though he was a much more defensive fighter when evenly matched.

He leaped towards me soaring off the ground almost twenty feet above me, and I crouched as the air around him began to warp as he heated it. His daggers were in his hands as he fell towards me, and I waited, conserving my strength until he was only a few feet away.

And I flicked my hand out, my only dagger appearing from mist and flying towards him as I rolled away. He had to twist to dodge the throw, but it still caught him in the shoulder, cutting through the cloak and leaving the slice a shining crimson.

When his feet hit the ground, the earth seemed to shake with his impact. My dagger turned to mist and reappeared in my

Princess of Shadows

hand as I crouched, waiting for his next attack.

Fire. He would use fire next. My control over the mists was worthless against it. I squatted down as I waited for him to attack. His face didn't even register the cut on his shoulder. It would be just another scar on his body. A trophy from killing the Prince of the Dark Court.

Nyx did not let his wounds heal in battle. It was why I didn't bother to dip my dagger into my sheathe to coat it in the iron shavings. Healing took power, and in the midst of battle, he wanted every ounce of power for killing his opponent quickly, overwhelming him.

He took a deep breath, and I braced myself, my hands touching the ground. Instinctively, I sought out a warren to jump to even though I knew that there were none nearby. This was why I'd placed the portal here. No one could get here quickly. Not without the portal that I'd hidden.

Instead, I pulled on my second power. Strength over stone. A power I used very rarely. It was more draining, and it came from my fairy side, a side far more common.

Nyx breathed out, and a blast of flame came rushing towards me. I pulled up on the stone under the soil of this field, and a door-sized piece of stone rose from the ground in front of me. A shield from the flames that threatened to burn me alive.

The flames whipped around the stone, singing my shoulders and my cloak. Pain flashed in my shoulders from my burns, but I knew the wounds were minor. My dwindling power flooded the burns and healed them, leaving me with only a burned cloak.

I quickly made two copies of myself and began my counterattack. I sprinted around the stone while one copy leaped over it and the other ran around the other side. Nyx would

Chapter 19

need a moment to recover from that strong of an outpouring of energy. Dagger in hand, I and my two copies raced towards him.

Everything suddenly became incredibly hot as Nyx raised his hands to either side. The air around Nyx began to waver, and I jerked to a stop, the copies continuing towards him.

They caught fire as they stepped five feet away from him, their bodies turning to mist and fading almost instantly. I threw my dagger once again, and Nyx couldn't dodge it as he held the power around him.

As it flew through the air, it seemed to slow as it passed that point where my copies burned up, and then it slipped through, hitting Nyx in the chest. He grunted as the tip buried into him almost an inch deep.

Unlike a normal man, it was not a fatal wound for Nyx. Nyx was born from the blood of dragons, and his flesh was stronger than that of normal Fae. The dagger slowly sapped him of his power, though. If I'd been holding it, I'd have been gaining that power, but I couldn't get close enough to him.

Finally, he let the shield down, and as he reached for the dagger, it turned to mist and reappeared in my hand. He began to race towards me, his hands firing burst after burst of fire at me, and I danced around them. Each one got closer, but so far, I'd managed to survive each blast.

The very air in the field seemed to be on the verge of catching fire with so much heat. This was not going well. I had to get close enough to fight him, but my powers were nearly useless against him, and he knew all my tricks.

Throwing daggers at him was only going to get so far. I danced closer to the stone that I'd raised from the ground, using it as a shield.

"Fight me!" he roared from twenty feet away. I tried to center myself. How could I get to him? How could I get through the fire to force him into an actual knife fight? I was at a disadvantage in a knife fight, but at least there was some chance of regaining some of my energy. The next time one of those fireballs hit me, I wasn't going to be able to heal myself or I'd be completely drained.

"Fine. Come fight me and quit throwing those fucking fireballs." He laughed and it sounded like rocks grinding together.

"So that you have a chance? No, Sebastian. You're already almost drained. You'll be dead soon enough."

I heard him take a deep breath, and I touched the stone in front of me. It broke at the ground level, and I heaved, picking it up. Then I threw it. Powering it with magic and using my power to enhance my strength, it flew through the air at Nyx. His eyes grew wide as the giant stone became bigger and bigger in his eyes.

I immediately sprinted towards him, my body following the stone. He couldn't follow through with his attack or he'd be hit squarely in the face by a three-hundred-pound stone.

He dropped to the ground, his chest pressed to the burnt and ashy grass, and I pounced in a last-ditch effort to get on his back. He rolled just as my dagger dug into his shoulder, ripping free of the blade.

He screamed as it tore through the flesh and blood spurted from the wound. Without hesitating, as he rolled, his arm shot upward towards me, and a flash of light blurred my vision.

Pain filled my chest. A fireball. He'd caught me squarely in the chest with a fireball. I had pulled only a touch of power from him with that strike. If I healed the wound, I would be

Chapter 19

nearly mortal.

I stepped back, blinking away the light blindness. And I saw her. Running into the field. Nyx saw my gaze shift and he followed it.

"Don't stop me, and I'll let you live," he growled, pain still tinging his voice.

I could barely move. Everything inside me screamed to heal and run. Jump into a warren and get away to feed.

But I couldn't. I gritted my teeth as Nyx stood up and began walking towards Rose. She stopped several hundred feet away from him and seemed to realize how bad of a mistake she'd made.

I tried to ignore my wounds and chase after Nyx to at least draw his attention long enough for Rose to get away, but my legs failed me. I hit the ground hard, and I screamed as my burnt chest slammed against the ground among the charred grass.

Nyx and Rose both turned to look at me, but Nyx turned away almost immediately. He knew that I would never be able to catch him with my current wounds. I put my hands against the ground wishing there was a warren under me. I could cross the space between us in an instant.

And I felt a hidden reservoir of power. Not my own. Something different. A Queen's power.

I looked up and saw Nyx leap through the air. Rose put her hands up, and her wings seemed to flash in the sunlight. Then a blinding light filled the air in front of her as she stepped to the side.

Nyx screamed and fell crashing to the ground beside her. She stared at him in horror and began to walk backward away from him, her hands going to her mouth. Nyx lay on the

Princess of Shadows

ground screaming as his hands covered the gauze over his eyes. Gauze that protected his eyes from white light.

Nyx was the son of a half-dragon, raised in a cave for more than a hundred years. His kind could see in the complete dark of a cave. Their eyes were only able to adjust to the fire that they controlled. White light was not natural in the world of dragons. At least not his kind.

He was the perfect hunter in the darkness, but in the light of day, his eyes would already be aching. That flash could have blinded him. He would heal it, but that was not something he was used to doing in the heat of battle.

I felt for that reservoir and realized that I couldn't pull the power into myself. Instead, it seemed to augment me, making me not just a half-incubus, half-fairy. I was something else. Part Queen?

I touched the ground again, hoping that the impossible would be made possible, and I felt for a warren. There was none.

But, just as a bridge pulled at you, wanting to be used, the Queen's power pulled at me, showing me the answer. I directed it through the ground towards Nyx. Towards Nyx's shadow as he stood up, rubbing his eyes and growling at Rose.

Then I felt it, the warren. Tighter than any I'd ever seen. As I slid through my own shadow into the warren, I saw that it was filled with a different mist. Black mist almost like smoke mixed with a white that could only be described as condensed sunlight.

I slid through the tunnel only a few feet long. My wounds ground against the stone as I slid through the tunnel that was barely wide enough for me to fit through. I groaned, knowing that no one could hear me, and I reached out to touch the end

Chapter 19

of the miniature warren.

The image of Nyx grasping his daggers in both hands appeared in my mind. His cloak trailed behind him on the ground as he prepared to rush Rose once again. I smiled as I slid through the nothingness between this space and the Immortal Realm.

My hand wrapped around Nyx's neck. My legs wrapped around his waist, and I plunged my obsidian dagger into the back of his neck with every ounce of strength I had left, slicing through his spine. His arms and legs seemed to collapse as he lost feeling everywhere below that point.

As he fell to the ground, I held the knife, feeling his strength drain into me. The power flowed into my burnt chest, healing it bit by bit. Nyx gasped under me, and I felt the power inside him fade until there was nothing.

Until the shell that had held the soul of the man who had raised me was empty. Until I knew that he'd gone back to the void. He'd been the only man who had seen me as something to protect and teach. He'd been the only one other than my mother who had seen the value in my bloodlines.

I hadn't wanted this, but he hadn't either. He'd be proud that he was bested by me, that the student had surpassed the teacher. I felt the sadness roll over me in waves, but I pushed them back. Not now. I would grieve later.

I pulled the knife out of his neck and rolled him onto his stomach. It was only then that I heard Rose screaming. I took a deep breath and let it out slowly, glad to be rid of the pain.

Then I bent down and picked up his daggers. They would be his only real possessions. Nyx, the greatest assassin in the history of the Fae was dead. I remembered when he'd shown me these same daggers a thousand years ago and begun teaching me how to use them. Then, I remembered the day that he'd handed two hartskin sheathes to me, giving me the most valuable gift I'd ever received. I could never have been a part of the Assassin's Guild, but that had been his way to say that I was worthy. That he was proud of the man I'd become.

He had not been my enemy, yet I'd been forced to kill him.

"Rest, friend. You'll be remembered. Seraphina will not get away with turning us against each other." I patted his chest. His scarred hands seemed to relax, and I stood up, holding his daggers.

Turning to Rose, I said, "It's done. We're safe now. Nyx didn't work with anyone else, so we shouldn't need to worry about any other assassins."

She ran to me, and I held her against me as tears fell down her cheek. "I thought you were going to die. I couldn't watch that and not do anything."

I took another deep breath and said, "I thought I was going to die. I should have died. Your being here is the only reason I didn't."

She looked up at me, her eyes seeing under the hood, and asked, "Because I distracted him?"

I shook my head. "Because you're a Queen. Because you should be sitting on the Dark Throne. A Queen can lend her subjects part of her power. That's the true power of a Queen. They can wield massive strength, but they're still vulnerable to physical attacks."

I held up a dagger. "I could kill you just as easily as anyone else with this if I could get close enough. Your powers let the rest of us do things that we couldn't do otherwise."

"Rose, I *created* a warren. I shouldn't have been able to do that. No one can do that. But together, we did."

Chapter 19

Rose sniffed and said, "I have to do this, don't I? I have to go to the Dark Court."

I released her and stepped back. "You don't have to do anything. I wish that you would. You could stop Seraphina's abuse of the Dark Court." I stood up a little straighter and said, "But you don't have to. No one can force it on you. There have been Queens who have turned down seats of power before."

Rose nodded. "I... Can I take some time to think about it?"

"Yes. Take all the time you need. But before we do anything else, you need to learn about your powers. I can't always be there to protect you, and if you do end up going to the Dark Court, there will be dangers everywhere."

She nodded, and I took her hand. "But first, I need some rest. A lot of rest."

She smiled at me, and I felt myself relax at least a little bit. She was a Queen. The Queen. The one who could set everything right again.

"Let's find this village of yours. I can't wait to meet everyone. Enivyn has told me so much about everyone."

"Yes. You can meet everyone, and I'll get some sleep."

Chapter 20

Seraphina

"What do you mean he's dead?" I screamed at the assassin. Nyx dead? At the hands of Sebastian? How was that even possible? Nyx was the best assassin in the Immortal Realm.

"Nyx carried a device on his person at all times that would activate in the event that his heart stopped beating. It sends a message to a connected device displaying the area around him as though we were seeing and hearing through him."

"I watched the Prince picking up Nyx's daggers and then hugging Nyx's prey. Sebastian believes that he has found a Queen to fill the Dark Throne. Is this true?"

I began to pace. That little shit. How had Sebastian managed to kill Nyx? Who else could I send to deal with him now? Sebastian and Rose had to die. They had to.

It had taken almost fourteen years to set this in motion. I couldn't let it all fall apart when I was this close to finally

Chapter 20

setting everything right.

The thought of Rose sitting on the Dark Throne was laughable at best. She was ignorant of everything magical. At least until three days ago. There's no chance that she could survive the Courts of the Immortal Realm. If she truly had the power to ascend to the throne, then she would need to contend with more than just me.

And until she was far more skilled in the use of her powers, there was no danger to me. I could deal with her if she ever came here, but Sebastian was another issue. He and those cursed daggers were a danger to everyone.

"Why would I know? I heard about an untrained Fae pulling magic into the Mortal Realm. That's why I sent Nyx and Sebastian after her. She pulled a significant amount which made her a threat to our secrets."

The assassin nodded, and I knew that he didn't quite believe me. I was a Queen of the Court of the Light, though, and there were laws against direct lies that not even I could break.

"Then the Assassin's Guild would like to formally request your permission to deliver retribution to the Prince and the fairy he protects."

My eyes became little more than slits as I stared at the man in the hood. "You're telling me that the entire Assassin's Guild would like to attack Sebastian and the fairy?"

"Yes, Lady. Nyx was the best of us, the most honorable of assassins, and his death is a tragedy. The Prince will pay for Nyx's death and his refusal to obey your commands with his life."

I tapped my nails on the table that separated us, letting the thought run through my mind.

"You have my approval and my protection if there are

repercussions from the Dark Court when you return with Sebastian and the fairy's heads."

The assassin nodded and turned quickly to leave my conference chamber. This should work out well. Even at his strongest, Sebastian wouldn't be able to fight off sixty assassins working together. And even though Rose was a Queen by birthright, she had none of the training needed to aid Sebastian.

I sat back down in the chair and let my frustrations fade. This was better. Nyx was a loss, but he was an acceptable loss. This way, the Assassin's Guild would be in my debt rather than I be in Nyx's.

I smiled softly. Yes, this was a surprising turn of fate indeed.

Chapter 21

Rose

It was early evening by the time that we could see the village. The days were short in the Dark Kingdom, only a third of each day. The opposite was true in the Light Kingdom according to Enivyn. He had chatted with me about the Immortal Realm during our hike through the woods while Sebastian stayed quiet.

Small little huts just like the one that we'd stayed in by the portal exit were clustered around a central fire ring. Enivyn walked as fast as his little gnome legs could carry him. He was so full of excitement at being the one to bring Sebastian to the village.

He needn't have worried about walking fast enough, though. Sebastian limped along beside me. He looked like he was about to stumble any second. His eyes were completely gray and filled with mists. They were unnerving, like looking at a blind man's eyes with all the color drained from them.

He just kept taking one more step, and my body stayed tense as I waited to catch him when he eventually fell. I was so intent on Sebastian that I didn't even notice the centaurs running out to greet us. In fact, the entire village seemed to pour out of their huts, but the centaurs were the first to get to us.

A very large female with silver hair and a matching silver coat and tail raised a bow towards me, and I stopped in my tracks. I didn't know what to say to keep her from shooting me after everything that had happened.

"Kasia," Enivyn said quickly, "this is Rose. She's a good fairy. I trust her." The centaur looked at me and then at Sebastian. Then, she finally looked back at Enivyn.

She snorted softly but then said, "A friend of Sebastian and Enivyn is welcome here." She slowly released the bowstring, putting the arrow in a quiver at her side. She slung the bow she carried over her shoulder.

"That was good." Enivyn's voice seemed more nervous than I'd expected. "Kasia likes to shoot first. Then she asks questions. Especially now. Babies do that to mothers." He patted my leg and smiled up at me. "The rest are easier. Don't worry."

Kasia walked back into the village, and her foals followed her, but they kept looking back at us. I didn't feel nearly as confident as I had before arriving. My nerves were so frazzled at this point that it didn't take much to make me lose what little confidence I'd found.

Surprisingly, the first non-centaur to get to us was another half-gnome. He looked nothing like the other two. Clean-shaven, he wore a relatively nice coat and normal shoes. He was still just as small as the other two, but other than that, he

Chapter 21

looked just like any other man. Under heavy eyebrows, two dark brown eyes that seemed to smile like the other gnomes watched me with a twinkle.

"Rose, this is John. He's my other brother." I raised my eyebrow in surprise. "John? That's... that's a human name."

"I know that all of you full Fae think of the half-bloods only by their Fae side, but some of us have embraced the human side. After my mother raised my two brothers, giving both of them proper Gnomish names, she demanded that I be given a human name. And a human upbringing."

He smiled then. "My brothers are like most of the half-bloods who have embraced their Fae side. I have decided to do the harder thing and embrace the human inside me."

He bowed to me and said, "It is a pleasure to meet you, Rose. A friend of Sebastian and Enivyn's is a friend of mine."

"And any brother of Enivyn's is a friend of mine," I replied with a smile. He was so well-spoken compared to his brothers. It made me question many of the assumptions I'd already made.

Until now, I'd met Fae who embraced their natural gifts and done the things that their race was best suited for. It made me think that maybe there was more to the Fae than I'd given them credit for.

John turned and headed back to the village. The rest of the members of the village saw us, and as soon as they noticed Sebastian, they retreated, making space for Sebastian to walk through the center of the huts.

Enivyn led us to a small hut in the corner. The door had no lock, but when Enivyn opened it, I could smell Sebastian's faint scent everywhere. This was his home within the village, and no one bothered it. Even though he'd been gone for a long time, nothing and no one had disturbed it, and so his scent still lingered.

Sebastian immediately moved to the small bed that had been made for him. For a village so far removed from both worlds, the hut seemed luxurious. The bed was made of solid wood with a feather mattress. A fireplace sat in the corner with chopped wood sitting next to it. There were even paintings hanging from the walls.

He was loved here. This man who snarled at everyone and anything. This murderer. A man who embodied the darkness was their hero. Their savior.

Enivyn left without a word, closing the door behind him. Sebastian tried to get his cloak off but couldn't manage it. I moved to help him get it off, and when it was over his head and lying in a heap on a chair, he sighed, taking slow breaths.

"Thank you," he said softly.

"What can I do to help you?" I asked. "Are you hurt?"

"I'm fine, Rose. I just need to rest. And eat something. Please bring me a plate of food when you find some."

He pulled his silk shirt off. The entire front of it was burned. His chest and stomach were still pink where the new skin had grown over the burned flesh. I'd watched it happen. It had been terrifying to see it, to know how badly it had hurt him.

He reached to untie his boots, but he seemed to struggle. I squatted down in front of him and undid the laces. "Sit on the bed. I'll get your boots off." He nodded and hobbled to the bed to sit down.

I pulled his boots off along with his socks. He seemed to hesitate and then said, "Thank you, Rose. Please let me rest until you find food."

"I will. And I'll tell Enivyn to spread the word not to bother

Chapter 21

you. I'm sure he already has."

Sebastian nodded and crawled under the blankets with some difficulty. I turned and with just one glance backward at him, I left the hut.

Enivyn stood outside the door and gave me an odd look, his thick eyebrows bunching together. Then it was gone, and he was back to being his generally excited self. "Come on fairy. You can help with dinner. Not the cooking part. That's Andryn's job."

"Okay, Enivyn. Show me what to do, but can you do me a favor first? Sebastian wants to be left alone. Can you let everyone know?"

"Everyone knows to leave him alone. He's low on power. He comes here a lot like that. Cara helps him with that sometimes. She's a good seamstress and Sebastian's friend." He started walking towards the center of the village.

"Come on, fairy." He still refused to call me Rose, but I guess I could get over that. At least he wasn't scowling at me anymore.

I followed his happy little steps as he brought me to the cookfire where a gorgeous man stood butchering a deer. "Yum. Look at all those potatoes from Helena's garden," he said pointing at a basket taller than him that was overflowing with different colored potatoes.

It was going to take some getting used to looking at all of these oddly-colored plants. I truly hoped that the potatoes tasted like the potatoes from home.

"Here's where you help, fairy. That basket of potatoes needs peeling. Andryn is going to cook them. You get to peel. It's a good thing to do for everyone. Fairies peeling potatoes is odd. An odd fairy could be good. If you sat and pointed at people.

Princess of Shadows

Do this. Do that. Then you'd be a normal fairy. Normal fairies are bad. Don't be normal."

He handed me a small knife, and I stared at the mountain of potatoes that I got to peel so that I could be odd enough for him. I blinked a few times as Enivyn walked away.

The handsome man butchering the deer said, "It's okay to use a little magic to help with that if you want. I promise I won't tell." He winked at me, and it was hard not to stare.

Where Sebastian was rough and dark and brooding, this man seemed to be his exact opposite. He was beautiful. Golden blond hair that seemed purposefully messy. A face that looked like he'd never seen hardship. And eyes that pulled you in.

His body was nothing like Sebastian's. Where Sebastian was big and strong, this man was lean with tight muscles. His movements were graceful. Even something as simple as trimming the fat off a piece of meat seemed to be beautiful.

He wore a dark green tunic without any sleeves that had golden embroidery over the edges. His pants were made of leather that had been dyed an even deeper brown than natural.

"I don't know how to use magic yet," I confessed. I guessed that honesty was the best decision in a place that was already skeptical of my intentions.

"Your wings still glisten," he said as though that meant something to me. "How long have you been in the Immortal Realm?" I thought back on everything that had happened. All the odd day and night changes.

"Two days? Maybe? I'm not exactly sure. It's hard to keep track."

He smiled at me and said, "Well, if you can't use magic, then you'd best get to work. That's a lot of potatoes." He looked at a smaller bucket and said, "That's where the peels go. The

Chapter 21

potatoes can go in the soup pot. Quarter them before you drop them in."

"I think I can do that."

"I'd hope so. If you can't peel potatoes, then what can you do?" He meant that as a joke, but it got me thinking. What could I do to help these people? What good was I to them? I knew nothing of farming or sewing or building or even of magic. This was probably one of the only things that I could actually do to help these people.

I set my jaw. I was going to live in this world. I wouldn't let my human upbringing keep me from being successful in this world of magic and assassins. I looked at the bag of potatoes again. And lots and lots of potatoes to peel.

Today, I would peel potatoes, but tomorrow, I would learn how to do something more. Something more valuable.

Chapter 22

Sebastian

I tossed and turned on the bed as the sweats set in. I was dying. Starving to death. It began as a fever like this. My energy was dangerously low. I doubted that I could stand at this point.

Food would help. It would be slow to help, but it was better than nothing. I didn't dream of food, though. I dreamt of Rose. Fever dreams of the mists surrounding us.

My dreamscape. Her naked under me. Screaming in pleasure. A violent and passion-filled dreamscape. For once, I was lost in the sensations just as much as my prey was.

A fantasy that had never happened.

The dreamscape was not a place for my pleasure. Only for food. Only for survival and strength. A place where I never failed in my hunt.

It was a wonderful fantasy. To enjoy the process of feeding

Chapter 22

beyond the power, beyond sating the constant hunger. To be able to find someone who could drive me to madness just as I drove them towards it.

My eyes snapped open as the door to my hut opened with a rattling sound. I sat up, groaning in pain as I did so. A beautiful mature woman with a stately presence wearing a robe of silk. Probably the only silk in the entire village. Long red hair the color of autumn leaves that flowed down to the center of her back. A lithe face and thin body.

An elf. *Cara.*

"Did Enivyn not inform you that I didn't wish to be disturbed?" I said and almost winced at the gravel in my voice. My throat was swollen already. I needed the food to be done.

"I did not need to hear from Enivyn to know that you were starving, Sebastian. Everyone knows how weak you are, and they all question why your friend has not satisfied your needs. She is a full-blooded fairy, surely she can survive a trip to the dreamscape."

I lay back down, letting my body relax as much as it could. "I haven't asked her. I don't plan on asking her. I'll survive on food just fine."

"Then why have you not asked for me, Sebastian? I have never refused you. I believe it to be an honor to help the one who has done so much for the people in this village."

How could I possibly explain it to her? Rose was a Queen. She would be *the* Queen soon enough. I was her only bridge to her past, and she didn't truly understand me. She didn't understand that everywhere I went, people expected me to feed on them. They begged me to feed on them. What was a little power that would come back in a few days in exchange for a night they would never forget?

"I can't, Cara. Not while Rose is here. Not while I'm caring for Rose." I could feel her eyes on me. Eyes that held the last memories of a forgotten forest in them. Eyes that had seen her entire people eliminated for resisting an invasion by other elves so that some city could mine something unimportant there.

"You care for the girl?" she asked.

"Yes, Cara. I do. And not just because she is powerful." There. I said it. The one thing that I hadn't even admitted to myself.

The door swung open again, and I sat up, hand outstretched and ready to summon my dagger.

Rose stood just outside the door with a massive tray of food blinking in surprise. "I'm sorry, Sebastian. Enivyn said that he'd tell everyone to leave you alone. I should have stayed by the door to keep people out."

"It's fine, Rose." My hand fell back to my side as I slowly adjusted in the bed. "Cara was just leaving. Is that venison I smell?"

Cara interrupted. "No Sebastian, I was not about to leave. If you care about her as you say you do, then she needs to understand what you require to maintain your strength. Do not refuse for her. Give her the choice. If she does refuse you, then seek me out and I will give you what you require to maintain your strength."

She turned away from me and smiled at Rose. "You have beautiful wings, dear. They suit your power." Her smile widened. "They remind me of your father." She glanced at me again and said, "You weave quite the knot to untangle between the two of you."

Then she walked out as Rose's eyes went wide at the mention of her father. When the door closed behind Cara, Rose

Chapter 22

whispered, "How does she know my father?"

"Cara is a seer. She sees multiple timelines in both Realms. I don't really understand how it works. No one but seers really understand, but it explains some of her eccentricities."

Rose nodded, looking at the door for a few more seconds before she shook her head slightly. She turned to me and brought the tray of food to the bed. It was loaded down with things that smelled delicious.

Nothing smelled as delicious as Rose, though. I had a difficult time keeping my eyes on the food as the scenes from my fantasy ran through my mind unbidden. The hunger inside me made me want to do things that I would regret more than anything I'd ever done before.

I picked up a piece of venison, not worrying with a fork or knife, and put it in my mouth. It was good. Andryn's food was always good. One of the only people from the Court of Light that had been invited to the village.

"What was she talking about, Sebastian," Rose asked as she sat down next to me in the bed.

I sighed and ate another piece of venison, giving myself some time to think of how to put this. Rose just kept watching me, patiently waiting for her explanation.

I finished chewing and decided to be blunt. "I'm on the verge of starvation. My power reserves are drained to nothing. Between the chase with Nyx and then the fight, I'm out of power."

"I do not constantly refill my internal power reserves like fairies. If I don't feed, my body consumes itself to refill the power supplies, and I slowly die. A full-blooded incubus *must* consume sexual energy, or they'll starve. I'm not quite that bad, and it's why I've survived longer than most full-bloods. I

Princess of Shadows

can eat food and very slowly recover my power reserves if I eat enough."

I looked Rose directly in the eye as I said the next part, "But it will take weeks before I'll be able to jump into a warren with you and possibly a year before I'm back to the level I was before Nyx caught up with us."

"Then what do you need, Sebastian? What is it that Cara was suggesting that I provide? Do you need to make me dream again?" She seemed to shiver, and I wasn't even sure what it meant. I couldn't feel her emotions at all.

"I can't feed like that right now, Rose. I can't pull you into the dreamscape. I'm too weak for even that. The only way I can feed right now is physically."

A blush fell over Rose's cheeks. "Why didn't you feed on Cara, Sebastian? I need to know. She's pretty. Probably prettier than me. I guess that you've done that with her lots of times." I could see that she'd just realized the one thing that I'd never wanted her to find out. I had been with more women than all the men she'd ever met combined.

I had known it would come up, though. I just hadn't ever found a way to talk about it. Honesty was my only option here. I couldn't dance around it. It was too important.

"Yes. I've fed on Cara many times. Most times that I've been in this village. I've fed on thousands of women, Rose. And that's exactly what it was. Feeding on them. Not for sexual gratification. In all the thousands of years that I've been alive, I've never found anyone who could make me feel anything more than a hunger for their life force. A hunger for power. For survival."

"But for some reason, I don't want that anymore. I don't want to feed for power. I'd rather eat food and be weak than

Chapter 22

to be with other women."

"Really?" she asked.

"I haven't fed on anyone else since I found you, and that has to be a record. I don't plan on breaking that streak."

Rose had changed so much in the past few days. She'd been such a pain in my ass, but now... Well, now I cared about her in a way that I didn't really understand. Incubi weren't supposed to care about anyone except themselves. It was against our very nature. Even a full-blooded fairy couldn't sustain an incubus by herself. Not if he were actively using his power for more than feeding.

But a Queen might, and that's what Rose was. A High Queen with more than enough energy to keep me at full strength. More than that, something inside me seemed to sing when she was close.

She sighed. "You know I'm a virgin, don't you?"

"That's why I haven't pressured you. Even though an intelligent Incubus would have. It seems that you've brought out the idiot in me."

"Can you give me a little time?"

I nodded and picked up another piece of venison. Meat, especially the rarer cuts, had the most power in them.

Rose picked up a piece of bread coated in honey butter and took small bites as she stared at the wall. "All of this is so much to take in, Sebastian. You. Magic. I'm a freaking fairy Queen. Everything. I don't know what to think about it all. I was just an ugly girl going to college a few days ago, and now you expect me to be the ruler of half a world."

"My life consisted of class, trying not to embarrass myself in front of my sorority sisters, and trying to spend an hour running through the forest. That's about it."

Princess of Shadows

"I just don't know if I'm ready or strong enough to be the girl you and everyone else thinks I am. I've nearly died so many times in less than a week. How does anyone do this?"

She turned to me, her eyes asking me the questions that I had no answers for.

"No one expects you to become Queen tomorrow. That's why I brought you here instead of the Dark Court. You need training. You need time. You need to get your bearings."

I groaned as I shifted. A pain in my back shot lightning through my body. "Eventually, you'll need to make some decisions. They won't be easy decisions." I put my hand on hers and said, "But you'll make the one that you feel is right, and everyone will just have to deal with it. Either way, I'll support you."

Rose gave me the best smile she could muster as she looked me over. I knew that look. She was trying to decide how badly I was hurting. I'd seen it enough times, though. Most of the time it was to determine if I was going to die anytime soon.

"Do you want to go out to the fire?" she asked changing the subject. "Enivyn said that they're going to tell stories."

"You'd like to listen to them?" I asked.

She nodded. "Enivyn sounded like they were the best part of the night."

"They usually are. Unlike mortals, we don't have all of your entertainment options. Our stories are told, not watched on television."

"I think that might be better. Like a book with other people."

"I'll go to the fire with you," I said, handing her the tray with shaking arms. "I can eat out there as easily as I can in bed."

She set the tray down and stood up, reaching her hand out to help pull me to my feet. I took it gratefully, but when I

Chapter 22

pulled on her, she couldn't keep her balance and fell on top of me, forcing us both backward onto the bed, her on top of me.

"I'm so so so sorry," she said as she tried to roll off me.

"Wait." The words came out as a whisper. Everything in my body ached, but having her weight on top of me felt incredible. Her warmth. My body buzzed with hunger, but it didn't seem to matter. I stared into her eyes and couldn't stop myself.

My hands went to the back of her head, and I rose up to meet her, my lips touching hers. Softly, tentatively. Nothing like in a dreamscape. Nothing like I'd ever done before. This wasn't the kiss of a man who was giving a woman her fantasy. This was the first kiss between a man and a woman, and for the first time in my life, I felt nervous touching someone like this.

She gasped but didn't pull away. My lips pressed against her harder, and my tongue found hers to begin the dance of lovers. A heady sensation ran through me as I stared up at her. Lust for another person. Not her power.

She pulled back, panting softly. "Not yet, Sebastian. Soon, but not yet. I'm not ready."

I nodded to her and smiled, the sensation of her lips against mine still making my heart race. "I can wait."

She climbed off me, and as she turned around, I looked at her, seeing those wings made of shadow made manifest. Then, my eyes ran over her body, and I felt a stirring between my legs. A stirring for her body and not her power. Even when I was starving.

She grinned at me as she faced me. "I can try to help you up again, but I think you'll just pull me on top of you."

"How else am I supposed to woo you, little fairy?"

"Most of the time, men are supposed to woo with dinner and

a movie. At least that's what I've heard since I've never been wooed before. Though, I guess rescuing me from an assassin, nearly dying to save me, and then taking me to meet all of your friends might work. And, I think I may enjoy stories around a campfire more than a movie."

"I'm glad that sacrificing my body and power for your safety is at least as impressive as buying you a dinner."

Her lips curled in a real smile and said, "Come on. You're going to have to get out of bed on your own."

I groaned as I pushed myself off the bed. "You carry the tray, and I'll do my best to get to the fire."

"You need to get healed up so that you can be chivalrous again. It might be worth crawling into bed with you just so that I didn't have to carry heavy things anymore."

She grinned at me, and I tried to smile back at her, but the pains that ran through my body were almost too much to take. She saw through my façade and didn't joke anymore as I hobbled out to the bonfire that had been prepared.

There were two spots on the logs that had been made into benches around the fire for us, and I tried to smile at everyone as they waved to me. I sat down on the ground, needing something to support my back, and I sighed as some of the pains receded for the moment.

Even though everything hurt, it felt just a little bit better. Had that kiss actually given me a touch of power?

John the half-gnome stood up and said, "Tonight, I'm going to tell the tale of how Sebastian, Prince of the Dark Court and only son of the late Dark Queen Catarina, saved my brothers and myself from slavery under the Court of Light."

Chapter 23

Rose

Something stirred in my mind. Something that I should remember but didn't.

"My brothers and I lived in the Mortal Realm at the time. My mother refused to go to the Immortal Realm, and my father accepted this." He began walking around the fire as he talked, drawing the eyes of the listeners.

I pushed myself a little closer to Sebastian, picking food off the tray and eating it slowly as we listened to the story. Sebastian wrapped his arm around me, and I shivered at his touch. Even now when I knew that there was no way that he was using magic, his touch made my body crave more.

"We were happy for the most part, living in a small town outside a larger city." He nodded to me and said, "A suburb is what the humans call it. We weren't able to live underground as my father wished, as all gnomes desire, but we lived near a forest. My father would take us through the forest nearly every day foraging for food. Mushrooms, nuts, bird eggs, and the like."

"It wasn't because my mother couldn't provide food for us. She was a nurse at the local hospital and made plenty of money. No, gnomes need to hunt and find their food. At least part of it. It's as important to them as gold is to goblins or running is to centaurs. They cannot ignore that side of themselves."

"This wasn't a dangerous thing because my father had already taught us how to hide in the forest. We foraged in places that we weren't supposed to go, but gnomes are excellent at staying hidden."

His voice, even as human as it sounded, still had a rhythmic quality to it, and his movements matched it. It made John's story entrancing.

"We were happy even as odd as it sounds. My father was able to teach us about being gnomes, and my dear mother taught us about the human world. We all learned to read and do mathematics as human children did, though we did it at home. As humiliating as it sounds, she dressed us up as children even after we were nearly adults. It was the only way to let us walk around in the world without fear of someone noticing us."

"We all shaved every day, and we kept our voices high pitched. It wasn't unusual for us, though. It was all that we'd known, and a person will do what it takes to be able to walk outside their door without fear."

"My father was the only one of us who refused to act like a human child. He had no desire to go to zoos or shops. He never wanted to get into any of the human vehicles. He was content to forage and come home to tell us stories of a world where magic was real."

Chapter 23

"Until the day that everything changed." John's voice became more somber, his words more staccato.

"We were riding home from a shopping trip when we were in a car accident. This was many many years ago, and Sinivyn ran to the nearest pay phone to call for an ambulance. He also called our father."

"The ambulance took my mother and us to the hospital. She was hurt badly. The car door had crushed her arm, and the doctors thought that they would have to remove it due to the excessive damage."

"They wanted to give her the option, though, so they didn't operate immediately. My father arrived at the hospital before she'd woken up, and he did the one thing that he'd told us never to do."

John the gnome paused, building a tension in the air. Then the words came flying out. "He took her arm and healed it. Gnomes can heal wounds, though it takes almost all of their power to do so."

"We had lived safe and simple lives for many years at this point. We'd enjoyed everything that humans and gnomes enjoyed. We'd never drawn attention to ourselves, and our ability to hide what we were kept us safe."

"Now... Now, my father had risked it all to save my mother's arm. I wouldn't have done anything differently. Neither would my brothers. We didn't have access to our magic yet because we'd never been to the Immortal Realm to claim it."

"We were released from the hospital as her arm had miraculously been healed. No one could explain it, yet no one tried to question it either. When we arrived home, the soldiers were already there waiting for us."

"So was Sebastian." John glanced at Sebastian with a smile.

"Climbing out of a shadow, he slipped through the group of four soldiers standing in their gleaming golden armor. Those black daggers of his laying waste to them. As we stood in the doorway of our family home, we watched the four of them die in our living room."

"My father recognized him as the Prince. Sebastian told us about how the soldiers had come to take us into the army and use us for our ability to hide troop movements."

"He offered us a solution. He could take us to the Immortal Realm and set us up in a safe place. My father declined, knowing that my mother would be unhappy in the Immortal Realm. We accepted the offer and have lived here since. Every year or two, we each spend a week in the Mortal Realm visiting my parents."

"We would have been enslaved by the Court of Light or dead if Sebastian hadn't saved us that day. He risked himself to save a few half-bloods and a human loving gnome that he'd never met."

"And that is the story of how we became the first citizens of this village. More were rescued by Prince Sebastian and brought here after that. Each person has their own tale of how he saved them."

Trust the Prince. The words echoed in my mind. The old woman. The day of the bus crash. That was what she'd said. *Trust the Prince.*

Sebastian was the Prince. He'd found the secret. Now, he had saved my life at the risk of his own. She had known all of this would happen. I looked at him and realized that if there were ever a man to be vulnerable with, Sebastian was the one. I took a breath. I would give him what he needed.

I looked up at Sebastian who had closed his eyes again. He

Chapter 23

was slowly chewing as he had been from the beginning of the story. Bite after bite, he was devouring the tray of food.

John sat down, and Kasia stepped into the ring of logs beginning a tale of a hunt she had gone on. One by one, stories were told until the fire was burning low. Still, Sebastian continued to slowly eat the food on the tray until I looked down and it was all gone.

Sebastian's eyes were still closed, but he had a smile on his face. "Want to go lay down now that you're done with your food?" I asked.

He opened his eyes and nodded to me. "Enivyn can show you to the visitor's hut," he said.

"I had hoped to share your bed as we did in your cottage." He raised an eyebrow, but he slowly got to his feet.

"I enjoyed the stories," I said, "but it's been a very long day and I need some sleep."

There were no chuckles or laughter as there would have been if I'd said that in the sorority house. In the house, I would have had to endure catcalls and all types of humiliation. Here, everyone was just worried about whether I would help Sebastian get better.

And I would. This man was not the cruel creature that I'd thought him to be. He was the epitome of nobility in the Dark Court. Cruel, hardened, and strong, yet fair and caring for those who deserved his protection.

I followed after him, leaving the tray on the ground by the fire. As he moved, I saw that he was already feeling a little bit better. He limped just a little less. His head was held just a bit higher.

He was still sick. I knew that. But he was stronger. I thought about the dream that he'd brought me into. A fantasy. He'd made me feel things that I hadn't understood. Now it was time to feel the real thing.

I moved to walk beside him, and he held my hand as we walked. When we got to the hut, I stopped him. "Sebastian, will you show me what it's like to be with a man?"

He smiled at me and said, "I'm not a man, but I'll show you what it's like to be with an incubus. I've heard that it's the preferred option."

Chapter 24

Rose

I was ready for this. Ready for him. I was. I was sure of it. Maybe I wasn't, though. Maybe I just wanted to be ready for it.

As soon as Sebastian stepped through the doorway, he pulled his shirt off and dropped it to the dirt floor. I couldn't stop looking into his eyes. Completely misty. Gray. Just like when he'd been in the dream.

They pulled me into them, a swirling cloud of need. Of hunger. I could feel him when I stared into those eyes. I reached out and put my hand to his chest, feeling the smooth skin and hard muscles underneath. I ran my fingers down his chest, feeling his muscles ripple at my touch.

"That feels good, Rose," he whispered. My eyes didn't watch my hand. They were locked in his gaze. Long black hair fell around his face, breaking his confident smile.

His hand reached up to touch my cheek. He felt like he was on fire. The warmth that flowed through his fingers brought a heat to my skin that hadn't been there even in the dream.

"I think I like this better than the dream. You feel different."

His hand moved down my neck, his fingers slipping to the back, and he pulled me to him with a sudden burst of strength. His lips fell on mine, hard and urgent. Passionate. Fire exploded inside me as he trapped me in the kiss. Trapped was a terrible word for it though, because there was nowhere that I'd rather be.

His need flowed through me like a drug. This couldn't be normal. I should have been feeling all the physical sensations, not his hunger. His hand holding my neck just a little too tight. His lips pressing too harshly against mine. His teeth coming down to chew my lip.

Instead, I stared into those eyes and felt the things that he kept behind the mists. The longing for a true companion. The hope that he'd found one. The hunger. Always the hunger. The desperate need to keep me from pushing him away.

And over all of it, his pure bliss at having found someone who was stronger than him. Someone who could handle him at his worst. Someone who he could be weak around.

I pulled back from his kiss. His eyebrows furrowed as he questioned if he'd made a mistake. I smiled at him and said, "Take off your pants." Without thinking about what I was doing, I pulled my shirt off, leaving my chest bare.

I should have been terrified by this, but something flowed through me that knew that this, of all the things in the world, was right. Sebastian moved faster than I'd expected him to, and I looked down at his maleness. Hard and ready for me.

Then he stepped up to me as I was about to tell him to lay

Chapter 24

down and whispered to me, "No, Rose. Not this time. You can command me every time after, but tonight, you'll let go. Tonight, you'll allow me to show you what this is all about."

He didn't give me a chance to argue as he wrapped his hands around me and picked me up. My wings fluttered, trying to give me balance as he carried me to the bed. As he held me, I looked him in the eye and got lost in those mists again. I barely noticed as he lay me down except the strange sensation of my wings sinking through the mattress, still there, yet immaterial.

His lips pressed against mine, but then they moved down to my neck. I closed my eyes, getting lost in the sensations of his lips and teeth on my body. Down my neck, he left a trail of kisses. His hand roamed over my waist and then up to my breast, squeezing it tightly while his lips found the other.

Teeth sank into my flesh, and they should have sent shooting pain through my body. Instead, my body felt only the passion that flowed from Sebastian into me.

And it drove me higher.

I let out a moan and put my hands in that jet-black hair as my body began to pulse with an energy that I'd never experienced. Even in the dreamscape, I'd never felt like this.

He released my breasts and moved lower, kissing my stomach and somehow drawing that throbbing from between my legs and pushing it through my body. His hands moved to my waistband, and he slowly pulled the leggings down.

I kept my eyes closed even as he lifted my legs to remove the last bit of clothing from my body, leaving me bare. I knew the need he felt now. I may not have been an incubus, but I was desperately in need of what I knew was to come.

It was a hunger that had never been satisfied. A hunger I'd never known until I'd met Sebastian.

Princess of Shadows

He began kissing my stomach again, and he spread my legs. At one point, I'd have been scared to be this vulnerable especially around a man like Sebastian. A man that knew how to twist my body to his whims. Not anymore. Never again.

Not with him.

His lips moved even lower, and his hands moved to my waist, holding me still as his tongue touched my most vulnerable spot and sent lightning bolts of pleasure through my body.

I bit my lower lip, but the low moan still came out. I'd never felt anything like this. Not even in that dream. Sebastian may not have had enough power to work his incubus magic, but this was magic just the same. There was nothing in the world so exquisite as his tongue between my legs.

I could sense the hunger in Sebastian being sated. His body no longer ached. His powers would return soon.

I let out another moan as he found my entrance, making soft circles. My entire body pulsed with my heartbeat, a drum that resounded through my entire being.

A pressure was building inside me that I'd known only once before. Once, in a dreamscape. A pressure that I knew would sate the hunger building inside me. In this singular moment, I wanted nothing except for him to continue doing this. His tongue and lips on me were the only things in the world that I craved.

And then they were gone. My eyes snapped open for the first time since the beginning as the pleasure began to fade. The desperate pressure inside me needed more. Why had he stopped?

I felt my wings flicker in anger, and a dark power flowed over my body, close to the skin. But when my eyes opened, they saw Sebastian's face over mine as he pressed his body

Chapter 24

over mine. Flesh to flesh, he surrounded me.

His own dark power flowed over his skin. I could feel it as clearly as my wings. It melded with mine as I felt him press against my opening as he looked down at me. His misty eyes less gray and more blue.

"Don't turn away," he murmured in a whisper that I couldn't have missed. Pressure began to build at my opening, and a sharp stinging sensation made me wince, but then it was gone.

Sebastian's hands ran underneath me as he filled me for the first time. I pulled him closer, my nails pressing into his back as he forced a pleasure I couldn't have imagined through my body.

That desperate pressure that had been building inside me poured out in a wave as I moaned and dug my nails in harder. Sebastian didn't seem to notice the pain as his hands never stopped moving over my body, pulling and pushing that power over me, and making all the sensations even more intense.

Wave after wave of bliss flowed through my body, and Sebastian gasped, his eyes turning an even darker blue as he stared down at me. His touch became more insistent, his nails digging into my back as well.

He began to thrust into me, and my back arched as he forced my body to take even more pleasure. The world seemed to disappear as I lost track of everything except the sensations. Only the sound of his body against mine, his hunger and mine finally being fed.

And his eyes staring into mine.

I could see him. All of him. In this moment, I felt everything that he was. The strength. The pain. The struggle. The loss. The power. The love.

He bent down and kissed me. The cautious softness was

gone. There was no exploring, no wooing. He pressed against me so hard that it hurt. His thrusts were desperate now, and the kiss was no different.

I felt that pressure building inside me again, different yet the same. Mists began to flow around me, caressing me in a way that hands could never do. Soft kisses all over my body. A cacophony of sensations.

The mists flowed under me, slowly lifting me off the bed, becoming a soft cushion underneath me and letting me float an inch off the bed. Sebastian's hand went to my throat. His lips found the crook my neck, and as he kissed me, his teeth bit down.

It was all too much. The sensations. The feelings that flowed from him to me. The pressure inside exploded outward in a scream, and my body shook, my legs tightening around him. Wave after wave of pleasure raced through my shaking body. I'd never felt anything so intense.

Sebastian groaned above me, and his thrusts finally stilled. The mists in his eyes receded, leaving crystal clear, deep blue eyes. Deeper than I'd ever seen them. "Thank you," he whispered, his chest heaving as he caught his breath.

"No Sebastian, thank you. That…" I took a deep breath, my head still swimming from all the sensations. "That was incredible. Is that how it always is?"

He smiled down at me as the mists that had supported us began to dissipate, letting us settle onto the bed again. "No, I was very weak that time. Next time, it will be much better."

I couldn't imagine it. There was no way that anything could top the sensations that I'd just felt. At least not in my mind. As I looked at Sebastian, I realized that I was almost certainly wrong. I just didn't understand how.

Chapter 24

Something had changed, and as he rolled over, I didn't cover up. Sebastian had seen all of me. He'd touched all of me. He lay on his side, hand under his head as he looked at me. His other hand ran over my skin, teasing me.

He wasn't shy about it either, letting his fingers trace my breasts and nipples. "Do you feel better?" I asked, and he grinned at me, his confident smile back in place.

"Better than I can remember. I'm not up to my full power yet, but you haven't ever known me at my full strength. I feel better than that, though. You have no idea how badly I've wanted to feel you like that."

I felt the blush come over me, but his hand went to my chin, stopping me from turning away. "Don't be ashamed, Rose. You're beautiful in ways that no other woman has ever been."

I tried to pull away, but he climbed on top of me, pressing my hands to the bed. His strength covered me, making me feel even more vulnerable as he pressed his lips to mine.

I felt him then, a joy that didn't make sense. He wasn't happy that he wasn't sick anymore. He wasn't just satisfied with me. He was happy. Like a child on Christmas morning.

I wanted to ask him about it, but once again, I felt like he could read my mind. "You made me feel different, Rose. I felt like a man instead of an incubus for the first time in my life. I wanted to see you in ecstasy. I wanted to be the one who showed you that even in this world of cruelty and pain, there are reasons to smile."

"And as I felt your bliss, I felt a happiness inside me that I hadn't felt in years. I don't want you to turn away from me, Rose. Ever. I don't want you to run or hide from me."

"Because you're the first person I didn't want to hide from."

I stared up at him, feeling every bit of his emotions as he

poured out his feelings. This was not the same man that had sat at a tree and watched me being chased by a unicorn. No, that had been the cold side of Sebastian. That had been Tinkerbell.

This was the man that was willing to fight a battle he was almost guaranteed to lose. The man who was willing to fight the most powerful woman in the world. For me.

I smiled. "Fine. I won't turn away from you, but that means you're stuck dealing with me."

A grin crossed his face, and he rolled over onto his back, letting me up. "Perfect. Now why don't you curl up to me like in the cottage? You slept well that night."

I narrowed my eyes at him. "You're bossy, and I don't think I like it. How about you curl up to me this time. I've never been a spoon, but I think I'd like to try."

"I don't know what that means, Rose." I sighed and turned away from him.

"Just curl up to me sexy fairy man." He didn't need any more coaching than that, and when I felt his arm wrap around me, I felt safe. After everything that had happened in the past few days, I felt safe here.

And I felt like I was home. Finally.

Chapter 25

Sebastian

I woke up next to Rose who was still softly snoring. The curve of her body sang to the male in me. Not the incubus. I wasn't hungry for her power. Somehow, after a millennium, I'd found someone who sang to the rest of me.

I tried to crawl out of bed to make coffee without waking her, but as soon as I stood up, Rose rubbed her eyes and looked at me with a sheepish glance. I hadn't bothered to put on clothes after last night. Neither had she, but while I was standing, she'd pulled the covers up over herself.

The fire had burned down low last night, and I tossed a few logs on to get it heated up again as I filled the coffee kettle from a basin. "How do you feel this morning?" she asked. I knew she was staring at me. Everyone stared at me, and normally, it annoyed me. She was different. I liked the way she was looking at me.

Princess of Shadows

I set the water to boil and turned back around. "I feel good. The real question is how do you feel?" I put my hand out to touch her, and she seemed to pull away, curling up tighter in the covers.

"I think I feel good?" she said, and I could feel the vulnerability. I felt the incubus inside me already ready for more, but I pushed the hunger back.

"You're not tired?" I asked, concerned. "Even most fairies are at least a little groggy the next day. I didn't hold back last night."

She shook her head and seemed to be breathing faster than normal, and her wings were fluttering regularly. She needed some space. Not very much, but a little.

I stood up and pulled my pants on, covering myself up and giving her some time to wake up a little before she had to confront what had happened last night. I squatted by the fire, watching the twigs breaking.

It was hard to see it and not think of Nyx even though I knew that I should be focused on Rose. I'd wished that I could control fire like him when I was young.

As I watched the fire, memories flooded my mind, and I bowed my head remembering. Then I felt Rose's hand on my back. "I'm sorry that you had to fight him, Sebastian." Her words were so soft. I looked up at her. She was wearing her clothes from yesterday.

"How'd you know?"

"You've never talked about caring about anyone except him. Now you're watching the fire and sad. What were you thinking about?"

"You don't really want to know. You probably wouldn't understand how he was."

Chapter 25

"Try me, Mister. I'm a Queen, and Queens know things. Or at least I think they do." She gave me a smile, and I couldn't help but smile back.

"I was thinking about the first time that Nyx hurt me. He was showing me how to fight. He was letting me use him as a target as he danced across a training ground while I shot stream after stream of mist at him. One finally caught him in the chest while he was jumping."

"He'd fallen hard, and I'd rushed to help him up, scared that I'd hurt him. I was young, maybe a hundred years old at the time which is extremely young for someone raised as a Fae. As soon as I was within a few feet of him, he screamed, and fire filled the air."

"It coated me from head to toe. I screamed as it burnt me. He didn't try to put it out. All he did was watch me as I slowly healed from it. When I could finally see again, my eyes healing, I looked down and saw an obsidian dagger at my throat."

"Don't trust me, Prince," he said. "Don't try to help me. I may be helping you now, but in the end, men like me only destroy things. If you stay near me, I'll end up destroying you too."

"He was right all those years ago. He'd have killed me yesterday. I cared about him, but I did kill him. When he told me that all those years ago, I didn't believe him. I didn't believe that he'd end up hurting me. But I did remember not to trust anyone else."

"It made me stay away from everyone, only coming out of the palace to feed." I looked up at Rose. "I don't want to be like that anymore. I want to trust you, and I want you to trust me. For the first time since my mother died, I want to trust someone again."

"I trust you Sebastian, and I hope that you can trust me." She smiled down at me, and for just a moment, everything was quiet. Then the kettle began to whistle, and I picked it up as I stood.

"I think I can," I said, feeling the moment that we'd shared begin to fade. "What do you want to do today?"

"I don't know. I'm kind of lost in all of this. What am I supposed to do?"

"You probably need to start learning about your magic. If you're going to survive the Immortal Realm, you're going to need to know how to defend yourself."

She seemed to think for a moment and then said, "I want to do more than peel potatoes." She stood up straighter and seemed to steel herself. I gave her a confused glance and began to put coffee into the kettle.

"I think that's more than reasonable for a Queen in training..."

"No, I want to be useful. All I could do last night was peel potatoes. I don't want to be known as the Queen Who Peels or some such nonsense just because I'm worthless in every other way. I want to be a contributing member of the village."

I shrugged. "That seems like a good task to set yourself to."

"And I want to learn to fight like you." I turned around, ignoring the coffee.

"I don't think you want to do that, Rose. People who fight like me end up killing people. Maybe you should surround yourself with people like me who can protect you. Then you won't have to fight. You won't have to kill."

"No. You just got done telling me that you didn't trust anyone. Why would I surround myself with people I can't trust? I may never be as strong as you, but I'm tired of being

Chapter 25

treated like a princess. If you won't teach me, then I'll find someone else. I doubt that they'll be as good as you, but at least it will be something."

I snarled, showing her my teeth. "You will not find someone else to train you to fight. They'll only give you bad habits. If you're bound and determined to learn to fight, then I'll train you. I have to warn you that it will involve me hitting you repeatedly. There's no way around that."

"I'm a fairy. I can heal. I already know that's possible."

I gave her a half-smile and reached out a hand as a dagger materialized from mist. "Not from this, and not from anyone else who is used to fighting fairies. They'll coat their blades in iron shavings just as I do. You won't be able to heal from a cut filled with iron."

"I'd hope you wouldn't be training me with those," she said as she eyed the obsidian blade.

"Eventually I will. If you're going to learn to fight, you'll learn to fight like me, and that will require you to wield an obsidian blade."

She took a deep breath and nodded. "Fine. Then let's get dressed and I can start training. God only knows when something will force me to race off and stop learning."

I nodded, but before I got up, I kissed her. A simple kiss on the lips to remind her that this was not the last time I was going to wake up with her. She blushed again as my hand ran over her breast. "Yes, let's get dressed, but when you're done being a good little fairy, I'm going to show you how to be a bad one."

Chapter 26

Rose

Cara stood next to me in her silk robe. Her eyes were a milky white as she stared into mine. Unnerving, I let her explore my soul with her powers. As I stared into her eyes, I felt a pull not unlike the mirror or the portal.

The forest surrounding us faded and I was standing on a lakeshore staring at a different forest. One that was on fire. Bodies littered the shore of the lake. Some in armor, most in simple leather clothing.

Blood ran into the lake, turning it a dark pink. The air was filled with smoke as shouts and screams came from the forest. A woman holding a baby in each arm ran towards me.

"Help me Cara!" the woman screamed. My body moved on its own, and I began to run into the water, trying to cross the narrow bit of lake. Then an arrow came from the forest and struck the woman in the chest. She didn't survive even long

Chapter 26

enough to scream in pain. Her eyes stared at me, dead already as she fell to the sand, her babies hitting the ground hard.

They screamed in fear and pain, and I began to swim, my robes heavy around me as they soaked up the lake water and pulled me downward. I continued to swim, desperate to get to the infants.

A man in gleaming golden plate stepped out from behind a tree, shouldering the bow. He walked towards the dead woman lying face down on the sand, unworried about me.

I would never get to the babies in time to save them from him. Never. I couldn't stop swimming though. I couldn't just give up on them. Something inside me knew that this one man was no match for me.

A shadow seemed to grow from the ground around the woman's body, and a man in an assassin's cloak stepped out of it. I kept swimming, my hope renewed that I would get to the babies in time now that the man in plate had a distraction.

As I got to the shore, the assassin flicked his hand outward towards the man in plate, and an obsidian dagger appeared from mist right before it left his hand. The man in plate raised his arm to block the throw, but the assassin was already rushing him.

The dagger hit the man's armored forearm, but when he moved his hand away from his face, the assassin was already too close, and his other dagger hit him right between the eyes, piercing flesh and bone.

He pulled it out immediately, and brandishing both daggers now, he approached me. I stared at him and saw the darkness inside him. A darkness that I knew.

Sebastian, the Prince of the Dark Court.

"Prince, please do not hurt the children. Let me take them

Princess of Shadows

far from here." My voice sounded differently. More flowing. More lyrical. And stronger.

"There's nothing we can do for the rest of them," he said, pulling back his hood and letting me see his face. He looked different as well. Younger. Leaner. Less burdened.

I tried to run to him, but I couldn't. Instead, my body went to the children and picked them up, tearing them from their mother's arms.

"Take my arm, and I'll get you to a place that is safe."

I looked into his eyes and knew that he was telling the truth. No lies. No falsities. No fairy truths.

I took his hand, and he reached down, touching the shadow of the dead woman.

And then the forest returned. Cara stood in front of me, and Sebastian was further away, sitting on a tree stump covered in his assassin's cloak.

"Interesting," she said, her eyes becoming green again. "You have a remarkable gift, Rose. A gift not heard of in a very long time. It was once called the Gift of Sacrifice."

"In times long past, dragons ruled the Fae Courts. A different dragon each millennium. They called it their sacrifice because they were never allowed to slumber as dragons tend to do. For a thousand years at a time, they were required to interact with the Courts as all rulers must."

"Dragons had many gifts just as fairies and all of the other Fae do, but a singular one was reserved for those who held the High Seats. It was their belief that to understand a person you ruled, it was necessary to understand their gifts and the curses that went along with them. In order to do this, these ruling dragons were given the power to hold the same powers as those around them."

Chapter 26

"What you just experienced was the gift of a seer. You saw into my past, a scene that always plays through my mind when Sebastian is around. I am sure you understand why now."

"That is my gift. You do not understand your own gift enough to understand my curse." She glanced at Sebastian and smiled. "But you may understand Sebastian's. Have you felt his hunger? A hunger for a person that does not begin in the loins?"

I thought back to last night. It was all such a blur. "Maybe?"

"Maybe it's too early for you to have felt the curses. It will come though. Be prepared. When you forge a connection to someone, an action that we'll practice, you'll get both sides, the gift and the curse."

"Regardless, that is something that we'll work on later. First, you need to learn to use magic at its most basic level. It's an instinctual action that you need to understand so that you can use your power on demand."

She said, "Your primary magic stems from light. As Sebastian weaves mists, you'll weave light and its opposite, darkness. Luckily, I have a similar affinity."

She smiled as she raised her hand and a light so bright that it seemed to burn shown from it. Directly at my face.

I put my hands up to stop it, but the light seemed to wrap around my hands. I tried to close my eyes, but it was so bright that it hurt even with my eyes closed.

"Stop!" I yelled.

"Stop the light," she commanded, but I didn't know how. It continued to burn me, growing in intensity until it all seemed to go dark. I opened my eyes, and everything was blurry. Pain was everything, like someone had stabbed my eyes with a hot poker. It felt like I'd never get over the pain, but seconds later

Princess of Shadows

it was gone completely.

"Can you see?" she asked as her form became clearer.

I nodded. "Excellent. At least your healing powers are in full effect. You would have been blind if they weren't."

"You blinded me?" I asked incredulously.

She nodded. "You didn't think this process was painless, did you?"

"Yes. Yes, I thought that learning magic would be like learning anything else. Namely, that it wouldn't require you to burn my eyes away."

"Those are mortal thoughts. Everything in the Immortal Realm requires sacrifice. Pain is an insignificant one. Ask Sebastian how much pain matters to him."

I bit my tongue to keep from lashing out at Cara. A darkness seemed to flow through me.

"Sebastian, come here. She seemed to value connections and there is a very strong one between the two of you. Maybe she'll act out of instinct when you're in pain."

He didn't hesitate as he hopped off the stump and made his way over to Cara. He removed his hood and put his hands behind his back, ready for her to repeat her actions on him instead of me.

His eyes open wide, he glanced at me. "No. This is ridiculous, Cara. There has to be an easier, less painful way to teach me magic."

"There is, but it takes time. That's a luxury you don't have, and you know it. We will gain time with the sacrifice of pain. Or, you could just move my light."

A grin crossed her lips as she raised her hand again. A beam of light so powerful that it seemed to burn the air flashed from her hand, and Sebastian began to scream.

Chapter 26

I moved instantly, putting myself between her and him. Pure shadow like that of my wings flowed around us, a barrier between the light and myself. I snarled at Cara, and a liquid blackness flowed from my hand towards her.

I saw inside her, as she must have done to me. Seeing that twisting, seething seat of power, and I knew that she did not control the shadows. Only the light. The liquid blackness coming from my hand covered her face, blotting out all the light around her.

She tried to penetrate it with her own control of light, to break the stream of blackness, but it was like a child trying to break down a door. I felt her throwing all of her magical force at it, but she could do nothing.

"Stop," Sebastian said softly from behind me, grabbing my shoulders. Suddenly, all that rage went away, and with it, the blackness evaporated.

She fell to her knees gasping. "What did you do?" she whispered between gasps. "That is not light manipulation. That was something different."

"I wanted you to stop hurting him," I said meekly. "Are you okay?"

She nodded as she slowly caught her breath. When she finally stood up, she said, "Good. Let's see if you can do it again."

I nodded solemnly, but a part of me became overwhelmed with excitement. I'd just done fucking magic. Not just a little thing. I'd just put a zillion year old elf on the ground with my magic. I was not going to be some fairy princess anymore.

I took a deep breath and felt those forces inside me. Ones that had woken in that moment. I felt the shadow shield inside me, and I pushed it outward, surrounding Sebastian and myself in a ball of shadow. Sebastian put his hand to the semi-transparent wall and slid through it easily.

Then he stepped out, and when he put his hand to it, there was a resistance. I could feel him pressing against it, but it took almost no strength to resist him. He pulled a dagger from his sheath and stabbed the shield.

Pain shot through my stomach as I felt the power inside me seeming to flow out of me as though someone had poked a hole in the bucket holding my very essence. I screamed and fell to the ground trying to find the source of the pain. The shield disappeared immediately, and the shooting pain began to fade.

"Guess it's like most shields. Not useful at all against an assassin's dagger." Sebastian's voice was almost unconcerned at the fact that I'd just fallen down in pain. I looked up at him as he slid the dagger back into its sheath. He'd known that was possible. More than possible. He'd known that it was likely.

He stared down at me, and I realized that he was analyzing my emotions. I'd felt that power when we'd been intimate, that sense of knowing exactly what the other was feeling.

"It's necessary to know the limitations of your magic," he said. "More than anything, you need to know if you have weaknesses. Assassins are a real possibility. Nyx was sent to kill you, and there may be others soon enough. You may be safe here, but eventually, Seraphina will find you. When that happens, if you throw up a shield, they'll stab it just as I did, and then they'll drain you completely. I had to know if yours was different."

I took a deep breath and pushed myself to my feet. It felt so callous. It was logical and important to know, but he'd hurt me, nonetheless. I glanced at Cara and saw her raised

Chapter 26

eyebrows. This was a test. A test to see if I could do what was needed. A test to see if I was strong enough.

"Fine. Tell me what to do next." Sebastian grinned.

"Fight me. With your liquid shadows."

He raised his hand and mist streamed towards me, rippling and curling in upon itself as it seemed to grow outward. It hit me square in the chest and somehow seemed solid. I had to step backward to catch myself from the impact, and then it began to wrap around me, solidifying as it covered my body.

I screamed as it began to tighten around my waist. I could feel it squeezing tighter and tighter, threatening to crack my ribs.

"Use your power," Cara said. "You have more power than anyone else. Don't try to be smart. Just overpower them."

The pain raged through my entire torso, and I screamed again, but as I did, I let the dark power flow out of my skin once more, sliding underneath the mist. The pain immediately relaxed, and I could feel my body reknitting the bones that had begun to crack.

With a loud exhale, I pushed the power outward until the mist began to snap and crumble as it broke away from the main line of mist coming from Sebastian's hand.

I smiled at him as I saw him straining to keep the mists together, and I reached my hand out just as I'd done before. Liquid smoke flowed through the air at Sebastian's face. Unlike Cara, he dropped his hand and rolled out of the way, my stream of smoke missing him and continuing past where he'd been.

Before he'd even finished his roll, he pressed his hands to the ground, and the world shook for a brief moment before I felt myself begin to fall as the very ground underneath me gave way.

"Your wings!" Cara exclaimed.

With nothing more than a thought, my wings came to life, moving faster than the eye could see behind me. I stopped falling and began to rise out of the hole in the ground.

"Holy shit, I'm flying!" I screamed in excitement. I looked down as I slowly floated down to the ground and landed. I could fly! I mean, I wasn't zooming through the clouds, but I was freaking flying. I'd get to zooming soon enough.

I looked up at Sebastian and he was grinning like a kid with a new toy. "You'll need to move a lot faster in an actual fight, but that was a lot better than I expected." Now he wasn't callous. He was a cat playing with a mouse, enjoying the game that he knew he'd win.

Then, I glanced backward into the hole in the ground and reality hit me. It was ten feet deep at least. Enough to break someone's bones. Sparring with Sebastian was not like sparring in some kind of gym here. He wasn't afraid to hurt me because he knew that I would heal. That didn't change how much pain I had to endure, though.

"I would have broken my leg at the very least if I'd fallen," I said as I steeled my jaw.

"You'd have healed. You'll never get out of a fight without being hurt. If you let the pain stop you, you'll die. If you ignore the pain and keep fighting, there's a chance you'll survive."

I took a deep breath and decided to stop playing nice. I'd see what light could do. I raised my hand into the air, and instead of darkness, I let pure whiteness flow through my body.

Sebastian pulled his hood down to cover his face as the first rays of light began to stream from my hand. He bent down and picked up a rock, casually as though we were just standing

Chapter 26

around talking. Without needing to see, he threw it at me.

My body reacted without thinking, twisting to the side. The rock clipped my shoulder, but more than that, the light stopped streaming from my hands. As I turned back to the fight, Sebastian was standing directly in front of me, his dagger an inch away from my throat.

"Never let anyone get close to you," he said. "You may be the most powerful fairy in the Dark Court from a distance, but once I get this close, you're just as dead as anyone else."

I swallowed hard as I felt a power radiating from the dagger. A power that terrified me. It pulled at me, seeking to draw my strength. Like the bridge, it called to me, begging me to touch it.

I stepped backward and nodded to Sebastian. "How am I supposed to fight someone like you? I'm supposed to be some super powered fairy who should be able to crush you, but you know how to deal with everything I do."

"You learn new tricks. You get faster. You learn how to guess what I'm going to do. More than anything, you need to practice your powers and learn what you can do. Your base powers aren't unusual. What you can do with them is going to be different, though." He smiled. "Especially if you learn to combine them."

"What do you think, Cara? Could you imagine how strong she'd be if she learned to combine earth and light? Or seeing along with my empathic abilities?"

"Unstoppable," she murmured. "There's nothing you couldn't do. With the right people beside you, you'd be able to do anything."

Sebastian nodded with a grin. "But first, you need to figure out how to work with your own natural abilities. You'll always have those regardless of who you're near, so you need to be as good with those as possible. We'll work on combining them with other people's after that."

I nodded, feeling at least a little bit of hope that I could become strong enough to survive the Immortal Realm and everyone that was trying to kill me.

Sebastian stepped back twenty feet, smiled, and pulled out his daggers. "Now, try to kill me."

Chapter 27

Rose

I wrapped one hand around Kasia's waist as she galloped across a field as fast as she could. She wore thick leather armor and carried a spear and shield as she galloped. A group of three dummies stood at the end of the field, and I held the silver sword with one hand as I tightened my thighs around her, doing my best not to lose my seat.

She'd refused to wear a saddle, informing me that if a rider couldn't manage to stay in their seat without a saddle, they weren't worthy of riding a centaur into battle. My arm didn't shake anymore. A month of steady training with sword, magic, and riding had strengthened my body and mind.

As we closed on the dummies, I released my hold on Kasia's waist, lifting my arm and focusing on my power as I prepared my swing. She struck out first with her spear, hitting the dummy square in the chest. A burst of power came from me.

Liquid shadows flowed through the air and hit the second dummy in the face at the same time that I swung the sword, connecting with the top section of the other dummy.

Kasia slowed and looked at the dummies. "You've grown, Rose. Do you remember when you dropped the sword and almost fell off at the same time?"

I couldn't help but giggle as I thought about the first time that I'd tried this exercise. What had they expected of a girl who had never done magic or held a sword?

"You have too. You don't complain nearly as much about how slow you are when you're carrying me."

"I have never complained," she said indignantly. "A centaur warrior does not complain about her tasks."

"You're right. They don't complain. Gnomes complain. Centaurs bitch." She snorted, the sound much more horselike than her other sounds.

There was still a light in her eyes that seemed to beam at me. Centaurs were notoriously difficult to work with until they respected you. I'd been an idiot fairy when I first arrived, and though she'd trusted Sebastian's judgement, she didn't trust me anymore than Enivyn had.

Now it was different. Just as Cara had done, each of the people in the village had tested me in their own way. They'd trusted Sebastian's word before, but none of them had trusted me.

"Race you back to the village," I said with a smirk.

"That is not a fair race. You do not use your feet."

I shrugged. "Fine. I'll use my two feet, and you can use any combination of two of yours. That way it's truly fair."

She snorted again. "Wings only. No magic."

"Sounds good to me. Go!"

Chapter 27

Kasia took off at a gallop. She would always win in an initial sprint. My wings began to flutter, lifting me off the ground. That was what I'd known how to do instinctually. What happened next was learned.

I leaned forward, my wings moving even faster, a blur of shadows on a sunny day. I could feel them working, the connection through the skin reverberated faster than anything I'd ever felt.

Unlike a muscle, my wings were made of pure magic, and they didn't tire, burning magic to move rather than physical energy. I had to hold my body up, though, and that was tiring. My stomach and back tightened, holding me in place, as I edged ever closer to Kasia whose hooves pounded the ground in a cloud of sparkling dust.

Lights began to flash around me, faster and faster. The same lights that had surprised me in that field with the unicorn. As I flew, they clustered around as though I were being chased by a swarm of lightning bugs. Wisps, the Immortal Realm's version of flies. Instead of consuming decaying flesh, wisps consumed the remains of spent magic.

Flying a little higher, I looked down on Kasia from above, and as I passed her, I tugged at her hair. She reached up and tried to grab me as we raced towards camp. I expected physical and magical testing almost constantly. The punishment for failure was pain, and I'd begun to accept that.

She missed my arm, and with her other arm, she tried to snag my leg. I twisted away, giggling as I passed her. "You're as bad as the gnomes," she snarled.

"You're as bad as a unicorn," I replied. "All snorts and snarls."

That seemed to make her run just a little harder. She was faster than any horse I'd ever heard of. It had been weeks even after I'd learned to fly before I could beat her in a race.

My muscles ached as we reached the village, and I landed on the outskirts, just a few feet away from the first hut. Kasia slowed down next to me a few moments later breathing hard.

"You are much faster now," she said, acknowledging her defeat in our little race.

"You were right," I said. "It's not really fair. My wings don't ever get tired. I have no idea how you can run that far as fast as you do."

"It doesn't matter if it's fair or not, little fairy. We all have the gifts that we've been given. It's the mark of an idiot to not use those gifts. I have four legs and a body built for running. You have wings."

I nodded and began walking into the village with Kasia beside me. Andryn was digging a hole, and I smiled at him. "Need a little help?"

"I wouldn't refuse it. It'd be nice to be able to eat a nice smoked boar tomorrow without having my back ache."

Kneeling down, I reached out towards Sebastian who was out hunting the boar that would eventually go in the firepit. He was close to the maximum range of my powers. Maybe a mile away.

I couldn't connect with anyone as well as I could with Sebastian. I was limited to a range of several hundred yards with the rest of the villagers, but Sebastian and I had a much stronger bond. I closed my mind, focusing on building the tether between the two of us. Silver lines that would connect our souls and powers temporarily.

Then, I felt the soil under my hands. With just a brush of power, I pulled the soil deeper, forcing it to compact in the circle that Andryn was digging. I looked up, and a round hole

Chapter 27

five feet wide had appeared.

Andryn was grinning at me. "Remember when you didn't even know how to peel potatoes without a knife?"

"I'll never forget. My hands still ache from that night. You could have told me that you could do it in a few minutes with magic instead of watching me struggle with them."

He shrugged. "You didn't ask."

"What are you wrapping the boar in this time?" I asked, changing the subject.

"Sinivyn's going to gather some fire fronds."

"One of the Fae could make a lot of money taking those back to the Mortal Realm. Who would have thought that any kind of greens would taste like chilis?"

"They wouldn't survive in the Mortal Realm." He began covering the bottom of the pit with wood that would smoke the boar. "Some plants like apples are simply different here. They're native to both realms, but they draw in some extra magic from the world here. Others like fire fronds require the magic of the Immortal Realm. Their flavors aren't developed from soil conditions. Instead, they get their spicy flavor from the magic that is in the very air that we breathe."

I nodded. I may have learned a lot of things about the Immortal Realm, but I was still lost in so many ways. Luckily, no one had any problem explaining things to me once I'd told them that I wanted to learn.

"Does that mean that there are different places with stronger types of magic than others? Like, would Sebastian's mists be weaker in some places than others?"

Andryn grinned. "That's a good leap, Rose. Sometimes I wonder if being human for so long helped you learn faster." He paused for a moment to think. "A good example is the

Princess of Shadows

Dark Court. It was built in a place where light magic was weak, a natural defense against the Court of Light. As it's been inhabited and changed by the Dark Court, it has slowly become even more hostile towards those who use light magic."

I nodded. "What about the Court of Light? From what I've heard, there aren't very many magics specifically common amongst the Dark Court."

He grinned again, enjoying teaching me. "The Court of Light saps the very essence of anyone associated with the Dark Court. Slowly, it drains them of their power, and if stay for too long, it can even kill them."

I blinked in surprise, but Andryn seemed not to notice. "On that note, have you been training with light as well as shadow?"

I sighed. "Yes, but it's a lot harder to use. Shadows seem so easy comparatively."

"That's because light is a Court of Light gift when you are obviously Dark Court. You somehow managed to get both which is uncommon, but Queens have strange powers. You shouldn't neglect it. Uncommon gifts are oftentimes some of the most powerful."

"It'd be better if you'd said all that in a Yoda voice, Andryn."

He raised an eyebrow. "What is a Yoda voice?"

"Don't worry about it. It's a human thing. Yoda's like a really old green gnome who uses magic and says things backwards."

He went back to stacking the wood. "That doesn't sound like a compliment and is extremely confusing."

"You just like to lecture me. I think it's a Court of Light thing." The light elf nodded and brushed his hands off.

"No, it's an elf thing." He stepped back and looked at the hole. "All prepped and ready for the boar and fire fronds. Now I have to make tonight's dinner. Unless you want to help make

Chapter 27

bread and stew, you'd better move along. I hear that the shifter pups need some playing with."

"I think I'll pass on the bread making." He nodded to me and I headed towards the shifter family's hut. I could already hear the curses from Cara. Shifter pups were notoriously difficult to control, but they were easy to entertain. Cara just didn't seem to understand how to be entertaining.

As I walked through the village, people waved and smiled at me. For the first time in my life, I felt like I belonged. When I'd first gotten here, everyone had been wary, but as I'd learned more about them and my powers, I'd found ways to help.

This was exactly what I'd always wanted. People who genuinely cared about me and appreciated me. A place where the forest was always nearby. A world where things actually made sense.

It hadn't been long since I'd come to the Immortal Realm, but now that I was here, I knew that I could never go back to my old life. I'd been an outsider there. This place, this village, this entire world made more sense to me. I may not have known very much, but every bit of information seemed to slip into place without any trouble.

I understood why the unicorn had attacked me, and I wasn't afraid of seeing another one. I understood the pecking order within a shifter pack. I understood the centaur's society and culture. Things just made sense.

The Mortal Realm was still a mystery to me even though I'd spent my entire life there. I still didn't comprehend why Sasha had dated Tony. I didn't understand why people made such a big deal about turning twenty-one. I still hated the idea of watching TV.

The only things that had actually made sense were the things that were closer to what happened every day in the Immortal Realm. Plus, I had magic here, and magic was awesome. I could fly! I could dig a hole in seconds. I could ride a freaking centaur.

I saw Cara pulling her robes away from the shifter pups in front of their hut. She'd been asked to take care of them while their parents were hunting with Sebastian. She looked absolutely miserable.

I smiled. I got to play with shifter pups.

My wings began to flutter with excitement. This was going to be fun. My feet lifted off the ground as my wings sped up. Silently, I floated through the air. The pups were facing Cara, and Cara was trying her best to keep them from destroying her robes.

Rushing through the air, an ear-to-ear grin on my face, I landed right behind them and pulled two of the four's tails hard, and they yelped, immediately turning around and trying to bite my hands.

I saw their faces light up as soon as they saw me. I leaped backward, fluttering a foot above the ground and said, "I've got them Cara."

"Thank you, Rose," she said, her voice filled with exhaustion. All four of the pups raced towards me, and I began to throw slow moving bits of shadow at them as I fluttered backward just a little slower than them.

They dodged the shadows which wouldn't have hurt them even if they were caught by it. Yipping at me as they ran, their tiny paws tore at the ground. A pack of miniature wolves chasing me as I flew through the air laughing.

Yes, this was the definition of a fantasy turned into reality. I'd never have found it in Mortal Realm. I was meant to be

Chapter 27

here. This was home. Finally.

Chapter 28

Sebastian

"We're doing what?" I asked as I took off my cloak, draping it over the chair in our hut.

"We're giving Enivyn a birthday party." I blinked and cocked my head.

"What's a birthday party?"

Rose grinned. "It's a human thing. How many candles do you think the village has?"

"How many candles…? I don't know, Rose. I don't live here, and I definitely don't do inventory for them. Why do we need candles?"

"For the cake, of course." She dug through the pack of clothes that she'd brought from London. "You need candles for a birthday cake."

"What are you talking about?"

She shook her head. "Nevermind trying to explain impor-

Chapter 28

tant things like birthday cakes to silly fairies. Just watch and don't try to do anything. Just be pretty. You can do that, right?"

"I can just be pretty. Eventually, you have to explain yourself though."

"Just watch and learn, old man. Sinivyn's got Andryn working on the cake. I hope he doesn't screw it up too badly. John's teaching the village the song. Kasia said that she'd make crowns since nobody keeps birthday hats on stock here."

I gave up trying to understand what this woman was talking about. Why would anyone need a crown for their birthday? And what did any of that have to do with a cake?

I watched as Rose took the necklace that I'd paid for with a dagger out of the bag that held her dresses. "Any idea if my dagger will cut this metal?" she asked.

"No idea, Rose. I don't even know what that metal is."

She shrugged and pulled her dagger from its sheath at her side. She set the necklace on the ground and slammed the dagger's blade against it. The metal snapped with a clinking sound. Over and over again, she cut pieces off the necklace, and I watched without trying to help. I had no idea what she was going to do with it.

Then she put two ends together, and I saw light flare between her fingers. She held the two pieces together as the smell of burning metal filled the hut.

"Fuck," she murmured, dropping what was left of the necklace and holding her finger. She winced as she pulled a droplet of the metal out of her skin. "Haven't ever tried melting metal before. Maybe I should have done it a different way."

She picked up the necklace that looked nothing like the original now and smiled. "What do you think?" she asked.

I hopped off the chair I'd been sitting in and walked over to her, taking the necklace in both hands. She had cut all the dangling bits off and shortened the chain until it was much smaller. Almost too small to fit around a neck.

"Kind of a strange necklace now. Why take off the sapphires? They were pretty."

"Wouldn't work for a crown. I didn't have much else to work with, so this is the best I can do for a real crown."

I blinked again, thoroughly confused. How could this woman confuse me when I was fifty times older than her?

"Alright, time to gather everyone together. If I teach you a song, will you sing it when it's time?"

"I'll do what you ask me to do," I said, not really sure what I was agreeing to.

She sighed. "Nevermind. You just look pretty, okay?"

"I can do that."

She took a deep breath and put the "crown" in a small pouch at her side.

"Let's go. And don't put that cloak on. This is a thing for friends, not creepy assassin guys."

I chuckled. "Fine. I'll be a friend today."

She hopped to her feet, her wings fluttering and making the movement much more graceful. Then, she opened the door and walked towards the center of the village where someone had tied Enivyn to a chair and blindfolded him.

"What are you doing, Andryn? You were supposed to blindfold him, not tie him up like a prisoner!"

"He kept taking off the blindfold and sneaking glances. This was the only way to keep the secret."

"Rose! You're here! Save me please? Andryn won't let me get up. I'm hungry. No one let me eat any snacks today!"

Chapter 28

"It's okay, Enivyn. I'm going to untie you, but you have to promise me that you won't take off your blindfold. We'll get you some food in just a few minutes, and it's going to be the best snack ever."

"Great! I love snacks! I won't peek. I promise."

Sinivyn walked into the village center carrying a candle, wearing a strange, braided vine on his head.

Then Cara followed him carrying a tray with a huge cake on it. It was a frosted, three-tiered cake with chocolate icing all over it. My stomach rumbled thinking about it. It had been years since I'd had a good cake. There hadn't been all that many good reasons to celebrate in the past fourteen years.

Rose finished untying Enivyn, and he sat still at the community table.

Kasia began handing out the strange braided crowns to everyone in the village, and she even put one on her and her foals. Only the shifter pups didn't wear them. Everyone put on the crowns and I saw smiles from many of the villagers. They all seemed to know what was happening. Even Cara cracked a smile.

Was I really the only one who didn't know what a birthday party was?

Rose put her fingers to the candle wick, and it burst into flames. "Okay, Enivyn. Take off your blindfold!"

As soon as he could see, he squealed in excitement. "Oh man. Oh man. Oh man. A birthday party? For me? John told you, didn't he?"

Rose raised her hand and the entire village began to sing. "Happy Birthday, dear Enivyn."

I stared in complete bewilderment as everyone sang the words to the song as though they'd sung it a thousand times.

When it was done, people brought small gifts to him. One of the foals brought him a pretty rock. One of the villagers gave him a new bag. On and on it went. Enivyn's smile seemed to grow with each gift.

Finally, Rose stepped up to Enivyn and said, "I don't have very much to give, Enivyn, but there is one thing that I can give." She pulled the crown from the pouch and put it on his head, adjusting it so that it wouldn't fall off.

"I'm a Queen so I get to do this. Today, I pronounce you Prince of Smiles as there's no one in the village who can smile as big as you."

The entire village seemed to laugh and cheer at the same time. Rose walked away as Andryn began to cut the cake. She seemed to have just as big of a smile on her face as Enivyn did.

"I think I understand what's happening," I whispered to her as she stood next to me watching the entire village laughing and talking.

"It's a human thing. We're born, we live some years, and then we die. So we count them and congratulate ourselves for living another year. More than anything, it's a good reason to be happy to just be alive."

"It's not a bad tradition for humans," I said.

"It's not a bad tradition for anyone to be happy to be alive, Sebastian." I looked at her and saw her watching the villagers.

"Maybe you're right. Maybe it's good to just enjoy the moment every now and then."

"I heard that chocolate's your favorite."

"You heard right."

"Then you'd better go get in line for some. I'm positive that those gnomes will gobble up every extra piece they can get their hands on."

Chapter 28

I laughed and grabbed her hand. "Fine. I'll stop worrying for a minute and just enjoy a bit of cake."

Chapter 29

Rose

I stood panting in the training circle that had been marked off. The villagers knew not to come near here as Sebastian, Cara, and I had slowly but steadily become more brutal in my training.

Mists crawled from the ground around my feet as I faced Cara. Using the Gift of Sacrifice, I followed Sebastian's movements as he stood behind me. I knew that he was working the mists. The black shield that coated my skin held the mists back, and Cara shined her light at me which the shield blocked.

I felt Sebastian leap towards me, his daggers being called from the mist. I twisted at the last moment, shoving him towards Cara. He screamed as I pulled the hood back and he stared into her blinding light.

Leaping over him, my wings fluttering to lighten me and

Chapter 29

carry me over his body, I stood in front of Cara and felt my dagger coalesce from shadows in my hand. Her eyes went wide as the dagger pressed against her throat at the same time that I raised my other hand and encased Sebastian's legs in stone.

"Dead," I whispered to Cara. Sebastian pushed the stone away from him with his powers at the same time that I threw the dagger at him, hitting him in the shoulder as hundreds of tendrils of light burst from my hand and sought him out, wrapping around his arms and legs.

He began to scream as the tendrils of light burned him as they immobilized him. I took a step towards him, pulling the dagger out of his shoulder and putting it to his throat. "Dead."

The tendrils of light evaporated, and both he and Cara were left panting as I put the dagger into the sheath at my side.

"Fuck, Rose. You're getting good. How did you manage to make the stone cover my feet without touching the ground?"

"I turned the mist into stone. It wasn't that complicated once I thought of it."

"You... You can't do that. It doesn't work that way. The power of stone only manipulates what is already there."

I grinned as he rubbed the healing burns. "The power of stone works that way, but the power of stone mixed with the power of mist doesn't. It's like how you replicate yourself."

He blinked. "That's genius. Why haven't I ever thought to do that?"

"Because you're male. Men are terrible at thinking."

"Those light tendrils are interesting as well," Cara noted. "I've never seen light manipulated that way."

"That's different. It's a combination of the power of mist with the power of light. Just like that first time that I covered you in liquid shadows was a combination of mist and shadows. Shadows don't have enough substance to do that, and neither does light."

Sebastian rubbed his shoulder where his wound was still bleeding. "When we're sparring, please leave the iron off the edge."

Concern filled me as I realized that this wound wasn't going to heal quickly like everything else. "I'm so sorry, Sebastian. I hadn't meant to. It was just already in the sheath."

"It's okay, Rose. Not the first time that I've had a bit of iron in a cut. I'd just prefer it if you remember next time."

He put his arm around me and pulled me to him. "I don't think that I can teach you very much more. You need experience, but you're finding connections that I've never even heard of."

I looked up at him, distinctly aware of Cara's eyes on us. She was afraid of me. Everyone was to some degree at this point just as they'd all been afraid of Sebastian.

"I'm proud of you, Rose. You're not the scared girl that I dragged kicking and screaming into the Immortal Realm anymore. I think it's time that we talked about what our plan is going forward."

"What do you mean?" I pulled back. Was this the discussion I'd been dreading?

"Where do we go from here? Seraphina may not have found us by now, but Rose, we're immortal. Eventually, she'll hunt us down and kill us unless you decide to step up and become Queen. Or if we convince her that she doesn't want us dead."

I sighed. Cara sat down on a log to watch and listen. She would inform the rest of the villagers of what we were talking about. Even though Sebastian was the founder of the village,

Chapter 29

we were both still outsiders. Esteemed and loved guests, but still guests.

"Can't we push this until later? Another month or two? I like it here. I'm happy."

He ran his hand over his smooth cheek. "No. You're ready. There's no reason to continue putting the people in the village at risk like this."

I turned around, looking out at the forest. Finally, I felt like I was home, and I was going to have to leave. I liked the people here. I cared about the people here, and they cared about me. Cara, Enivyn, Sinivyn, John, Kasia, her foals, the pups, Andryn, and everyone else.

This was everything I'd ever dreamed of. Sebastian thought that I needed to leave it all behind to take my seat on the Dark Throne. To go into another brand-new hostile world and have to prove myself all over again. To set myself in an opposing seat to the very woman who wanted me dead.

There would be no peace for me there. No happiness. At least not like this. I took another deep breath. He was right, though. We couldn't just postpone things. That bitch Queen wasn't going to stop looking for us.

"Why do you want me to take the Dark Throne, Sebastian?" I asked without looking at him.

"Because if you don't, then there's no one who will keep the Dark Court safe. If there was a Queen of the Dark Court, the Assassin's Guild wouldn't have been sent to kill you. No one would send me anywhere other than my Queen. The people will be safer if you're there to be the wall between the Court of Light and the Dark Court."

I snarled. "I don't want to do that. I don't want to spend my life ruling people and fighting. I want to play with wolf pups

Princess of Shadows

and ride centaurs and maybe find unicorns to chase me. I've spent my entire life being miserable. Do I really have to go in search of misery when I've found the perfect life?"

His presence hovered behind me, and I leaned back against his chest. "There's no one else to do it, Rose. No one in thousands of years has had the power you have along with the correctly twisted bloodlines. You were created for the throne. A Dark Queen to hold back the light."

I felt his hands on my waist, and I wanted to melt into him. I couldn't, though. Not right then. I pulled away and turned to face him. "Sebastian, maybe one day I can be Queen, but not now. I'm not strong enough. I still don't even understand the world. I've met a handful of people and barely understand them. I need more time. Much more time before I consign myself to that role."

"I cannot force you to take the seat regardless of how much I want you to." He set his jaw, frustration running through his face. I reached out and felt his emotions, using his powers to augment my own. It wasn't anger like I'd thought it would be. Pure sadness. He was heartbroken that I wasn't willing to take the throne.

"We'll need to go to the Court of Light to see Seraphina, and I'll have to do what she's always wanted. I'll give up my own seat, and along with it, the power that goes with the seat. You'll also give up your seat. Formally. That way she has no reason to hunt us."

I nodded, knowing how badly it hurt him. "You won't be able to be Queen after that. Ever. No matter how bad it gets, you'll never be able to sit on the throne."

"I understand, but I can't do it. I can't be in charge of that many people. I'm still just beginning to understand the

Chapter 29

Immortal Realm. I can't be the ruler of half of it." The decision was made. A decision that didn't make me feel any better.

Sebastian gave me a fake smile. "Then we'll be free to live out our immortal lives in this village."

Somehow, I knew that this decision was going to make him even more miserable than going to Court would make me.

But the decision was made.

Chapter 30

Sebastian

Tomorrow I was leaving for the Court of Light. I bit my tongue to keep from screaming. I must have done something wrong. Maybe I should have kept her running, never letting her settle down or find happiness. She had to be Queen. It was what she'd been made for.

Yet, if I'd kept her from the village, she'd never have become strong enough to take the throne. She'd never have learned just how strong and how incredible she was. No, I could think of nothing that would have changed this result. If we'd stayed with Astriel, she'd have fallen in love with people there. It was who she was.

A Queen who loved the people that would serve her and whom the people would love in return.

I looked at her. Wearing a simple linen dress with her long brown hair in a braided crown, she held a bowl of hunter's

Chapter 30

chili. She was beautiful. And I was about to do a terrible thing. A thing that she may never forgive me for doing.

I put my hand on her thigh, and she looked at me with a smile. "So, tell me about this Court of Light. I tried to talk to Andryn about it since he lived there for a while, but he didn't want to talk about it."

"It's a palace made of gold and white marble. Everything shines there, and the people shine as well. Just a touch of a glow. Their wings are made of pure light, bright and shining."

"The palace is set on the top of a mountain to be closer to the sun, and a crystal-clear river runs around it. Everything about it is beautiful. Some of the Fae theorize that humans developed the idea of heaven from visits to the Court of Light."

"It sounds kind of intense. Like, maybe it'd be nice to visit, but it probably isn't all that fun to live in. How does anyone sleep when it's always so bright?"

I grinned. "A question I've had for many years. I assume it involves excessive amounts of wine since that's the only way I could imagine being there for more than an hour at a time."

"That sounds terrible. What about the Dark Court? Is it just pitch black all the time? Because that's what I imagine. Do you know how many times I would stub my toes if there was no light?"

"There's light, Rose. We're not the same as the Court of Light. Many of the Dark Fae live in the light, and we're very welcoming of differences."

I stretched my legs as we sat on the log. "The major differences between the Court of Light and the Dark Court don't really have anything to do with how much light we enjoy. The split is two-fold. One, we care very little for bloodlines. Nobility is based on strength, not on who your grandparents were. Two, we don't put very much emphasis on the past. We care about the now."

"But the Queen of the Dark Court has to have both dark and light bloodlines, doesn't she?"

I nodded. "That is the one position where bloodlines matter because she must be respected by both Courts in case the Queen of the Light dies and she must rule both Courts as Seraphina has been doing."

"How is the Court of Light different?" I moved my hand higher on her thigh, and she smiled a little sheepishly at me. She was still more than a little embarrassed about our nightly enjoyment of each other.

"Bloodlines are the only thing that matters for the Court of Light. If you're born of high nobles, you will be a high noble whether you are the strongest or most deserving of the spot or not."

"Strange. I wonder why it's like that, but that's a question for another day." She stood up and carried her bowl to the stack of dirty dishes that someone was in charge of cleaning. The job was changed every night, and not long ago, even I'd had to wash the dishes.

"Let's get some sleep. Tomorrow is going to be a very tiring day," she said with a half-hearted smile.

Yes, it was going to be a very tiring day for both of us. But it would be for different reasons.

I followed Rose to our hut and felt the people that we passed watching us. They knew what we were going to do. Some sided with me and others sided with Rose on what was the right decision for her, but all of them had kept their opinions to themselves. It was not their place to tell a Queen what she should do as they would never have to make that decision.

Chapter 30

I walked into the hut after Rose, and she immediately closed the door, sliding the latch into place to lock it. Her hands slid under my shirt, pressing against my chest. Her touch was the purest magic I'd ever known, pushing my doubts and fears away as her fingers brushed against my skin.

"I need you," she whispered. "If everything goes wrong tomorrow, at least give me one more night with you."

I didn't answer her with words. Words would never have been enough. Her lips called to me, and I answered them, bending my head down and pressing my lips to hers. I built the tether between the two of us that would allow me to feed and pull her into the dreamscape.

Lifting her, I felt her wings begin to move, lightening her until she weighed almost nothing. My fingers went to the back of her dress, untying it slowly as my other hand supported her weightless hips.

My lips never left hers as our tongues danced. A flurry of passion. She thought that we might die tomorrow, and she wanted to show me exactly how she felt about me. If only she knew that tonight was going to be our last night together.

She slipped the dress off her shoulders and let it fall to the ground. Her hands pulled my shirt off, and then she pressed her body against mine, skin to skin, power to power. I pulled back from the kiss and felt the mists rise around me, filling the room until she could see nothing but me.

I pulled on the tether that connected us, to connect the dreamscape to the physical, and her reality began to blur. I stared into her eyes, watching them dance between green and blue, the power of the fairy rising from inside her as I pulled at her very soul.

She felt so good in my arms, and the last thing I wanted was to leave her, but it was the only way. Power flooded my body as I transported us to the dreamscape and brought her to the four-poster bed in a recreation of my rooms in the Dark Court. Physically, I carried her to the simple bed that we shared in the hut. Laying her down, I controlled the dream that she experienced.

My lips clamped down on her neck in the dreamscape while I took off my pants in the physical. My teeth sunk into her flesh, and she moaned. Every sensation was heightened there, and all of them were pleasurable. Her body was mine to control, from the way she moved to the way she felt.

Mists wove around her, each tendril teasing her skin with soft kisses. In the dreamscape, even her wings could feel the embrace of the mists. She began to glow, shimmering between light and pure blackness, and I brought her back to the physical as I crawled between her legs.

How had I lived before her? I may have survived, but I'd been so cold. Her very touch warmed me. I'd survived for a very long time, but it was only after I'd found this annoying fairy that I'd found life.

My lips found her breast as I ran my hands under her, my nails digging into her hard enough to bring tiny droplets of blood to the surface before healing over. Gods, I needed her. I pulled back again, panting because of the need flowing through me. Not hunger, but a desperate need to be closer to her. I was never hungry anymore. She gave me everything I could want and more.

Moans escaped her lips as I found her entrance. "Sebastian," she cried out as her wings began to move, pushing her closer to me. The feel of her skin against mine was a fantasy turned reality. A fantasy that I'd never dreamt.

Chapter 30

A fantasy I could never have imagined.

"I love you," I whispered as I began to thrust. She didn't need to say it back. It didn't matter. This was not a game we were playing. There was no power exchange in this relationship. All I needed was for there to be no doubt about the way I felt for her. No question that I was willing to do *anything* for her.

Her hands ran over my body, and I brought her back into the dreamscape, letting the mists cover and tease her again. She began to shine with a light that eclipsed even the Fae in the Court of Light.

She screamed out a moan, and the wave of power flowed through the tether to me, stronger than I'd ever felt before. My thrusts continued, pushing her deeper into her bliss. Yes, I'd found the woman that had awoken my numb heart.

I bent down and kissed her again, not ready to be done. I would never be ready to be done with Rose, but I would be happy with at least a few more hours.

At least I would leave this world knowing that I'd finally found love. Finally found the only thing that was worth dying for.

Chapter 31

Rose

I awoke in a dreamscape that I'd never seen before. A field near a cottage. It was based on the Immortal Realm without a doubt. The smell of citrus filled the air as I looked out on the twilight scene. Tall trees that were shaped like evergreens had varying shades of pinks and purples that seemed to glow under the purple moon. The grass was so dark, it was almost black here.

Sebastian stood watching a woman and a child doing magic very similarly to how he'd begun teaching me. She moved his hand slowly, and I could feel her pulling on his power with her own. It was so lifelike. I could even smell her scent. A mix of lilacs and clove. Strangely intense.

The edges of the vision were frayed, turning to dark mists. This was a memory, and he'd pulled me here for some reason. Sebastian had told me that he didn't sleep. As an incubus, he

Chapter 31

wandered dreams instead of sleeping, letting his body rest while his mind wandered.

"You were tired," he said softly without turning to look at me. I walked closer to him, seeing the vision laid before him.

"Who is it?" I asked as the boy pulled a thin stream of mist from the ground.

"My mother and me a very, very long time ago." His words seemed sad. Nostalgic.

"You've never talked about your mother before."

"My mother was the last Dark Queen, and her death still hurts. Even nine hundred years later. She was the only one who understood me. My father was a full-blooded incubus, and he was her consort, a position like a husband in the Mortal Realm. He never strayed from the bounds of his position. They were inseparable until he died."

"How did he die?" I'd never heard Sebastian so melancholy. What was it that I didn't know?

"I don't know. I was too young. It isn't uncommon for a full-blooded incubus to die suddenly. Their powers are almost exclusive to the dreamscape. Any assassin could have killed him if he weren't protected while dream walking. Glass cannons, they can cause incredible damage if they decide to, but they are easily killed by people in the physical."

He shrugged. "I didn't know him well, but my mother knew him well enough to be able to teach me about my powers. And about my curse."

Sebastian sighed. "I miss her, Rose. She'd know what to do. She'd know how to handle everything, and then we could live in the Dark Court in safety and peace. We could visit the village anytime we wanted without fear."

"You don't have to leave the village, Sebastian. We have to

talk to Seraphina tomorrow, but then we'll return here and live like we've been living. We'll be happy here."

He turned to me, his eyes full of sadness behind the mists. "I am the last of her line. The last of the strongest blood in the Dark Court. Seraphina wants you dead, but she wants me dead even more. She blames me for her husband's death. Tomorrow, I'm going to give her what she wants."

"I'm going to lock you in this dreamscape. Then, I'm going to break the portal before you wake up, and I'm going to give myself to Seraphina to kill. There was never a way to convince Seraphina not to hunt us. Not now. This is the only way."

"No! You will not sacrifice yourself like some martyr to save me. That's not the way that this works. Sebastian, I love you. You're bossy and annoyingly male, but I fucking love you, and you don't get to die on me. Especially not like this! Stop trying to save me, and we'll figure something out."

He gave me a sad smile and said, "It's either this or Seraphina hunts us forever. Everyone you care about dies. Everything in the world that brings you happiness will be taken from you. No Rose, I'm not going to let you lose everything you love."

"I love you more than anything. Including myself. My life has been one terrible experience after the next. Until you. You're obnoxious and talk too much, but you're also the only good thing left in my life, and I'll be damned if I let you end up miserable like me."

Tears began to fall as I looked at him. No! No! No! This was not happening. This was not the way that things were supposed to turn out. We were supposed to live out our immortal lives in peace in the place that finally felt like home with friends.

"You'll find happiness without me. Enivyn, Sinivyn, Kasia,

Chapter 31

Cara, and everyone else will help you. Goodbye, Rose. I love you."

He pulled me to him, and I tried to speak, but my mouth wouldn't open. His magic stopped me. I couldn't even tell him how I felt about him. That he was my world. That I'd rather watch the world burn than see him do this. That I'd go through any kind of hell to keep him with me.

He wrapped his arms around me, bent down, and I felt his lips press against mine as he turned to mist and faded away.

The dream didn't end though. I was left screaming, with tears running down my face, as I was forced to watched little Sebastian and his mother moving a stream of mist between them.

Chapter 32

Rose

I woke up screaming as I twisted and turned in the bed. My power clung to my skin, a shadowy shield coating my body. Eyes wide, I flailed in the bed, trying to find Sebastian. He was gone.

That bastard had purposefully ignored teaching me about dream magic so that he could do this if he wanted to.

On a table was one dagger in the hartskin sheathe. A second to my one. He'd left it for me. He wasn't going to fight her. He was going to die. I screamed in anger and sadness.

Andryn broke open the door, tearing the latch from the wall as he came in, a golden sword in his hand. I pulled the sheet over my body. "What's wrong?" he asked as he glanced around the room, his eyes trying to find the source of my pain before finally looking at me.

"Sebastian's gone," I whispered as the tears began to fall

Chapter 32

again.

"Yes, he said that he was going settle things with Seraphina. Isn't that what the two of you had planned?"

I shook my head. "*We* were supposed to settle things with her. Not him. He's not strong enough to protect himself against her. He's not going to settle things. He's going to sacrifice himself to protect me."

Andryn sheathed his sword. "Did you think that there was another way? Seraphina will not stop hunting him. Ever. The only reason he is still alive is because he'd never given her a good reason to have him executed or assassinated. The Assassin's Guild would never have fought him without a reason. He was their Prince."

"She has her reason now. He didn't assassinate you as she ordered, and he killed Nyx while Nyx was under her orders. Both of those things were worthy of an execution."

"Now, unless you became responsible for him by taking the throne, she would never have stopped."

"Then why didn't he tell me that?" I screamed, the tears falling even faster. The portal would already be broken, and there were no shadow walkers in the village. There was no way to get to the Courts fast enough to stop him from becoming a martyr.

"He didn't want to force you to become Queen for his sake." Andryn said it as though it made any kind of sense. Why couldn't he have just told me? We could have talked about it, could have figured out a way to make it all work.

"It wasn't his decision to make. How could I make a decision without knowing all the facts?" I sobbed.

"Because he was protecting his Queen. Whether you sit on the throne or not, you're all of our Queen. Even me."

Princess of Shadows

I gritted my teeth. I was not going to let this happen. I was not going to let Sebastian die for me. Or anyone else.

"Get out," I said, my tone of voice no longer full of anger or sadness. "Sebastian is not going to die. Not like this. I may kill him when I find him, but Seraphina certainly isn't going to."

Andryn nodded and tried to close the door, but it hung at an odd angle after he broke into the hunt. As soon as the door was closed, I pulled on the linen dress that Sebastian had pulled off me last night. I didn't know how I was going to find him or save him, but I was going to.

Then the sound of screaming rose above my anger. I reached out with my powers, touching the villagers. I felt their emotions and knew that Sebastian hadn't left yet. If he'd gone through the portal, I wouldn't have access to his empathy.

The first thought I had was that I still had a chance to catch him, but then I realized what the emotions of the villagers were. Fear. Pure and utter fear.

I stepped out of the hut and saw black cloaks fluttering in the moonlight that we lived in. The assassins had found us.

Chapter 33

Sebastian

The portal was nearly invisible here. Just a piece of tinsel wrapped around a rock. I stood next to it, looking at it with a set jaw. This was it. Go through the portal, break the portal, shadow walk to the Court of Light, and tell Seraphina that Rose was dead, that I'd finished the task.

She wouldn't believe me, but it would make it harder for her to have me killed. I'd be imprisoned undoubtedly. She'd starve me, torture me, and maybe eventually, she'd have me put to death in front of the Dark Court to show that even the Prince of the Shadows was fallible and subject to the law.

Regardless, she wouldn't know if she were right or not. As long as I didn't break from the torture. I took a deep breath. Rose was worth it. She was worth every last ounce of pain, every bit of molten iron that Seraphina would pour over my body, permanently scarring my body so that I would never have willing prey again.

I should already be gone. The dream was only meant to last until twilight when the first moon would shine its silver light across the land.

I bent down toward the rock, but I was interrupted by a voice. A voice I remembered clearly. One that should be dead.

"Prince Sebastian, why are you here?"

I turned around and saw the old Queen of the Light, Aurora. The one that Seraphina had taken the throne from. There was only one way to unwillingly lose the throne as a Queen: death.

Dressed in a simple silver dress, she stood just as tall as she ever had. Barefoot, she walked across the field towards me. Sadness filled her face. She'd always been a kind Queen. The kind of Queen that I'd hoped that Rose would be.

"You should be in the void, Aurora. Seraphina killed you." The woman smiled, but sadness tinged her lips.

"She believes this to be true, but she is not as clever as she thinks she is. It does not matter, though. The Princess of Shadows needs you, Prince. For many reasons, but this night holds many dangers. You would let your future Queen stand against Seraphina without you?"

Her eyes were daggers as she questioned me. The intensity that her eyes burned told me that her powers were not gone. She was no spirit.

"I have to do this, Aurora. Seraphina will hunt me until I'm found. She will never forgive this grudge."

"How do you know that she has not already found her quarry?" A shiver ran through me.

"They're here?" I stepped towards Aurora, rage and fear filling me with the need to move.

"A battle has already begun, Prince of Shadows. A Queen

Chapter 33

holds the forces at bay, but she is young still. She needs your blade beside her own."

I blinked, letting the words fill me. Rose was as good a warrior as any in a spar. In place with no real repercussions for failure. She was good when she knew the wounds would heal and no tears would be shed. When no lives hung in the balance.

I took off at a sprint, burning through my power as I enhanced my speed. No. It wasn't supposed to be like this. I was supposed to keep her safe. No matter what, she had to be safe.

What had I done?

Chapter 34

Rose

Black cloaks fluttered as the assassin's ran from the forest edge. Fear filled my body, but my training with Sebastian reminded me that fear had no place on a battlefield.

Kasia ran by me, spear and shield in her hands, and I leaped onto her back as she passed, my wings carrying me towards her. "Get me to the front," I hissed at her as I prepared myself.

There were too many for me to fight alone. Cara stood next to the fire that always burned. Her eyes had turned sorrowful. She was remembering the day that she had saved those children while her village burned.

"To battle, Cara," I commanded. "Andryn," I yelled as I passed him, "gather the others. Have the pups and foals gather around the fire. Keep them safe, and send everyone else to me."

Cara began running behind me, her eyes turning milky white as she saw the future. Andryn turned around, belting out

Chapter 34

people's names. I couldn't think about what to do. Battles weren't about thinking. They were about knowing, about doing.

The shifters were already arrayed in the front of the village. Four of them. They'd be cut down immediately. They were faster than the assassins, but the assassins had magic and blades that would keep them from healing. They were the foot soldiers of the supernatural world, and there simply weren't enough of them.

Touching the ground, I smiled at them. They yelped in surprise as stone flowed up from the ground like molten steel. Wrapping around them and coating their bodies in the thinnest layer of granite I could manage. Nearly weightless to them, it would shield them from much of the magic and the blades.

The gnomes showed up next, and I felt for their magic, combining it with my own. The shifters seemed to become pure shadows, hidden even while in plain sight. As they moved, you could see flashes of them, but otherwise, they were as close to invisible as I believed possible.

"That's great! Now do me! Armor. A sword. I'll keep you safe, Rose." I glanced at Enivyn and took a breath.

"Stay behind me, Enivyn. Keep your back against mine and don't touch anyone except assassins."

Light swirled from me to the gnomes, wrapping around them, covering their bodies in the same blinding white brilliance that Cara had used on me. They glowed so brightly that many of the assassins had to pull down their hoods as they approached.

"Watch for the elements of water and fire twinning," Cara said from beside me.

I nodded. A combination I'd never used or seen used. There was no one with control of either of those elements in the village. The only person to control fire that I'd ever seen was Nyx.

I glanced back and saw that Andryn had his golden sword out and was standing in front of the children of the village.

I pulled on the stone in front of us and right before the assassins reached us, I pulled a ten-foot tall wall out of the ground. Using the combination of mist and stone, I created stairs to the top.

"Deal with any that make it around the wall," I said to the shifters.

I heard yips but couldn't see them. Leaping into the air, my wings came to life, carrying me to the top of the wall. Two of the assassins were fairies, and they'd begun to fly over the wall.

I put out my hands and glowing tendrils of light flew from either side of me, ignoring the assassin's bodies and clinging to their wings. They were unprepared for the attack and did their best to not let the tendrils hit their bodies, but they had never fought a Queen who could burn their wings.

Their daggers were in their hands almost immediately, but they were too slow. With a single burst of power, I felt their wings burn. Screams rang in the air, and the tendrils disappeared as the fairy assassins fell to the ground, their shadowed wings red hot and burnt. Their bodies crumbled as they hit the ground. They weren't dead, but I'd felt every ounce of their power burn up as they tried to heal their wings.

Others were climbing the wall, and I let loose stream after stream of liquid shadows at them. Some hit. Others didn't. It slowed them down as the shadows stuck like glue to their

Chapter 34

faces and bodies.

A commotion came from behind me, as several of the assassins had sprinted around the wall. The shifters were tearing them apart. Completely unseen, they'd waited for the assassins to approach the gnomes, their eyes closed against the blazing white shields I'd given them. Then the shifters had lunged, taking them unaware.

Searing pain shot through me as an explosion hit me from behind. The smell of burnt flesh filled the air as I fell to the ground. As I fell, the ground under me turned to ice, and I slid, the edge getting closer and closer.

I tried to scramble to catch myself, but the ice was slicker than anything I'd ever felt. Combining mist and stone, I created a wall in front of myself. I hit it hard, and my vision blurred for a moment.

Without looking, I knew another fireball would be coming. I'd replayed the fight between Nyx and Sebastian over and over again in my head. Raising my hand, shadows expanded outward, and the fireball hit it with an explosion.

Arrows began to rain on the two assassins who had managed to climb the wall. I looked down and saw several of the villagers firing hunting bows at the assassins. Two arrows hit the one that controlled fire in the chest. He pulled them out, but he wasn't fast enough.

Wings propelling me forward, my daggers appeared from shadows just as Sebastian's would have, and I flung the first at his chest, but he dodged, twisting out of the way. A blast of water came towards me, but that meant nothing when I had my shadow shield.

I stabbed the flame assassin in the chest and felt his powers drain. He pulled his dagger from his sheath, but with a burst of power, I ripped the dagger upward through his chest and into his skull. He dropped to the ground, blood pouring from his body.

The water assassin stared at his comrade for a moment too long, and an arrow caught him in the chest. He grunted in pain, and as he began to pull it out, I'd already stuck a dagger in his neck.

As he crumpled to the ground, I sighed and looked over the wall. There were another fifty assassins. We'd killed less than a dozen, and I was fighting as quickly and efficiently as I could.

We were going to lose. No one here was a warrior but Kasia, and she was powerless against people able to throw fireballs. I was the only chance, but I could only do so much.

I set my jaw. I had to try. These were my friends. Closer than any family I'd ever had. I wasn't going to let them die without a fight.

Chapter 35

Sebastian

I was out of breath when I got to the village. Screams filled the air, and over everything, the scent of death lingered. This couldn't be happening. I could see Rose on the top of a wall that hadn't been there this morning.

She ducked as lightning struck nearby. Dead assassins littered the ground around the wall she stood on. Two villagers were bleeding on the ground with knife wounds while Cara stood over them. Kasia was stabbing as someone sat on her back with a bow, firing arrow after arrow at assassins as they tried to surround Kasia.

Between the warriors and the center of the village stood three gnomes who glowed like the sun.

I sprinted towards them, and I felt the well of power that resided inside Rose. It was draining. Too quickly. Tapping into it, I shadow walked into a warren that I created, something I'd practiced regularly in the past month.

I flowed out of the shadow next to Rose and immediately threw back my hood. Rose lashed out with her dagger as I'd expected, but I dodged. Her hand came up to use her powers, but she stopped as she noticed that it was me.

"Protect the people in the village," I commanded, and without waiting for her response, I shadow walked through my personal warren. I touched the stone and reappeared right behind an assassin. My obsidian blade sank into his head, and I was already shadow walking before I'd even had a chance to pull the blade out.

I called the dagger back as I stepped back into the Immortal Realm, and it reappeared as I was stabbing upward into a different assassin's head. The first body dropped only a moment before the second.

In that moment, I was death like never before. These were some of the greatest duelists in the world, in any of the worlds. Yet, I killed with an ease that made them look like children before a soldier.

Their bodies littered the field, single stab wounds in each of them. Dozens were dead in minutes. It was an impossibility. This was just one more way that Rose had made me better than I could be without her.

Then I heard Rose scream. One of the assassins had realized that there was a warren beneath us. Rose's body fell from the wall. In an instant, I shadow walked to her side, but it was too late for me to stop the assassin as he leaped from the wall.

I reappeared in the Immortal Realm, sliding into existence a foot away from Rose, and I watched as if everything was in slow motion. Enivyn, glowing like a star stepped over Rose's body right before the assassin hit her.

Chapter 35

The assassin screamed as he looked down on the light, his eyes burning out as he saw the light in its full brilliance. Enivyn looked up at the same time, and the obsidian dagger found the one weak spot in the armor that Rose had created for him, his face, slicing through flesh and bone like butter.

My dagger slid across the assassin's throat only a moment later, but it was already too late. The half-gnome's body collapsed on top of Rose who pulled his limp body to her, his light fading out and leaving spots in my vision.

The rest of the village continued the fight, but in that moment, only Rose mattered to me. Tears began to fall from her cheek as she stood up, cradling Enivyn in her arms.

I could feel her emotions. Pure rage mixed with more sadness than I'd ever felt. I could do nothing for her, and for that short moment, I was frozen on a battlefield for the first time.

Her eyes turned black. Not dark. Pure black, the same color as her wings that burned with power.

A sphere of shadows snapped up around her as she walked onto the battlefield, carrying the half-gnome. The shadows seemed stronger somehow, denser. Another assassin used the warren, and he plunged his dagger into the shadow shield. Without even a scream, he died, his eyes seeming to smolder and smoke. His body fell to the ground, but the dagger stayed locked into the shield that surrounded Rose.

She didn't scream as she should have. She should have been in immense pain from the dagger strike as it pulled her power from her. She was so cold. The only pain that she seemed to recognize was the sadness of her fallen friend.

All of the other assassins approached her and saw their dead companion with burned-out eyes. A group of the surviving fifteen surrounded her, their weapons drawn, but all of them hesitated to use them against this shield they'd never seen before. A shield that could kill.

"Die," she whispered, and mist rose from the ground, slowly climbing up the assassins' bodies. They began to scream almost in unison, but none of them moved.

As the mist climbed, slowly covering them, the screams got louder and louder until they just stopped. Slumping sounds filled the air as everyone in the village stood silently watching the woman that we'd all fallen in love with.

Rose's shield dissipated as she walked back to the center of the village with Enivyn still in her arms. I followed her, and she approached Cara. "Can we do anything? Is there any magic that can bring him back?"

I wanted to reach out and hold her, to comfort her, but I knew that right then, the only person that Rose cared about was Enivyn.

"No. There is nothing that can be done once the body is dead." Rose blinked back more of the tears and lay Enivyn down next to the fire.

"There will be a funeral tonight for Enivyn," she said. "I don't know if that's the way things are done here or not, but we are having one. You'll take care of this, Cara."

Cara nodded, and Rose turned to me. "There are wounded, Sebastian. Help them. I need time to rest."

"Andryn, I am sure that you are in no mood to cook, but I need food, and everyone needs something to eat at the funeral tonight."

"Yes, Lady," he said with a bow.

"Kasia, gather whoever you need to build a pyre for the assassins. Build it far enough away from the village that we

Chapter 35

don't need to see it during the funeral."

My mother had been a Queen. The Queen. She'd always had an answer. She'd always had a plan. She'd been in battles, and she'd turned the tide in many of them. That had been nothing compared to this.

My mother had been the Dark Queen for a hundred years. The only one that many had ever known. She had been a wonderful Queen, but Rose was stronger than she ever was. I'd never heard of anyone who could kill like this.

I glanced back to where the mists had stood and saw piles of bones sticking out from under cloaks. Nothing on them as though they'd been picked clean by insects.

No one understood the power of a Queen until she sat on the throne, but I knew that I would rather fight Seraphina and every person in her guard at the same time than to fight Rose alone.

Somehow, that only made me want to protect her more. I glanced at her as she walked to our hut. There was nothing in the world that could make me leave her side ever again. Nothing.

I took a breath and let it out slowly. She needed time to come to grips with her emotions, and I had my orders.

Chapter 36

Sebastian

A pyre burned the remains of the entire Assassin's Guild far to the north in the area that Kasia enjoyed running with her foals. The faint smell of burned flesh and hawthorn wood lingered in the air. That area would never be the same. It would be a haunted place, a place of evil in their minds.

For the ten years that this village had existed, they'd had peace. Now, they knew fear, and everything would change. Never again would they feel the same simple happiness. They would train as warriors from this day onward. They all knew that if Rose and I hadn't been here, the entire village would have died to that assault. They now understood just how fragile their peace was.

I'd collected the obsidian daggers and their sheaths and put them in a bag. The Guild was gone, but the weapons were too valuable to destroy. These would be the weapons that the

Chapter 36

village would train with. A bag of weapons that was worth more than most palaces. Weapons that could kill Queens and Princes. Weapons that would pierce shields and put them on a much more even footing against more powerful enemies.

Andryn's stew was cooking, and a second, much smaller pyre had been built just outside the village for Enivyn. His body had been cleaned, and he'd been dressed in the nicest outfit he'd owned, a simple foraging outfit covered in pockets. The gnome's pockets had been filled with snacks by Sinivyn. All of his favorites. Honeyed walnuts, sugared berries, some small pieces of chocolate, and roasted seeds. He would go into the void with as many treats as he could carry.

The battle that had been his death had been strangely one-sided. There had been wounded, but none were life-threatening wounds. Mostly, they had been accidents while untrained Fae used powers in ways they weren't used to. There were a few dagger wounds, but after the iron had been cleansed, they healed quickly.

Scraped hands and knees from tripping in their hurry. Bumps and bruises from running into each other. A few cut fingers from improperly handling weapons. The shifters had wounded mouths from biting hands that were wreathed in fire or were carrying blades.

All so minor in comparison to the atrocities of normal battle. There were no severed limbs or corpses that had been burned beyond recognition. There was no need to mercy kill anyone. It had taken less than an hour to decimate one of the strongest fighting forces in the world.

The fact that only one person in the village had died from an attack by the entire Assassin's Guild was a miracle. A miracle in the form of a woman who was approaching the fire now.

She no longer wore the simple linen dress that she'd worn the past few weeks. Tonight, as both moons shown brightly in the night sky, she stepped down the pathway through the village in a black dress made of something that seemed to shimmer with darkness instead of moonlight.

As she approached the cookfire, I realized that her dress was the same pure blackness of her wings. It was magic made manifest. An extension of her power that flowed like any other dress, but as she stood near the fire, the light seemed to be repelled by it.

"John and Sinivyn, please carry your brother to the pyre." Her words did not ask. They commanded. The girl that I'd stolen from the Mortal Realm was gone, and a Queen stood in her place.

They did as she bid, picking up the wooden board that held Enivyn's body. Even in death, the gnome was smiling. There was a small gash across his forehead where the assassin had killed him, but otherwise, he seemed to be sleeping. Small sobs filled the air as many of the villagers began to cry.

Rose followed them with me behind her, and the rest of the village followed behind us. She didn't even seem to notice me as I stood beside her while they lifted their brother onto the pyre using step ladders that had been placed on either side. Her gaze and focus were on the one that had been lost.

When they had retreated, Rose stepped up to the pyre and put her hand against the wood. Smoke began to rise, and as she pulled her hand away, I saw a flash of light so bright it would have blinded anyone nearby. Then it was gone.

The wood had been coated in oil, and as the oil caught fire, the flames spread. A plume of smoke rose into the air as the wood was slowly engulfed. Rose stepped back beside me, and

Chapter 36

I could see tears falling down her cheek.

"Enivyn is the kindest person I have ever met. He was the first one to trust me, the first to welcome me into the Immortal Realm. He was a friend. Always quick with a joke, and always ready to help when there was work to be done."

"I've never felt at home anywhere, but Enivyn showed me that this village could be home. He showed me that the people here were not the same as everywhere else. They could be more than friends. They could be family. I will never forget the first person to show me that I could have a family. I will never forget Enivyn."

As she stepped back, I stepped forward. "Enivyn was a gnome, and gnomes are not warriors. They're not soldiers or guards are even assassins. Gnomes hide and find things. Yet, when our Queen was in danger, he did what I couldn't do. He protected her. He kept her safe so that she could keep everyone else safe."

"Without Enivyn, everyone in this village would have died. Even me. He's not just a gnome. He's a hero. And, no one will ever forget his name. I think that he'd like to know that. Even while he rests between worlds."

John stepped forward, tears streaming from his face. "I will miss my brother's smile most of all. He was always there to brighten my day with his smile and laugh. He was the Prince of Smiles. I don't know if there's anyone in the world who can smile as well as Enivyn."

Sinivyn said, "He was an annoying gnome, but I loved him. He stole my food, but I didn't even mind very much. The world is worse now. I wish my brother had not died."

One by one, each of the villagers stepped forward to remember Enivyn. We all stood and watched as the fires consumed his body. The smell of burnt rowan wood filled the air.

Tears fell, a gift to the departed. This was the first person in the village to die since I had built it. He was also the first person that I'd brought here. Without Enivyn and his brothers, this village wouldn't have been safe. They'd have been found by seers or sensed by passing Fae.

"This will never happen again, Sebastian," Rose said, turning to me. Her eyes glowed with an inner fire, dancing from black to ice blue.

"People die, Rose. Even in the Immortal Realm, everyone dies eventually." I wanted to reach out and hold her, to comfort her, but she wasn't sad. She was furious.

"Not like this. Enivyn never did anything to hurt anyone. He didn't deserve this, and I won't let it happen again."

"You can't stop bad people from doing bad things. No one can." I could feel the rage boiling inside her. So much anger. I'd never felt anyone so filled with it.

"The Queen can."

I stared at her for a few seconds and nodded. "Yes, the Queen can stop a lot of it."

"Then I'll become Queen." She turned away from me and looked at the fire that released her first real friend.

In this moment, I was sure that touching that fire would hurt a lot less than touching the one that burned inside the woman I loved.

Chapter 37

Rose

The pain of losing Enivyn was still there. Every time I ate. Every time I saw John or Sinivyn. Every time I went into the forest. It was getting better, though.

I wasn't going to let this happen to my friends again. I would let Queen Seraphina target me instead of the ones I cared about. I would be the wall standing between her and the Dark Court, and if that wasn't enough, I would destroy her and any who stood with her.

Sebastian had tried to explain that the Courts thought of things like this as games. Build the better army. Eliminate rivals. Trick people into disgracing themselves. Slowly move up the hierarchy.

I wasn't going to do that. I was going to crush the hierarchy. I felt the power inside me. I'd seen what I could do. From what Sebastian said, there was no one in the world who would be able to stand toe-to-toe with me in a battle. Not even Seraphina.

But there were new rules to play by. Yes, I could start a war, but that would cost many lives on both sides. Instead, I was going to have to play their games to some extent.

Sebastian promised to teach me, to guide me. He had friends in Court that would help as well. But before we could do anything, we needed to travel to the Dark Court.

I wasn't going to let this village become a bargaining chip for them. We would break the portal and only after I could protect the village would we open it back up. That meant years most likely.

"We'll miss you," Cara said. Her eyes turned milky white as she held my hand. "There is a room that you will find before it is too late. A room where lies do not exist. A room filled with pain and anguish. Find it and the truth will be yours."

A goodbye from a seer. Advice that I knew that I'd never understand until I needed it. I tried my best to set it in my memory, but already, the words seemed to fade as all prophecies did.

"I'll miss you too, Cara. Keep them safe and don't let the pups run you too ragged."

She smiled and nodded. The entire village was lined up to see us off. Tears filled many of their eyes, but exultation filled others. They knew what I was setting off to do. Finally, someone would keep them safe.

I just hoped that I could be that person. I'd managed to make this place my home. I'd managed to learn to fight, to learn to kill. But could I learn to be a politician? Could I really be a Queen?

I waved goodbye to them and took Sebastian's arm. I wore

Chapter 37

a silk dress that Cara had made for me in the three days since Enivyn's funeral. Sebastian wore his cloak, but under it, he wore a silk shirt as well. His pack was slung over his shoulder, and we were well supplied for a journey.

He didn't know what the Dark Court would be like when we got there. If Seraphina had heard that the Assassin's Guild had failed, there would be repercussions. At least until I took the throne.

We began to walk the path that would lead to the portal. I couldn't stop thinking about what I'd done to those assassins there at the end of the fight. It had been one thing to fight them. They'd had a chance then. I'd been expecting to have to fight eventually. That's why Sebastian had trained me so forcefully.

What happened after Enivyn died was different, though. I didn't know exactly how I'd done it, but I'd combined magics into triples. Shadows, stone, and light to create the shield. Then mist, light, and stone to kill.

I'd tried to reproduce it again, but I couldn't. Even when I thought about holding Enivyn's body, I couldn't get back to that place of anger that had let me destroy an army in seconds.

I glanced at Sebastian and wondered how he felt about me now. Instinctively, I reached for his magic and felt his emotions. There was such a mix of them. More than I'd ever felt in him. Fear, uncertainty, excitement, and lust as always.

But more than anything, there was pride.

He was proud of me for becoming a Queen. I still didn't understand how he could think that I would be a good Queen when I'd only known I was a fairy for a little over a month.

I knew that I was powerful, but having power and knowing how to rule were two different things. I would be able to lean on Sebastian though. He was wiser than he let on, and he'd lived under a great Queen. Hell, it had been his mother. She would have talked to him about all of this stuff.

At least I hoped so.

We found the stone that had a piece of tinsel wrapped around it. "Ready?" he asked with a smile.

I nodded. It was time to see the Dark Court for the first time.

He held my hand and reached down to touch the piece of silver. I felt the draw of power over the bridge, and I let it pull me through the world in an instant.

I felt myself falling as soon as I was out of the portal, and Sebastian's hand held me tight, stopping my fall. I looked up at him and saw him clutching a tree branch. I'd forgotten that the portal was at the top of a tree.

"Glad you didn't go through without me," he said, chuckling.

"Just put me on a branch." It was hard to keep from laughing.

He swung me to the side, and I grabbed onto a large branch. Only then did I remember that I had wings. It was like going through that portal had put me back into the mindset of the girl who knew nothing and needed everyone to protect her. Well, that was done. That girl was gone.

I hopped down and let my wings slow my descent. Sebastian landed next to me, his feet sinking into the ground just a little bit.

In his hand was the silver wire that had been the portal. "Burn it," he said as he handed it to me.

I wadded the wire up until it fit into my clenched fist, and I let light explode across the silver. I could feel it heating up, smoke rising out of my clenched fist, and then it caught fire. I dropped it into the grass and let it burn itself out.

Chapter 37

I looked down at the ash that coated my hand and couldn't help but remember the ash that had come from Enivyn's funeral pyre.

I closed my eyes, banishing the vision from my mind, and took a deep breath. "Take me to the Dark Court, Prince. It's time to find out if I'm everything you think I am."

Chapter 38

Rose

The Dark Court was not at all what I'd expected. I'd thought it would be a giant building or something. Some kind of dark version of the White City in Lord of the Rings.

No, this was a massive, sprawling city filled with people. Lanterns hung from tall poles, spreading light and shadows across the twilight landscape of a city that never saw a sun. Only the two moons had ever illuminated this place.

Outside of it all was a wall made of black granite with sparkling crystalline pieces embedded in the stone. Massive catapults made of ebony wood stood amongst men in black plate.

Different banners hung from poles at each guard tower. Sebastian had explained that each noble family was required to staff a separate guard tower. I hadn't expected there to be so many of them. At least a hundred different banners flew,

Chapter 38

and I was going to have to learn everything I could about each of them.

In the center of the city stood a tower made of sharp and jagged obsidian that looked as though it had been carved from a single piece of stone. Rising high into the sky, it rivaled the size of some of the tallest buildings in the Mortal Realm.

"The palace," Sebastian said as he pointed at the tower. "That's where you'll live. It's where most of the fairies live. At least most of the full-bloods do."

I nodded. "Why didn't we simply shadow walk into the palace?"

"There are no warrens under the Dark Court. It's not safe to allow shadow walking into a city. It would be difficult to move an entire army through warrens, but being able to shadow walk into the gatehouse with a team of elite troops would be the fastest way to win a battle."

He led the way down from the cliffside that we'd appeared on. We walked down a twisted path towards the gate. The gate rose high into the air above us, guarded by a group of thirty men in black plate. They held spears that seemed too long to wield with sharp points that could only be made of steel.

Two of them had wings sprouting from the back of their armor, and I was surprised to see just how different they were compared to mine. Where mine was a black that seemed to glow, theirs were varying hues of gray.

"Stop! Assassin!" one of the fairies said as he floated to the front of the group carrying a silver sword that was at least three feet long. "Queen Seraphina demands that you report directly to her on your mission."

I could feel Sebastian tense at the order, but he flung his

hood back. Immediately, the guards held out their spears. "Prince, you're a wanted man. Why would you come back?" the fairy asked.

Sebastian grinned. "I no longer take orders from Queen Seraphina. We have a new Queen, and I obey only her."

The guards looked at me, and I let my wings lift me into the air. Their eyes followed me. "Pure black," one of them whispered. "Darker than black," another one said.

"Take the Queen to the tower, Prince."

Sebastian nodded and put his hood back on. He whispered, "Hide your wings unless someone else stops us. We don't want anyone to notice you until you make a formal claim for the throne."

I took a deep breath as I walked through the gate and willed my wings to dissipate. They would come back in an instant if needed, but for now, they were gone. It was easier said than done. They wanted to be there just like a bridge wanted to be used.

We walked through cobbled streets. Old stone buildings pressed against the walls of the city, and hooded people walked beside us. Many of them looked nothing like humans or fairies. Things of nightmares.

We passed a shadow standing tall like a man wearing only a burlap robe. Another creature was covered in scales, its hands ending in long claws. Then there were men covered in scars or even open wounds who walked as though nothing were wrong.

Not all of the citizens of the Dark Court were even that close to human shaped. A half-naked woman with the wings of a bird folded against her back shoved me out of the way, and I'd have fallen if Sebastian hadn't caught me.

Chapter 38

"What was that?" I asked seeing that the woman's hands ended in claws rather than fingers.

"Harpy," he said softly. "Let's hurry. You can ask me all the questions you want once we're safely inside the tower."

He pulled me behind him as we moved through the crowds, turning into alleys when the crowds became too thick as we moved closer to the center. The shadows seemed deeper here. The walls, cracked and breaking. "Things don't seem to have changed too much since I left," he murmured.

In front of the tower, four fairies stood in gleaming gold plate. They all carried golden shields and golden swords. Their wings were of yellows, oranges, and reds, and they seemed to radiate a soft glow even through their armor.

"Stop," they commanded. "Queen Seraph..." Sebastian threw his cloak hood back and didn't stop as he approached the tower.

"You no longer belong here. Tell your Queen that the Dark Court no longer bows to her rule."

One of them laughed, a tinkling laugh that sounded almost like a bell. "You are a dead man walking, Shadow Prince. Your mother will be happy to be reunited with her son in the void. She has waited too long for you to please her again."

A simple flick of his hand sent an obsidian dagger flying through the air. The soldier tried to block with his shield, but he was too slow. The dagger slid through the armor like a knife through butter, embedding deeply into his chest.

He fell to the ground, his hand struggling to pull the obsidian dagger from his chest. Two of the others stepped in front of Sebastian while the third tried to pull the dagger out.

Sebastian held both hands up, daggers appearing. "Go tell your Queen that she no longer rules the Dark Court, or I will

Princess of Shadows

be forced to find others to go instead of you."

The men glanced at each other, and they gathered up their fellow soldier before rushing off. "We'll need to move quickly, but those men will struggle to find a shadow walker to help them. Especially since the Assassin's Guild was where most ended up going."

Sebastian pulled the massive door open, and as we stepped inside, he barred the door behind us. This was the true Dark Court. Everything around this tower was affiliated with it, but this was the real thing. Flames of black similar to my wings rose from braziers set around the room and contrasted the normal fire in the center of the room.

Shadows and light danced what seemed to be an eternal dance as the two opposing flames flickered. "The royal dance hall," he muttered as he led the way up the first set of stairs.

Cold black stone was everywhere, but in the stone, gold and silver veins wove pathways creating beautiful contrast. The more that I saw of the Dark Court, the more I realized that it wasn't the opposite of light. It was the combination of opposites.

Where the Court of Light was about purity, the Dark Court was about completeness.

Stairs. So many stairs. Sebastian seemed to almost run up them, and I could feel the excitement in him. I tried to match his pace, but he quickly outpaced me with those damned long legs of his.

"To Hell with this," I muttered. Leaping upward, my wings appeared, and I floated next to him as he began to take the stairs two at a time.

"Wondered how long it would take for you to think of that," he said.

Chapter 38

"You told me to hide my wings. I was trying to be good."

"Well, you don't have to hide anything anymore." He stopped at a door. Two floors below the pinnacle of the tower. He smiled at me and pulled the door open. A four-poster bed stood against the wall. Wings were carved into the poles. Sheets of black and silver.

It was the dreamscape. The place that Sebastian had taken me over and over again.

"We're home." He pulled me to him and began to kiss me as he shut the door behind us.

I pulled away from him. His eyes were already turning misty. "Sebastian, don't we have to do things? Don't I have to claim the throne or something?"

"Yes, you have to do that, but you have to claim it in front of Seraphina and a group of seers."

I pushed off him, still floating above the floor. "Then what was the rush?"

He grinned. "I've never wanted to share *my* bed with anyone before. Now I want to."

I raised an eyebrow. "You're telling me that you just tried to make me run up a zillion stairs so that we could have sex in your bed?"

He shrugged. "When you say it like that, it does sound a little silly."

"Not at all," I said with a smile. "The only thing silly is that you didn't tell me ahead of time so that I would be just as excited."

He pulled me to him, pressing those beautiful lips against mine. I'd thought that the village had been home, but now I realized that home was where my love was.

Princess of Shadows

* * *

I stared at the Dark Throne. Obsidian, smooth as glass and black as night. It stood at the end of the Dark Hall. The ceiling was made of glass, exposing the entire night sky. The pinnacle of the Dark Tower.

This was my throne. As soon as Seraphina arrived, I would claim the throne. Sebastian would guide me in becoming a good Queen. I would protect the people. I would rule with strength and compassion.

At least that was the plan. Now that I saw the throne, now that the plan was drawing to an end, I wasn't so sure I could do this.

"You'll stay with me?" I asked Sebastian.

"I'm never going to leave your side, Rose. Whether you want me or not, you're stuck with me."

"At least you're pretty. I mean, you're an ass most of the time, but you sure look good."

"I could say the same about you, Lady," he said with a grin.

"You promise that you won't leave me?" I needed this reassurance. "Even if I'm not as good of a Queen as your mother?"

"I swear on my powers that I'll never leave you." His hand ran across my back and pulled me to him.

"But, you don't have to worry about being a better Queen. You just need to worry about being you. I've seen who you are. I've seen the woman who will stand up against insurmountable odds and fight, and I've seen the woman who will cry at the death of someone they'd only known for a month. You're everything we need."

He leaned down and kissed the top of my head. "I hope

Chapter 38

you're right, Sebastian. I can't do this without you."

"I love you, Rose. Not because you're Queen. I love *you*. You woke something up inside me, and for the first time in a very long time, I want to be alive."

"I love you too, Sebastian. I just want to love you for eternity, and I can't do that if you leave me like everyone else has."

"For eternity. I like the sound of that."

Epilogue

Seraphina

The mirror shimmered as I touched it. There was no silver mirror in the Dark Court. No one was that stupid. That didn't mean that I couldn't use mine to look in on things that happened there now that the barrier dividing the two kingdoms was cracking.

The city was slowly becoming lighter. "Prince Sebastian," I whispered.

The mirror fogged for a moment, and then a room came into view. The throne room. Prince Sebastian stood beside Rose and stared at the Dark Throne. The throne that had been empty since I'd had his mother killed.

How had they managed to survive the assassins? No one could have survived that. Not even me. Not without guards at least. They'd had no guards. It had been Rose and Sebastian and a bunch of incompetent villagers against sixty assassins.

Epilogue

I took a deep breath and let it out slowly. I was not some human, powerless and helpless in the face of my enemies. Not anymore at least.

Sebastian was going to die. Soon. Rose would too. She was the reason everything had fallen apart. If she'd never been born, everything could have continued on forever in perfection.

Light began to radiate from my skin, white hot. I took another deep breath and let it out, my anger flowing. A Queen must be in control of herself and her surroundings. A lesson I'd learned in childhood.

Well, it was time to take control of the situation. I'd given everyone else a chance to end these two problems, and they'd all failed. Now it was time for me to get my hands dirty.

At least this time, I'd enjoy it. They wouldn't die quickly. There would be no damned obsidian blade to drain the life from them. They would scream. They would beg for mercy. They would beg for death before it was over.

A smile crossed my face as I looked at Rose. "It's time that I see my daughter again after all this time."

Get the rest of the story!

I hope you enjoyed reading Princess of Shadows as much as I enjoyed writing it! If you'd like to get up to date information on my latest books, sales, and other news, follow the link below. As an added bonus, you'll get to read bonus chapters from Aurora's perspective about what happens in the village after Sebastian and Rose leave.

https://dl.bookfunnel.com/gchd1gizgw

OLIVIA HART

COURT OF LIES

BONUS CHAPTERS

About the Author

Olivia Hart is a new author in love with all things fantastical and paranormal. She writes about the darker side of fantasy romance with sassy heroines and flawed heroes.

You can connect with me on:
- https://www.amazon.com/Olivia-Hart/e/B08WWLLTFH
- https://twitter.com/AuthorOHart
- https://www.facebook.com/AuthorOHart

Subscribe to my newsletter:
- http://eepurl.com/hqokzr